Brothers of the Fire Star

a novel by

Douglas Arvidson

CrossTIME
an imprint of the Crossquarter Publishing Group
PO Box 23749
Santa Fe, NM 87502

Brothers of the Fire Star
Copyright © 2012 Douglas Arvidson
Cover Illustration Copyright © 2012 Rob Scarborough
ISBN: 978-1-890109-91-2

Printed in the USA

Library of Congress Cataloging-in-Publication Data

Arvidson, Douglas, 1946-
  Brothers of the fire star : a novel / by Douglas Arvidson.
      p. cm.
  Summary: When Japanese soldiers invade the island of Guam at the start of World War II, thirteen-year-old native Napu and American Joseph, nearly as old, escape in a small sailboat, guided by the "Spirit of the Voyage" and learning the secrets of ancient navigators as they go.
  ISBN 978-1-890109-91-2 (pbk.)
  [1. Sailing--Fiction. 2. Survival--Fiction. 3. Spirits--Fiction. 4. Navigation--Fiction. 5. World War, 1939-1945--Fiction. 6. Guam--History--Japanese occupation, 1941-1944--Fiction.] I. Title.

PZ7.A754Bro 2012
[Fic]--dc23

2012012488

Other Books by the Author

The Face in Amber
The Mirrors of Castaway Time
A Drop of Wizard's Blood

Dedication

This book is for my grandsons, Konrad Douglas Scarborough and Kiernan Robert Scarborough. May they embrace lives of learning through adventure.

Acknowledgments

Traditions About Seafaring Islands (TASI) is an organization on Guam dedicated to helping keep alive the skills of the ancient Pacific navigators. I am honored to be a long-time member and I hope this book will, in some small way, be helpful to TASI's goals.

When I set about to write it, I drew on the many hours of instruction and encouragement I received from TASI Board Member and Advisor, Manny Sikau, a seventh-generation *pwo*, and a master navigator from the island of Puluwat. To Manny, a quiet and patient man, I owe much. Thank you.

Dr. Larry Cunningham, TASI founder and a noted educator and author, read the manuscript and took the time to sit with me and make suggestions and corrections.

And thank you, Sandy Yee, archaeologist and TASI member, who took the time to communicate with me, answering questions and passing along valuable information. To all the other TASI members with whom I shared a sea adventure or two, thanks.

Guampedia is Guam's online encyclopedia, a labor of love for its creators, Shannon Murphy and others, who seek to increase the world's understanding of the island's history and culture. For me it was invaluable as a resource as I wrote this book.

Thank you, too, Susan Hokanson and Jenny Tedtaotao, former colleagues of my teaching days on Guam, for providing the wonderful name "Napu" and other Chamorro names I used in the book.

And finally, I would like to thank my long-ago Scoutmaster, Douglas Cranson. As a boy and later as a Scoutmaster, Scouting was an important part of my life and Doug taught me many lessons about self-reliance and wilderness survival that have helped me throughout the years. Such a legacy is what Scouting is all about.

Introduction

This is a story about two boys, Joseph and Napu, who get caught up in the great and terrible whirlwind of World War II. It is a story about surviving by learning to live together despite differences in race and culture. It is a story about brotherhood and courage and how important it is to be self-reliant and to stay connected to nature. It is a story about how we are a very real part of a very small planet and how that very small planet is connected to a very big Universe.

The peoples of the vast Pacific Ocean have been sailing among that ocean's seemingly infinite number of islands, atolls, and archipelagos for over three thousand years. To do this, they developed a brilliant method of navigation that uses only the stars, sea life, and the ocean itself. The years of study necessary to master this system result in a powerful spiritual connection to the natural world.

While once widespread, this ancient method of wayfinding is quickly dying, replaced at first by compasses and sextants, and now by the Global Positioning System (GPS). While modern methods of navigation are easier to use and certainly easier to learn, there is a danger that if we forget the ancient skills we will lose something profound—that vital connection that all humankind once had to the Earth and the sky. We must never lose sight of the fact that we are made of the same stuff as the Universe; we are in the Universe and the Universe is in us.

When the Spanish reached the islands of the western Pacific in 1521, led by the Portuguese captain, Ferdinand Magellan, they attempted to destroy the culture of the indigenous peoples. This devastation resulted not only in great loss of life but also in the loss of the ancient knowledge of navigation as practiced by seafarers on Guahan (Guam) and in the Mariana Islands.

And so we begin our story: In December 1941, the same day the forces of Imperial Japan attacked Pearl Harbor and began World War II in the Pacific, they invaded the island of Guahan. When the bombing begins, Joseph is alone, out exploring in the jungle. He seeks shelter deep in the embracing roots of a great and sacred tree. When night falls, the spirit of an ancient navigator appears and tells Joseph that he must not die; he must find a boy named Napu and together they must escape to the sea and bring the secrets of the ancient seafarers back to Guahan.

Douglas Arvidson
March 22, 2012
Onancock, Virginia

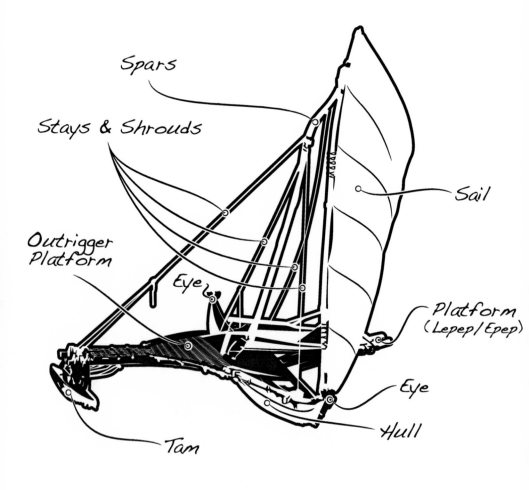

Spars

Stays & Shrouds

Sail

Outrigger
Platform

Eye

Platform
(Lepep / Epep)

Eye

Hull

Tam

The Proa: A Carolinian Voyaging Canoe

Douglas Arvidson

Part I
Escape and Survival

Brothers of the Fire Star

Chapter 1

The boy was deep in the jungle when he heard the planes and then the distant thunder of bombs. The earth shuddered beneath his feet and the quiet, moist air seemed to bend and stretch and then split open with the power of the concussions. For the first time in his life he felt the sharp, searing pain of fear. *The war is here*, he thought, *it has started. It has been everywhere else in the world and now it has found us even on this tiny island in the middle of the great blue ocean.*

He did not run. He had been told he must come home right away if anything happened, even though his uncle had insisted the war would not reach them. The Japanese, he'd said, would never dare attack the United States—and the island of Guam was American territory.

Joseph, nearly thirteen, had not believed his uncle's words because even as they were spoken, his uncle was building a small air raid shelter inside their house. It was a tiny room inside another tiny room and had thick walls and was filled with food and jugs of water. It was a stifling hot place and Joseph hated to go into it when his uncle held air raid drills.

So now instead of going home, driven by fear, he went deeper into the forest until he could not see the sky through the thick, intertwining branches above. The shadows cast by the trees protected him; the long, winding branches embraced him. He knew the pilots could not see him and that he was safer here than out in the open running through the village streets or even in his uncle's air raid shelter.

He tried to ignore the sounds of the bombs by focusing on the spiders. The jungle was filled with them. He could feel their webs sticking to his face and arms but he could not see the creatures themselves. It was as though they, too, had sought shelter when the air had become filled with such terrible energy.

He found himself standing at the base of a huge banyan tree. Its long roots, growing downward through the air and along the tree's trunk, were like a thousand writhing, twisting, gray snakes. He had been told that this was called a nunu tree and that the spirits of the islanders' ancestors lived inside it. He had been told to treat it with respect, to ask permission to walk near it. His uncle had frowned at such stories the way he frowned at almost everything.

But now Joseph had no choice but to hide deep among the nunu's branches and roots. He crawled into a place where he was protected on nearly all sides and curled up inside it. He held his breath and listened. The roar of the planes grew louder and the sound and concussions of the exploding bombs came closer. He knew they were hitting the village next to the harbor. His uncle's house was near his job at the trans-Pacific cable station. Joseph knew the man would run from the station to the house and crawl into his hot, dark shelter. He would be calling for Joseph and maybe looking for him, but Joseph had not told him that he was going to the jungle. His uncle disapproved of his exploring. "What if you trip and break a leg? What then," he would say, "How would we find you? You would die there and the spiders would eat you."

But here, among the tree's great roots, there were no spiders. The air was very still and he could smell the sweet, mysterious odor of things that had died and things that were being born. That was what he loved about the jungle, why he loved to lose himself in it.

He made himself as comfortable as he could. He cleared away some broken branches and dead leaves and found he could move deeper into the tree until he would not be seen even by someone walking close by. Slowly his fear subsided and after a long time, he began to feel sleepy. The bombs now seemed far away and the faint, acrid smell of things burning, slowly diminished.

*****

He awakened to a touch and a whisper. In the dark, he couldn't remember where he was. He started to jump up but now something seemed to be holding him down, refusing to let him go. He wanted to scream, to fight, but he remembered something he had read once in a Boy Scout survival manual: never panic. There is always time to think, if only for an instant.

And in that instant, he remembered where he was and what had happened. He forced his body to relax and his ears to listen. The bombing had stopped but the smell of smoke was still in the air. He looked up, but could see nothing. He tried to figure out what time it was. There was no way to know how long he had been sleeping. The sun was gone, so it must be past suppertime, maybe much later.

Again he heard the whisper, not much louder than his own breathing. The jungle hummed very softly all around him. There was the chirping and buzzing of insects and, as always, the rich, damp odors of rotting vegetation. He inhaled slowly and felt himself relax. It was nothing. The whispering was nothing.

Something touched him on the shoulder. He jerked away, hitting his head on a root. He swung at the invisible touch and called out, "Who is it? What do you want?"

He could hear fear in the cracking and shaking of his own voice. He tried to fight his way out past the roots but they seemed to hold him tighter and he heard the whispering voice, close to his face now, and this time he understood its words: "You must not die yet. You must escape to the sea."

"What? What did you say. Who are you?" Joseph hissed.

The voice repeated, "Do not let the war kill you now. Escape to the sea."

"The sea? How?"

"I am the spirit of your voyage. You must bring me with you."

"The spirit of my voyage? I don't know what you mean."

The air near his face moved, as if whoever was speaking to him was close enough to breathe on him. He groped but felt nothing. Small lights danced in the dark before his eyes, and at the same moment, the embracing roots opened up and he was free from their grasp.

He moved outside the tree and stood up. There were lights all around him. At first they were just the small lights he had seen inside the tree, but then these lights joined together in the air until they were flames and he saw that they were torches, torches being carried by a procession of people. They stood together in the jungle and he could see that they were part of the jungle itself; the trees and vines grew through them as if their bodies were made only of the cool night air.

They were looking at him, holding their torches high. One of them, a powerful old man wearing only a piece of cloth around his hips, stepped forward. He reached out and grasped one of the thick gray roots of the nunu tree that grew down from the upper branches. When he pulled on it, the root seemed to come alive in his hand, writhing and twisting in the dark air, but the old man held onto it and broke it off from the tree. A moment later the root, now transformed into the shape of a small human figure, stopped moving. The face and body of the figure were dark brown, its hair black, its lips a bright red. Its arms were folded across its chest and its bulging eyes were closed as if it were sleeping.

The old man held it out towards Joseph. "Take me with you. Take me to Napu. Take me to sea with you."

"What is it? Who's Napu?" Joseph asked, not touching what the old man offered.

"I am the spirit of voyaging. I have been living in this nunu tree, waiting for you," the old man said. "Every sea voyage has a spirit. You must take me with you. I will protect you."

"But who is Napu. Why would I go to sea? Where would I go? There's a war now, right here, a big war."

"You must escape the war. You must help Napu learn the ways of the ancient navigators. You must learn to use the stars and the sea and the sky to find your way across the waves. You must help him bring that knowledge back with you, here, to this island, to Guahan, where the old ways have been taken from us."

"What do you mean? Who is Napu? I don't know what you're talking about."

"I am the Spirit of the Voyage. I will guide you and protect you."

"But I don't have a boat."

The old man ignored Joseph's pleas. He reached out with the root and touched Joseph with it, once on each shoulder and once on the top of his head, and Joseph could feel the heavy shock of something enter him and move through his body. Then, despite the flames from the torches and the warmth of the night, he felt a coolness rush over him. Without thinking, he reached out his hands and took the root from the old man.

Before Joseph could ask any more questions, the old man turned into a cloud of luminous vapor and disappeared into the root. Then all the people in the procession began to fade away and a moment later they had become only bright points of light that dissolved into the black jungle night.

Chapter 2

When they were gone, Joseph saw that the light the ghosts had taken away with them was being replaced by another: the dawn. The dim early glow, the color of dark pearls, was just beginning to come down through many layers of leaves to the floor of the jungle. It was still too dark to see much, so, clutching the Spirit of the Voyage to his chest with both hands, the boy began to feel his way out.

When he emerged on the road that led down to the village, it was nearly full light. He was exhausted and hungry and his legs felt weak. He began walking slowly. He heard nothing but the soft calls of a few birds and the familiar sound of the wind rustling the tops of the palm trees. *Could war be so quiet?* he wondered. *Is it over already? Maybe there wasn't a war. Maybe it was just a dream.*

When he reached the top of the hill, when he could see the village with its big church and above them the barracks where the American soldiers lived, when he could see the blue water of the harbor and the sea spreading out far below him, he knew that he had not been dreaming, that the war was not over. The barracks and much of the village had been destroyed. Smoke poured from burning buildings and people were wandering in the streets. No, the war was not over; the war had just begun.

And then he saw that smoke was coming from the cable station where his uncle worked and he began running toward it. He ran down the road toward the village and the water, toward the smoke and the fires. While his head told him to go back, far back into the jungle, back to the protection of the nunu tree, his legs kept moving, faster and faster. He could feel the stones under his bare feet, feel the grass along the side of the road whipping at his legs, but most of all he could feel the hot air going into his lungs and around his heart and his heart was burning, as if it, too, were on fire.

He began to meet people coming up the road from the village, people he knew. Their faces looked as strange as the faces of the spirits he had seen in the jungle. It was as if they, too, were ghosts, as if they had been drained of blood. Only their eyes seemed alive, huge and round and moist, stunned by the horror they had seen.

There were young women and children and old people, too, and sometimes a young man would be carrying an old person on his back, but they all looked the same, their faces blank, their eyes dazed.

They didn't speak as he ran by them, nor did they appear to even see him. When he spoke to them, when he asked them what had happened, if the soldiers had come, they stared at him for a moment and then away, not answering him but walking upwards, toward—toward what? There was nothing up there but jungle.

Then he met a young man he recognized, an altar boy at the village church. Joseph spoke to him: "Have you seen my uncle?"

But Tomas's eyes had seen terrible things and now could see nothing.

"It's me, Tomas—Joseph. Remember? I came from Massachusetts to live with my uncle. You remember my uncle. He works at the cable station."

Tomas seemed to look at Joseph without seeing him, as if he could not focus on his face.

"Are the soldiers there?" Joseph asked, moving close to the young man's face. "Did they come to the village yet?"

Finally Tomas said, "Don't go there. There are dead people there. The planes will come back." He lurched away and resumed walking up the road.

But Joseph continued on down the road toward the village. He had to find his uncle; he would know where they should go, what they should do.

When he got to the village, everything was covered with drifting smoke, and the sound of crying and sometimes moans came from what was left of the burning houses. The streets were filled with bomb craters and littered with stones and fallen palm trees and scattered coconuts. While some people had escaped to the jungle, many of them simply sat by the burning embers of their homes holding some odd possession, like a pot or a rolling pin. They held them to their chests as if they were sacred objects and one old woman held what Joseph realized was her grandchild and the child was very pale and did not move.

The cable station was mostly gone. There was nothing but a shell of it left and it was on fire. Pieces of broken cement were scattered about and the earth was torn up with bomb holes and the trees were ripped apart and lying everywhere. He did not see his uncle but across the street he saw that their house was still there. Its corrugated metal roof had protected it from falling embers and some vagary of the wind and the chaotic luck of falling bombs had left it unscathed.

He rushed in the open front door and called out his uncle's name but the house answered him with the same shocked silence he had seen in the faces of the people on the road. His uncle was a hard man who had insisted on living a spare existence, and now Joseph's voice echoed off bare walls and the few pieces of simple, homemade wooden furniture. His uncle was gone.

Joseph went through the house and out the back door. Below the house was a small hotel for passengers flying in and out of the island. This, too, had been bombed and was on fire. He ran down past it toward the harbor where the big Pan American seaplanes landed. Then, at the edge of the water, he saw his uncle.

Something terrible had happened to him. He was lying half in and half out of the water, his feet hanging in a patch of vines, his shoulders and head floating face up in a glimmering pool. Joseph scrambled down the bank and fought his way through the vines and fallen trees until he was standing in the water next to him. He reached down and touched his shoulder and called out his name, once, twice, and then again but there was no response. For the first time Joseph could remember, his uncle's face was serene, as if just before he died he had witnessed the angels he so fervently believed in.

Though he had never seen a dead person, Joseph knew the truth, knew what had happened, that it was impossible and yet it was true. But now he felt nothing. Even though the village lay burning all around him, even though his uncle lay dead before him, even though tears ran hard down his cheeks, he felt nothing. It was as if he had left his own body and was floating in the air looking down on it all—on the harbor, on his uncle, on the burning village and on himself.

In his hands, lying across his chest, his uncle held a thick book that Joseph thought must be the old Bible he'd carried with him everywhere. But then he realized it was not the Bible but *A Boy's Picture History of the World in One Volume,* a book Joseph had brought along when he had come from Boston to live with his uncle almost a year ago. Could his uncle, in his panic, have picked it up by mistake, thinking it was his ragged holy book?

Without understanding why, without thinking, Joseph knew that he must take it with him. Later he would realize that what had made him reach down and lift the book from his uncle's arms was the same thing that made him run toward the war when he wanted to run away from it: It was the ghost of the old man in the root of the nunu tree. The Spirit of the Voyage was already guiding him, helping him. He reached down with the end of the stick—the end that held the face with its closed and bulging eyes—put it under the sodden book, and lifted it from his uncle's body.

*****

He went back up past the burning hotel. He saw the bodies of two men he recognized, young island men who had been kitchen workers at the hotel. They had been nice to him, giving him special treats when he and his uncle stopped by, but now they lay among the smoking wood and ashes as if they had fallen asleep. Joseph wanted to yell at them to get up and hide. *The war is here now,* he wanted to say, *we've all got to go someplace and hide.*

He went through the front door of his house, into the small living room. It was quiet and dark and a warm breeze blew in through the windows, carrying the smoke with it. Joseph sat down on a bench at the wooden table where he and his uncle had eaten their meals. He lay the Spirit of the Voyage and the book down in front of him. His eyes could see them clearly but he could no longer understand what they meant. The face on the nunu tree root was silent, its eyes closed; the book was soaking wet, its cover torn. He forced himself to read the title on the cover: *A Boy's Picture History of the World in One Volume.* He knew it was filled with pictures of great men and stories of great things the great men had done. He knew it was filled with stories of wars, other wars fought far away and long ago. Reading it had always filled him with wonder and envy; he had wanted to fight in a war and be a hero, like Teddy Roosevelt or General Custer. Now, though, he felt nothing. He thought he should be crying, but the tears no longer came. He felt numb, empty of everything.

For a long time he stared at the Spirit of the Voyage and at the book and then he began to feel strange. He was getting cold. This was the tropics and it was always hot, but now the cold moved through him slowly and got colder and colder until he was shivering and then he began shaking and he could not stop it. He got up from the table and went into his bedroom. He lay down on the bed and curled up in a tight ball and pulled a blanket over him. He pulled it up over his head and closed his eyes but he could not stop the cold and could not stop the shaking and the smell of the smoke came in through his bedroom window and in through the blanket.

Chapter 3

He lay curled up around himself all that day. Then another night seemed to come and go and then another day, but he could not be certain. He did not eat or drink, he did not think or dream. Had he slept? He couldn't remember. Yet he was aware of himself and he knew where he was and what had happened. After a while the feeling of being cold had gone away and his body had stopped shaking. He knew that time had passed, but how much? How many hours? How many days?

Then he heard a familiar voice that seemed to echo off the walls of his bedroom. He pulled the blanket down from his face. The room was dark but there was a dim light coming in through the windows and it seemed like the breeze carried the light in with the smoke and mixed them together. *It's them*, he thought, *it's the smoke and the light and the breeze that are talking to me.*

But what were they saying? He could not understand the words, even though the voice was clear and strong. He got up and walked out into the living room. Here there was more light and he saw the nunu tree root in which the Spirit of the Voyage lived and the big book lying on the table and then he noticed his uncle's calendar hanging on the wall behind the table. He moved closer to it. Every night before going to bed, his uncle had crossed off the day he had just finished. The last day he had crossed off was December 7. So it was now maybe December 8th or maybe the 9th. It could have even been the 10th. December 10, 1941.

He looked out the window. It might have been either late evening or early morning. But the breeze was increasing and then he remembered that this window faced the east and the sky was growing lighter. It was morning.

As he watched, the soft brightness increased and the sky began to turn pale pink and then out of this brightness there was also an increasing sound of something heavy in the air, as if the rising sun itself was growling its anger. It grew louder and louder and then, out of the quickening sky, the planes came again, passing low over the village, and the howling roar of their engines and the rattle of their machine guns cut through Joseph's nightmare and ripped it away from him like a ragged, bloody, old coat. And when the nightmare was gone, his fear was gone, too, and everything became very clear to him; he knew what he must do. He grabbed the Spirit of the Voyage and *A Boy's Picture History of the World in One Volume*, and ran out the door into the shattered air of the morning.

*****

The old ghost had told him he must go to sea, but which sea? Even though this was an island, there were two seas, because the one that crashed against the windward side was very different from the one that washed the shores of the leeward side. Again he remembered the ghost's words: "*I am the spirit of your voyage. I will guide you.*" But the image in the nunu tree root was silent, its eyes closed in a perpetual grim serenity.

The villagers made the decision for him; they were leaving their homes seeking refuge on the other side of the island, in the distant mountains, where there were deep ravines filled with dark jungle. Joseph knew, too, that the other side had no big harbors, no ships, and no large villages to be bombed and burned. That side of the island was scoured by waves the trade winds sent piling up against its shores. Yet a small part of this coast was protected from winds; there, small rivers flowed into small, snug bays. It must be here that the Spirit of the Voyage meant for him to go, it must be here that he would find the boat the Spirit of the Voyage said would be waiting for him. So he turned his back on the burning harbor and began to make his way through the streets of the village.

He had gone only a few hundred yards when he saw the soldiers. They were far off in the distance, coming out of the smoke that hung over the harbor as if they had been born from the fire itself. They were dressed in gray-green uniforms and carried long rifles and they scurried here and there, sometimes raising their rifles and shooting. Joseph turned away from them and began running though the smoking ruins of the houses.

When he reached the edge of the village where it backed up against a sharp, sheer rock cliff, he did not see any more soldiers and he knew he was close to the road that led up into the hills and back into the jungle. He kept moving along the bottom of the cliff, jumping over fallen coconut trees and crouching low as he scurried across open spaces. All around him there were fires and everything was shattered. Dust floated in the hot air and the wind carried it away toward the sea. Then the cliff ended and the road, steep and narrow, opened up before him.

Once on the road, he found he had joined a parade of shocked and terrified villagers. As they walked, they dropped things they could no longer carry, and so it was that Joseph found an empty sack lying in the grass. He put the Spirit of the Voyage and the book into it and slung it over his shoulder and began walking with the villagers up into the hills.

He walked for a long time in the sun and the dust, for many hours, and then, without warning, came a sudden and powerful feeling of thirst. It overcame everything, blotting out the constant, nagging fear of the soldiers, the visions of burned houses, and the face of his dead uncle that seemed to float in the air behind him, following him, haunting him. Now he could think of nothing else but finding something to drink.

He sat down alongside the road in the shade of a coconut tree. He wiped the sweat off his forehead with his arm, lay back in the grass, and now, looking up, saw that the top of the tree was filled with nuts, big, green nuts that he knew were filled with sweet, cool water. But the tree was tall, and the nuts were at least thirty feet above the ground.

He studied the trunk. It was smooth and branchless and curved outwards over the road. Maybe he could climb it as he had seen the village boys do, by tying his ankles together and hugging the trunk to him and using his feet to push himself up. But he had nothing to tie his ankles together with, and what would he do once he reached the top? He did not have anything to cut the coconuts off with. He would have to let go of the trunk to grab at a nut, and then what? It was a long way to fall.

But he was desperate. His uncle had told him about men who had collapsed and died from the tropical heat when they did not get enough to drink, and he had read in *A Boy's Picture History of the World in One Volume* about explorers who had died terrible deaths from thirst when their tongues swelled up and choked them. He felt his tongue and wondered if it was starting to get bigger.

Then, off in the grass on the other side of the road, something caught his eye, something glinting in the sun. He stood up and walked over to it. It was a machete. The handle was wrapped tightly with twine and the blade had been well sharpened. He glanced around to see if its owner might be nearby, but the people walking on the road ignored it. He picked it up. It hung heavily in his hand, but it felt good there and he knew that it was now his.

When he walked back to the shade of the coconut tree, he saw that the sack in which he was carrying the book and the Spirit of the Voyage had opened up at the top and the face of the Spirit of the Voyage was poking out. It appeared to be looking at him and, without knowing why, Joseph held out the machete and said, "Look what I found..." But the face did not change its expression, the sleeping eyes did not open.

Even though he had nothing to tie his ankles together with, he tried to climb the tree as he had seen the village boys do. They made it look very easy. He put the blade of the machete in his mouth and held it with his teeth. It was heavy and tasted metallic and sour, but he bit down on it hard. Then he grabbed the trunk with his hands and put one foot at the bottom and then, with a small jump, put the other foot next to the first.

But before he could push himself up, he lost his balance and fell sideways. The machete twisted out of his mouth from its own weight and fell into the grass and he almost landed on top of it. He cried out and then tried to spit the taste of the metal from his mouth. He sat down and rubbed his face with his hands. He was very thirsty and breathing hard but the villagers walking past on the road ignored him.

After a while, he tried again. He put the machete in his mouth, grabbed the trunk with his hands, and jumped on the tree, planting his feet together. This time he quickly pushed himself upwards before he could fall sideways, but his feet slipped and he fell against the trunk and the blade of the machete hit the trunk and was knocked sideways from his mouth. He slid down the trunk and felt the rough bark tearing at his skin and he tasted blood.

He spat the blood out and lay down in the grass next to the tree. He was very tired and he lay there a long time as the people from the village moved past him. He knew he would not be able to climb the tree to get the coconuts, but he could not make his mind concentrate on what to do next.

When he finally sat up, the sun was high overhead and heat shimmered on the road and the hills around him. The trade winds were blowing but the air felt harsh on his skin and the sky was full of haze and the air filled with the sound of planes—the terrible buzzing, burning sounds of war. He knew he had to move, to get away, to hide somewhere. He stood up, picked up the machete and slipped it into his belt, and then picked up the sack and slung it over his shoulder.

Again he joined the others on the road. These were the stragglers, people with wounds, old people carrying a few possessions in sacks on their heads, the remains of families—young mothers with small children and men walking alone or leading water buffalo. They walked slowly, sometimes looking up toward the sky, but they walked quietly—even the smallest of the children did not cry.

The road meandered upwards until it reached the top of the island. All around him Joseph could see the ridges of the sharp-topped hills covered with the yellow green of the sword grass and between the ridges were the dark valleys. And in the far distance was always the blue sea now gray with the haze and on the surface of the sea were the shadows of many ships.

When they reached the top of the island, they started down the other side but now the throngs on the road diminished as people moved off into the jungle to seek shelter in caves or in the bottoms of ravines. The road was hot and the wind picked up the dust and swirled it around Joseph's face. He squinted in the sun and the hot air made his thirst into something painful that lived inside him. His tongue had become thick and dry and he found it was difficult to swallow.

He heard the rumble of a motor. It was not a plane; a truck was moving slowly up the road from the village. He could see the plume of dust it left behind as it negotiated the curves, and then it appeared around a bend just below him. The glare of the sun off the glass of the windshield hid the driver's face, but Joseph could see soldiers sitting in the back holding rifles up at the ready. As it got closer, he saw that there were other people in the back of the truck, too—islanders were crouched or lying down, their hands and arms tied behind their backs, and some of the soldiers pointed rifles at them.

Joseph froze. For a moment he forgot the pain of his thirst. The truck rumbled slowly toward him and he saw the soldiers pointing to him and he heard them calling out to him in a language he did not understand. He turned and ran and heard the loud report of a rifle shot, felt a hard tug at the sack on his back, and lost his footing. He had been standing at the edge of a steep gully cut in the side of the mountain by thousands of years of rain. The jungle grew up this ravine, reaching toward him as if calling to him and now he knew what he had to do: he jumped out into it as far as he could and then he fell, tumbling over and over, unable to stop his body as it crashed downwards through the grass and trees and vines.

Chapter 4

He tumbled through the tops of trees and his body smashed against their trunks and against the steep sides of the hill. On and on he fell, but instead of trying to stop himself, he clutched the sack to his chest and allowed himself to hurtle downward, deeper and deeper into the ravine. Branches ripped at his face and tore into his sides and finally he slammed so hard against a rock it knocked the wind out of him. The sack flew from his arms. He lay on the ground writhing and gasping for breath.

For a long time he struggled to take in air, his chest heaving, his inhalations shrieks. Then the pain started to subside and his breathing became easier and he found himself staring upwards at the nearly solid roof of the dark, green jungle overhead. There was no sound, no hum of insects, no birds scolding, no whispering of life coming and going. For once the jungle was silent; all he heard was the soft rasping of his own breathing.

He listened for the soldiers in the truck, for rifle shots, but there was only the still, strange peace of the green forest that closed him in on all sides. Then he heard something else. He sat up. Just beyond a pile of brown, dried-out coconuts, a thin stream of water trickled out from a crack in a rock ledge. He pushed himself up and crawled over to it on his hands and knees, put his face against the rock, and began sucking at it. The water was sweet and cool but it took a long time for him to drink his fill and he had to stop often to breathe and to look around him in case the soldiers had followed him.

When his belly was hard and full with the water, he leaned back against the ledge. The first thing he saw was the sack. When he had crashed against the rock, it had flown from his arms and now lay in a pool of water a few feet from him. The top of the sack had come open and the book had been flung out against the muddy bank of the pool. The root of the nunu tree—the Spirit of the Voyage—lay on the pile of dried coconuts and palm fronds.

He stood up slowly. His back and sides were stiff and he found a large bruise forming on the side of his chest. He winced in pain when he bent down to pick up the book. When he reached for the

Spirit of the Voyage, he saw that something had torn a ragged piece out of the side of the sleeping figure. He remembered the soldier and the rifle and the shot, and then the sharp tug at the sack. The bullet had missed him and hit the Spirit of the Voyage. He rubbed the gash with his finger as if to soothe the Spirit's pain before he put it back in the sack.

But where was the machete. It had slipped out of his hand as he fell and now how would he find it, after falling all this way? But he knew he must find it, somehow, and he began the slow, painful crawl back up the steep slope. He had not gone far when he saw it lying on the ground against the bottom of a coconut tree. He grabbed it tightly by its handle as if it were alive and might try to get away from him again.

The ravine continued downwards and Joseph began to make his way along the edge of the small stream that was forming from small rivulets that came out of the rocks. It was slippery with mud and he had to choose his footing carefully. Still, he slipped often until he learned to support himself by hanging onto palm fronds and balancing his feet on dried stalks that littered the ground.

Soon the small trickle had gathered enough other rivulets and dripping water until it became a larger stream and now, instead of trying to straddle it as he walked, he stepped into the water and walked down the middle of it. The mud sucked at his old canvas shoes and the water felt cool and good on his feet.

In many places he had to climb over fallen coconut or iron wood trees or scramble over ledges where the stream plunged over small waterfalls. But always he went downward and always the air around him was thick with its silence and with heat and with the jungle's dark shadows.

He came to a place where the stream moved more slowly, forming deep, clear pools. He started to see small creatures darting around his feet and when he stopped to look at them, saw that they were tiny shrimp. He walked more slowly now, his feet sometimes sinking into mud up to his ankles, and then the stream became deep enough so that he had to move out of it and walk along its banks.

Finally, when the land flattened out, the stream became a small, sluggish river moving slowly under a thick canopy of trees and in the distance Joseph heard, not airplanes or bombs, but the soft, distant roar of the ocean on the reef.

He sat down on a log to rest. He put the sack on the ground next to him and, for just a moment, closed his eyes. Immediately he heard a voice. He jumped up, his eyes searching the jungle around him. He saw nothing but he knew he had heard it. It was a boy's voice, a voice not unlike his own, and it was singing. He sat down and closed his eyes again. He heard the silence of the jungle broken by the faraway ocean's hiss and rumble and then an airplane passed low overhead, invisible above the tops of the trees.

Then there it was, the sound of a boy singing, and this time when he opened his eyes, it was still there. He stood slowly and walked down the river toward the sound. As the stream spread out, before giving itself up to the sea, it formed a small delta and this is where Joseph saw him, the boy standing in the boat that floated in the middle of the broad, quiet pool.

He was not older than Joseph and smaller, with brown skin and long, straight black hair that shone in the shadowed light. He was barefoot and wearing only a pair of ragged shorts held up by a thick brown leather belt and on the belt was a big knife in a leather sheath. As he hummed to himself he appeared to be tying something to the boat.

Before Joseph could speak, the boy said, "Don't think you can sneak up on me! It is impossible, you see?"

He did not look at Joseph as he spoke. His voice was both challenging and taunting. "Come help me. I'm getting the sails ready and loading the boat with coconuts and other things to eat. Once that is done, we can leave."

Then he did look up and stared hard at Joseph. "I have to take you with me. I don't want to. But if I don't, the soldiers will chop your head off." He frowned. His eyes were large and very dark.

"Where are we going?" Joseph asked.

The boy did not seem to hear him. He went on, his voice quiet but hard. "I don't want you to come with me because my boat is too small and I don't have enough food for both of us. And you probably don't know anything about sailing—or even fishing. And it will be dangerous to have you with me. If the soldiers catch us, they will shoot me, too—or cut my head off—because I was helping you because you are white."

"They would cut off my head because I'm white?"

"Yes, of course. That's what they do. My grandmother told me. Of course, they will cut *your* head off first because you are probably a spy."

Joseph looked up the river behind him. He did not see any soldiers—only the deep green and shadows of the jungle.

"But," the boy said, and his frown deepened, "even though you don't know anything and will probably cause a lot of trouble and maybe even get us both killed, I must take you because I cannot leave you here. But you got to do everything I tell you to do. No arguments, okay? I'm the captain of this boat—I'm the boss." He did not wait for an answer. "So, come on, help me."

Joseph hesitated for a moment, but then, without saying anything and with the sack slung over his shoulder, he stepped down into the water. The pool was too deep to walk across, so he held the sack up over his head with one arm and swam to the stern of the boat. The boy reached down and took the sack from Joseph's outstretched hand.

"Can you climb in by yourself?" he asked.

"I think so," Joseph said, and he put both hands on the side of the boat and kicked hard while he pulled himself up. He got the top part of his body over the gunwale and then one foot, and then he was able to roll into the bottom of the boat where he lay for a moment to catch his breath.

The boat was made of wood and was maybe twenty-five feet long. It had once been painted blue but now most of the paint was gone except in a few places and the bare wood was almost black. It was filled with green coconuts and woven baskets filled with fruit. small, green bananas, yams, and breadfruit.

The boy was tying a piece of heavy cloth onto a long, thick pole. When he was finished, he seemed to study his work, to think about it, and then, when Joseph was standing next to him, he said, "You see, I have a boat filled with food and the sail is ready. And you have a machete. That is good for us, hey? I've got one, too. We will need both of them, I think. What else is in the bag?"

"I have a—a carved stick and a book." He said carved stick because that is what the Spirit of the Voyage looked like—like someone had carved the face and body into the wood—and he did not want to try to explain about the old ghost and the nunu tree.

"A what? A carved stick? And a book? That's all? No food, no fishing line or hooks? You can throw them away. We don't need sticks or books."

"It's my favorite book," Joseph said. "It's called *A Boy's Picture History of the World in One Volume.*"

"We need fishing line and hooks, not books," the boy said. Then he stopped what he was doing and studied the sack for a long time. "Okay," he said, and he shook his head and sighed. "See? You're causing trouble already. Put them in the boat. We can use the pages of the book for starting a fire when we reach the islands. And what is this carved stick?"

Joseph took it from the sack and held it out toward the boy. "I found it," he said. "I think maybe it's good luck."

The boy took the stick from Joseph's hand. He carefully examined the sleeping face and the raw gash on its side. "What happened here?"

"It got shot."

The boy stared into Joseph's eyes. "It got shot? Really? Who shot it?"

"A soldier. Up there on the road." Joseph motioned with his arm upwards toward the hills.

19

"Was he trying to shoot you?"

Joseph thought about this for a moment and said, "I guess so. He was in the back of a truck. There were some people tied up in the back and the soldiers were pointing guns at them. I was standing along the side of the road and there was nowhere to go, so I jumped over a cliff and fell down into the jungle."

"This means we got to leave tonight," the boy said. "They will come looking for you." He handed the Spirit of the Voyage back to Joseph, who put it back in the sack.

"Where are we going?" Joseph asked, looking at the boat.

"We are escaping to another island—where there are no soldiers. What is your name?"

"Joseph."

"They call me Napu," the boy said, pronouncing it, NAH-poo. "Because I am a very good sailor—very brave. I am not afraid of the sea like other boys. Napu means 'wave' in our language—in Chamorro. Like a wave on the ocean. I'm thirteen—almost a man. How old are you?"

Napu—Napu. Joseph repeated the name to himself and then everything the old ghost—the Spirit of the Voyage—had told him, came back to him: he must escape to the sea, he must take the Spirit of the Voyage with him, he would meet someone named Napu.

But he did not tell Napu this—it would all sound too crazy. Instead he said, "I'm thirteen, too," and it was not much of a lie; he would be thirteen in February. "We're going to escape in—in this boat?"

"Yes. It is my boat. I got it from my uncle when he died. I fish in it every day. I am a very good sailor and a very good fisherman. Every day I go out to sea and catch many fish. I caught fish for my grandmother until she went to join the ancestors."

He reached into the boat and lifted out a coil of line and a battered metal box. "You see, this is my fishing line and here are my hooks." He opened the box and held it out for Joseph to see. Inside were half a dozen rusty hooks. "It's hard to get good hooks," he said. "These are very valuable."

There was a roar overhead, sudden and loud, and Joseph winced and ducked down. Napu, though, just glanced up at the branches that hid the sky and said, "They are here. My grandmother said they would come and she was right. She was always right. So now we must escape. We will leave tonight as soon as it is dark. Are you ready?"

Joseph looked past Napu at the boat. It seemed very small and underneath the coconuts and woven bags of vegetables, he could see water in the bottom of it. He shrugged and said. "Yeah, I guess so."

Chapter 5

Once the sun had turned red and dropped into the dark, gleaming sea, night came quickly. Napu said the moon would not rise until much later and it would be a dark night—a good night to escape. He picked up a long bamboo pole and handed it to Joseph. "I'm going to pull up the anchor. The current will take the boat. You can steer it with this pole. We must be very quiet. No splashing, no loud talking. When we reach the end of the trees, we'll be out in the cove and I'll put up the sail."

Napu bent low and moved carefully over the coconuts and bags of vegetables until he was in the bow. He began pulling up a line that went over the bow into the water and as he pulled it up, he coiled it at his feet. A minute later, a small anchor emerged from the water. Napu dropped it on the top of the coil of line and turned around.

"Okay," he said, "use the pole to steer us."

Joseph knew what he was supposed to do. He had seen pictures of people using long poles to move boats through the water. Still, he had never done it himself and the pole felt long and clumsy in his hands. He hesitated.

"Get the pole in the water," Napu said, "Right now or we'll run aground on the riverbank."

Joseph knew he had to do something or he might look stupid and Napu would change his mind and not take him—and then the soldiers would shoot him or cut his head off. He took a small step to the side of the boat and put one end of the pole into the water. He pushed it down, further and further until he felt the bottom of the river. He looked around to see in which direction the boat was moving and saw that it was turning sideways in the current and drifting toward the shore. He pushed on the pole and felt the end of it dig into the mud and felt the weight of the boat against the pole as the boat began to turn. Slowly it seemed to be moving away from the shore and back into the middle of the river.

"Good," Napu said as he moved back to where Joseph stood in the stern of the boat. "Here, let me have the pole now."

He took the pole and Joseph watched as he guided the boat down the middle of the stream, pushing on the pole or lifting the pole out of the water and putting it back in on the other side of the boat and pushing on that side. He made it seem easy and the boat was now moving quickly across the pool.

Joseph began to see stars through the branches above their heads and then the trees were gone and the gentle sound of the ocean washing up on the reef became louder. He could see the white glow of the breaking waves and feel the cool evening breeze on his bare chest.

At the same moment Joseph felt the breeze, the water became too deep for poling and Napu lifted the pole out of the water and dropped it into the boat. He searched for a moment in the dark and came up with what Joseph recognized was a paddle. He handed it to Joseph.

"We are out in the bay now," Napu said. "We need to paddle to get us farther away from the reef and then I will get the sail up."

The wind was on Joseph's face and the night was dark but he could see a sky filled with stars and the glow from the surf breaking close by. He took the paddle from Napu. It felt heavy and solid, its handle smooth from much use. He had never paddled before, either, but, as with the poling, he had seen photographs of people doing it in *A Boy's Picture History of the World in One Volume.*

He reached over the side and dipped the paddle in the water and pulled. He felt the blade grip the water and his arms took up the strain. He pulled and lifted and dipped the paddle.

Napu had picked up another paddle and was paddling on the other side and together they moved the boat away from the reef and away from the shore. When Joseph glanced back, he saw the black shadow of the island rising behind them. Here and there were the orange glow of small fires and sometimes he saw what must have been a truck's headlights as it drove along the coastal road.

"Don't stop paddling," Napu whispered. "The wind is against us here. It will blow us back. We need to clear the reef and then I can put the sail up. We need to get as far away from the island as we can before the moon comes up."

Joseph took one more glance back. The island loomed over them, both forbidding and inviting. It offered safety from the dark sea that was now ready to sweep them away, and danger from the soldiers who wanted to kill them. His arms were already getting tired, but he once again dug his paddle into the water and pulled hard.

After what seemed like a long time, when Joseph's arms ached and he knew he could not paddle anymore without resting, he felt the motion of the boat change. The bow would rise up and then dip down and rise up again in a long, slow rhythm. Napu stopped paddling and whispered to Joseph to stop, too.

"We are clear of the reef," he said, "we can put up the sail now." Then he stopped talking and sat quietly listening. "Get down!" he ordered, "Lie in the bottom of the boat and pull the canvas over you. And make sure your feet don't stick out."

Joseph did as he was told. He dropped down into the bottom of the boat and slid under the canvas tarp. The woven baskets were cool and smooth against his skin and the bottom of the boat smelled of fish and stale salt water. He felt Napu force his way in beside him and then he heard what Napu had heard: the rumble of a big engine—a Japanese patrol boat. It grew closer and closer until it seemed it must be right over them and then their little boat pitched up sharply and then dropped and they were rolled around in the bottom and the baskets of fruit rolled against them and then it happened again and again until Joseph was sure the little boat would tip over.

Then the sound of the ship's engine began to fade and the boat's violent motion slowed. A moment later, the regular, rhythmic movement of the sea had returned.

"They're gone. Let's get the sail up now," Napu said as he slid out from under the tarp. "We can run with the wind."

Joseph crawled out from under the canvas and watched the shadowy figure of Napu working in the dark. He seemed to be able to do it all without seeing much and he worked quickly. In a few minutes he said, "Help me now. We will get the mast up. I had to take it down so I could hide the boat up in the river."

"What do you want me to do?"

"Go to the bow. When I lift up this end of it, put that end in that hole up there. It's tied to a block near the top of the hole, but you need to get that end over the edge of it so it will drop in when we lift this end up. Then come back here and help me."

It was dark and the boat was rising and falling on the swell, but Joseph made his way across the canvas tarp to the bow. There was a small raised deck here and he could just make out the hole in it that Napu was talking about. As Napu had said, the big end of the mast was tied to a block at the edge of the hole. He kneeled down and waited. The mast was a long, heavy wooden pole with the canvas sail bunched up and tied along its length, and when Napu started to lift his end of it in the stern, Joseph could hear him grunt with the effort. Joseph grasped the thicker end and guided it until it was on the edge of the hole.

"Do you have it at the hole?" Napu asked and Joseph could hear the strain in his voice.

"Yeah, it's there."

"Hurry up and come back here and help me then."

Joseph scrambled as quickly as he could back across the tarp. The boat was rising and falling and he saw that Napu was struggling to hold the end of the mast up and to keep his balance.

"Now, lift it up," Napu said. "Push hard."

The boys both lifted the end of the mast and pushed it upwards. When they had it up as far as they could reach, Napu said, "Hold it! Hold it there." He let go and scrambled across the tarp and then grabbed the mast again and lifted and pushed.

The mast was now nearly vertical but Joseph could not reach any higher. Without having to be told, he moved up on the tarp next to Napu and together they gave it one last push. The mast rose, teetered for a moment as the boat rode up on a wave, and then, with a heavy thump, the end of it fell into the hole and the mast stood up tall and straight.

Both boys fell down into the boat and lay on the tarp while the boat pitched and fell.

"Good," Napu said, and for the first time his voice sounded excited, even happy. "That was close. We almost lost it. Now we need to unfurl the sail."

"What do you want me to do?" Joseph asked.

"Nothing. It's easy."

He untied a line at the bottom of the mast and gave it a sharp pull, whereupon a long line that ran up the mast came loose and the sail billowed free. Quick and agile as a cat, Napu slid to the stern, put the end of the line through a heavy metal cleat, and pulled it tight. The sail had started flapping madly in the wind, but now Napu was able to pull it in and when he did, it filled with the breeze and Joseph felt the boat come alive. Sitting in the middle of the boat, by the faint light of the stars, Joseph could see Napu's shadow in the stern holding onto the tiller and steering the boat down the waves.

Chapter 6

They passed several ships and saw the lights of many more floating in the distance. Now, with the darkness and with the wind behind them and his boat dancing across the waves, Napu seemed bolder. He steered the little craft around the ships while he sat up tall in the stern, not ducking down into the bottom as they passed.

After several hours of this, Joseph had to ask the obvious question. "How do you know where you're going?"

For a long while Napu's silence seemed to increase the rhythmic sound of the water against the hull and the creak of the tiller in its gudgeons. Then Napu said, "My grandmother told me many stories of our ancestors who could navigate across oceans using only the stars and the waves."

Joseph gazed up at the sky, brilliant with stars from horizon to horizon. There were millions of them, clouds of them. For the first time that night he shivered, both because he was getting cold and because he could feel the cold loneliness of the vast heavens above them.

"So your grandmother taught you to steer by the stars?"

Again there was silence, this time even longer. Then Napu said, "No, my grandmother did not know how to do this. It is a manly thing, this navigating by the stars."

"So," Joseph asked, "how did you learn how to do it?"

Napu sighed and answered, "No one taught me. It is in my blood. That's how I know. I am an island boy and almost a man."

Joseph heard himself say, "Oh." And then he was quiet because he remembered what the old ghost had told him that night in the forest when war had come to the island, the night he had first heard Napu's name: *"You must help Napu learn the ways of the old navigators, learn to use the stars to find your way across the waves... the old ways have been lost..."*

But he said nothing about this to Napu and while Napu steered them through the night, Joseph rested in the bottom of the boat. At first he was reasonably comfortable lying on the tarp among the coconuts and fruit. He took the Spirit of the Voyage out of the sack and folded the sack around *A Boy's Picture History of the World in*

One Volume and used it as a pillow. Curled up and lying down low out of the wind, he was no longer cold and soon his eyelids began to feel heavy.

*****

Though he had not dreamed, when he opened his eyes he knew he had been sleeping. His body was stiff and cool and when he stretched, he felt the pain of his bruises. He gazed up at the sky. The stars were still there, wheeling vast and cold in their endless dome; the little boat was still riding the waves easily, and the sail loomed above him fat with the breeze. And he could see Napu sitting in the stern silhouetted by the small crescent of moon rising behind him.

"The moon is coming up," Joseph said.

"I know."

"Napu, do you know where we are?"

"We are sailing south from the island."

"Oh," Joseph said. "Do you know when we'll get there? To the islands you talked about?"

"It is a long sail. Go back to sleep."

"Do you know the people there? Are there soldiers there?"

"I have heard of the people there. They will give us food. There are no soldiers."

"Did your grandmother tell you this?"

"Yes. My grandmother was very wise."

"Where is she now?"

"Her spirit has joined those of our ancestors."

When Napu said this, his voice seemed to break, just a small quiver. Joseph stopped asking questions. He had been holding on to the Spirit of the Voyage and now he began to rub the sleeping face, feeling its smooth features. Then he said, "I need to tell you something—if you promise not to laugh at me."

"I will not laugh." The moon was rising over his shoulder and it sent a narrow path of light directly at the canoe.

"It's about the carved stick." And now Joseph hesitated and almost changed his mind. Should he tell him his strange story? Maybe Napu would think he was crazy.

"So, tell me," Napu said.

"I was in the jungle when the bombs and the soldiers came. I like to explore. I'm very interested in science and nature—history too. And when the bombs came, I hid inside a big tree—a nunu tree I think it's called. It has big roots that come down from the branches."

"Yes," Napu said, "that's a nunu tree."

"After a while, I fell asleep and when I woke up it was dark and I heard voices. I saw—I saw people. They were walking toward me and carrying torches that lit up the jungle. Except they weren't really people—at least not living people. They walked right through trees. They—I think they were ghosts."

In the dark, Joseph felt Napu's eyes on him, but the boy did not say anything.

"One of the ghosts was an old man. He grabbed one of the branches growing down from the tree and—and it turned into this. He said he was the Spirit of the Voyage and I must escape to sea and take him with me. He said I must help someone named Napu—help him learn how to navigate by the stars and bring that knowledge back to the people of the island."

Napu did not respond to Joseph's tale. He continued to sit tall in the stern of the boat, the wind whipping through his hair, the moonlight making him, too, look more like a ghost than a living person.

"Do you think I'm crazy?" Joseph asked.

"I think you are lying," Napu said.

"Lying? I'm not lying!" Joseph said and his voice rose against the wind. "I saw them, just like I said I did." And now he wished he'd never said anything about it, wished he'd kept his mouth shut about the ghosts and nunu trees and let Napu form his own opinion about the Spirit of the Voyage.

"Why would the spirits of the ancestors—the *taotaomo'na*—talk to a white boy who comes from across the sea in America?" Napu asked, his voice hard. "I have been living on the island all my life. The *taotaomo'na* are *my* ancestors, my grandmother is with them—and they have never spoken to me like that."

"I don't know why they spoke to me," Joseph said, "but they did. You can believe it or not—I don't care."

He was gripped by the urge to throw the Spirit of the Voyage overboard into the dark waves. He raised it above his head and pulled his arm back but before he could move further, he felt a sharp pinch in the hand that held the stick. He yelled out and dropped the stick into the boat.

"What's the matter?" Napu asked.

"It—the stick—never mind. It wasn't anything."

Joseph lay down again in the middle of the boat just behind the mast and closed his eyes. He let the Spirit of the Voyage lie where it had fallen.

Chapter 7

They did not speak to each other again for the rest of the night. While Napu sat up straight, stoically holding tight onto the tiller and steering the boat down the wind, Joseph slept. When his hunger woke him, the sky was brightening in the east, igniting the sea and the sky with a dim glow. All but the brightest stars had faded away. He was cold and sore and his muscles were stiff.

Before saying anything, he watched Napu for a while. He was afraid to admit that he was thirsty and hungry, afraid the boy would think him a weakling. Napu was still at the tiller, but Joseph noticed that his body appeared to be drooping. His head would drop and then snap up again; he would lean to one side and then the other.

Without sitting up, Joseph said, "I think I can steer, you know, if you showed me how. It's your turn to sleep. On the big ship I sailed here on, the crew set watches so everyone could sleep. I know because I asked them about it."

The sound of his voice seemed to wake Napu. He sat up tall and said, "A great navigator must steer for days without rest."

"But...." He was going to argue but maybe it was true, maybe great navigators did not need to sleep. Instead he asked, "Aren't you hungry and thirsty?"

"We have to eat and drink to keep our strength," Napu said. "Open a coconut and we can drink it and eat the meat. There are bananas there, too." He pointed to the dirty canvas tarp Joseph had been lying on.

The tarp was tied down with a long line and the boat was plunging in the seas, but Joseph finally managed to untie one end of the line. He took out a coconut, a large green one, and lifted it to show Napu.

"Is this a good one?" he asked.

"Yes," Napu answered, but said nothing more.

Joseph knew what he was supposed to do. He had seen people on the island use a machete to open a coconut. He set the coconut down and took his machete from where it lay in the bottom of the boat. It was difficult to stand because the boat was rising onto the top of one wave and then diving down the front of the next, but he tried. He stood quickly and started to lift the machete over his head to swing the blade down on the nut, but before he could even get it up in the air, the boat twisted in the sea as it rose up on a wave and tossed him sideways against the gunwale. He dropped the machete and grabbed at the side of the boat with both hands to keep from falling overboard.

Napu laughed. "You see? I was right. You don't understand the sea or coconuts. Now I will have to show you how to steer so I can show you how to open a coconut with a machete. Come here."

As the sun rose, so did the wind. The boat was lifted high on the crests of the waves, where it seemed to hesitate for a moment before racing down the fronts of them. Each time this happened, part of the wave slapped against the hull and a little seawater sloshed in.

With the boat lifting and falling under him, Joseph had to crawl through the water on his hands and knees along the bottom of the boat to where Napu sat holding the tiller.

"Come up here," Napu said. "Sit next to me. Watch me. Look at the sail."

Joseph did as he was told. He pulled himself up and sat on the small board seat next to Napu. When he looked forward toward the sail, he could now see all of the boat and what lay beyond it and it was then, for the first time, he realized that the boat was very small and the sea was very big. When the boat rose on top of a wave, all he could see were more waves sparkling away forever in the bright sunlight; there was nothing else, this was their whole world, and he and Napu and the little boat were inside it, part of it.

"Do you see how the boat is going through the water?" Napu asked. "The wind is coming from almost behind us and the waves are coming from there, too. We must keep the sail full and the boat sailing in this direction. To do that, keep the wind right here on your body and keep the waves right there on the boat. Do you understand?"

But Joseph had not been listening; he had been watching the sea. He had never seen anything like it, had never felt so lonely. When he had sailed across the ocean to the island on the big ship, he was far above the water, high up on a steel deck, not sitting wet and hungry down among the waves in a tiny wooden boat.

"Put your hands on the tiller," Napu said. "Here, next to mine."

Joseph watched Napu's face without seeing it and then felt Napu pulling at his hands where they were holding tightly onto the back of the boat. He let go of the wet wood of the transom and grabbed at the long, smooth wood of the tiller and gripped it tightly.

"Don't pull it!" Napu yelled.

But it was too late. Napu was not ready for Joseph's strength and for a moment he lost control of the tiller as Joseph pulled it toward him. The boat was just beginning to slide down the steep face of a wave and now, as it was lifted high, the stern swung around sharply. There was a loud sound like a gunshot as the wind got behind the sail and snapped it around to the other side of the boat and then the boat began to go over on its side as the next wave began to lift it up.

"Let go of the tiller!" Napu said, and he jerked at it, trying to pull it out of Joseph's hands.

But Joseph hung onto the tiller because there was nothing else for him to hold onto. The next wave lifted the boat higher and higher and the boat went over on its side further and further until water starting pouring in over the gunwale.

Then two things happened at almost the same moment: To keep from falling overboard, Joseph let go of the tiller and grabbed onto the upward side of the boat, and there was a dull popping sound as the line that held the sail broke. The sail flew outward and began snapping and flogging in the wind with a sound as loud as a gun being shot over and over again—bang! bang! bang!

As the boat went over, Joseph clutched at the side and felt water slapping at his legs and feet. He saw the waves rising up over them and felt the little boat struggling under him. There was nothing to do but wait for the sea to flood into the boat and swallow them up.

But then boat seemed to find her own way. She stopped going over, and when she rose on the next wave, she began to level out. Joseph glanced over his shoulder. Napu still sat where he had been all night, high and straight on the little seat by the tiller. Somehow he had not fallen overboard and somehow he had managed to push the tiller far over, stretching his arms out as far as they would go. With a lurch, the boat came upright and Joseph let go of his grip on the gunwale and fell down into the water that sloshed in the bottom.

"Get the sail back in," Napu said. His voice was hard and it carried above the snapping canvas. "Hurry, before it gets all torn to pieces."

Joseph did not move and could not speak. He lay in the bottom of the boat, his head against the canvas tarp, staring up at Napu.

Napu repeated his order and his voice was sharp with desperation: "Get the sail back in! You've got to do it, Joseph! Now! Now!"

Joseph's body felt numb. His ears were ringing with fear and he wanted to vomit. But then he felt a quick, sharp pain in his side as if someone had poked him. He pulled himself away and looked down. When he had fallen into the bottom of the boat, he had landed on the Spirit of the Voyage. But there was something different about it now. Instead of sleeping with its eyes closed, it was now staring at him, its open eyes bulging out of its head, huge and white.

For a moment Joseph stared back at it and then he shot a glance at Napu and then back at the stick. But its eyes had closed again. It lay quietly, half floating in the water in the bottom of the boat.

Now, somehow, Joseph understood what he must do. It was as if with the pain, the Spirit of the Voyage had given him something else, had somehow taught him something important. He got on his hands and knees and worked his way forward toward the mast. When he reached it, he grabbed it and pulled himself up until he could grasp the bottom of the sail. The sail was flapping wildly in the wind but he managed to grab the bottom of it and began to pull it in toward him.

Twice, with the boat plunging underneath him, he lost his grip and the sail pulled away from him, but on the third try, he was able to gather it all in and wrap his arms around it. He then found the line that was attached to the corner of it and held it up for Napu to see.

Napu, holding onto the tiller, nodded and yelled, "Wait. Hang onto it. Don't let it go. Wait for the right moment and then bring it back here to me."

The seas were lifting and dropping the boat, so Joseph would have to wait until a wave passed under them and the boat rode on the back of the next one. From his position at the bottom of the mast, he waited and watched the ocean rise and fall behind Napu. The waves came on, endlessly, some of them breaking and sending white foam up into the air, where it was carried away on the wind.

It seemed like a long time before the moment was right, and then, for just an instant, it was. A wave lifted the boat and, as it passed under it, the boat was steady in the seaway. Hanging on tightly to the line, Joseph jumped down into the bottom of the boat and scrambled back to Napu, who took the line from his hand and wrapped it around a strong, smooth, metal post on the boat's frame. Then the sail filled with the wind and the line went tight and the boat surged ahead.

Chapter 8

For a long time they sat this way, side by side, watching the ocean and watching their little boat plunging down the seas. Now that the sun was well up, long-winged seabirds appeared, soaring on the wind, nearly touching the water and turning and wheeling on their wingtips. The birds eyed the boys and the boat, circling them again and again.

"They are fishing," Napu said, breaking the silence. "We need to fish, too. You will need to steer now, so I can get the fishing line out and open some coconuts to drink. And we need to bail the water out. The boat is too heavy."

"I can do it now," Joseph said, "I can steer." And for some reason he knew he could, for some reason he now understood how the boat worked, how the tiller steered her through the seas.

"Take the tiller carefully," Napu said. "Don't pull on it, don't push it. Just hold it. If you make another mistake, we will both die."

Joseph had been holding onto the sides of the boat, but now he put one hand on the tiller next to Napu's. As Napu slowly released his grip, Joseph felt the power of the water against the rudder and felt the movement of the boat and how she rode in the sea down the waves. He soon learned to anticipate those movements and to move the tiller just enough to lead the boat where he wanted her to go.

Finally Napu said, "Good, you almost have it." Then he slid down off the seat and into the bottom of the boat, where he dug around under the tarp until he found a dented, rusty bucket and began to bail water. Fifteen minutes later he was finished — the bottom of the boat was wet, but most of the water was gone.

Next, he chose a big, green coconut and, holding it up in one hand, lopped its top off with six or seven quick strokes of the machete. He took a long drink and then handed the nut to Joseph.

Joseph had to release one hand from the tiller to take the coconut, but found he could now do this and still keep the boat on course. He lifted the open end of the nut to his mouth and tipped it up. The liquid that rushed into his mouth was cool and fresh and sweet and he gulped it until the nut was empty.

"It is the best thing to drink," Napu said, "It's better than water, better even than milk." He opened another one and repeated the process, taking a long drink before handing the nut to Joseph. They drank four nuts before they were full.

"Now we need to fish," Napu said. He opened his rusty metal tackle box and brought out a thick stick wrapped with fishing line that was tied to a black rubber tire tube. He selected a hook that had a bright piece of metal attached to it and tied it onto the end of the line and tossed it into the water. He let it trail far behind the boat, tied the rubber tube and the stick to a metal cleat, and then, without speaking again, took a long look at the sea around them and lay down on the tarp. In a few minutes he was asleep.

Then, even though Napu was sleeping close by, Joseph felt alone. He was alone with a sail full of wind and a small boat he could barely control. And Napu now trusted him to steer the boat and it seemed that the boat trusted him, too, running down the seas with an easy, eager motion. He watched the seabirds circling the lure on the end of the fishing line as it flashed just below the surface of the waves, he watched the puffy white clouds moving along in the bright blue sky, and, when the boat rose up on a wave, he watched the far horizon, a sharp, gray-blue line where the sea and the sky touched each other.

It was at one of these moments, just when the boat had climbed to the top of a wave, that he thought he saw a movement in the bottom of the boat. But it was not Napu moving—had it been the Spirit of the Voyage? Had it really moved? He took his eyes off the sea and watched it for a moment but saw nothing. It was only when he looked back out over the sea that he saw it again, from the corner of his eye.

Something was happening to it, as if the root of the nunu tree had come alive and was teasing him. Joseph took his eyes from the sea again for as long as he dared and watched it. And as he watched, it began writhing and twisting like a snake in the bottom of the boat and a cloud formed around it, a cloud that the wind could not blow away. Then a face formed in the cloud, a face he had seen before—the face of the ghost of the old man who had given him the stick.

In the bright sunlight the cloud shimmered and the old man's face shimmered with it. The blue of the sea was reflected in his face and then his body formed from the cloud and it seemed to move with the rhythm of the passing water. But the Spirit of the Voyage did not look at Joseph. Instead, for just a moment, the old man seemed to gaze down at the sleeping Napu and then gathered himself up into a small whirlwind and disappeared into Napu's open mouth.

For a moment too long, Joseph watched, entranced. The boat rose up on the top of a sea and then, as she began to run down the front of it, started to turn herself broadside to the wind. Just in time, Joseph felt the familiar movement of the boat change and he looked ahead. Without having to think how to do it, he moved the tiller in the proper direction and the boat came back around and once again found her path through the seas. *Napu was right*, he thought, *I almost have it now. Maybe the Spirit of the Voyage came into me, too, while I was sleeping last night — maybe he is still with me now.*

For the rest of the day, while he sat at the helm guiding the boat across the ocean, Joseph watched Napu. The sun was full on his face and he breathed deeply in his sleep. He had not stirred when the Spirit had entered him, nor had he moved when the boat had lurched from its course. Joseph wondered when the Spirit would come out of him — or would it stay inside him?

I will be like Napu, Joseph told himself; *I will steer the boat for many days without resting, because I, too, have the Spirit of the Voyage inside me.* Then he thought, *The old ghost told me that I must help Napu learn how to navigate. So maybe Napu does not know how use the stars to steer either. Maybe he does not know where we are going. Maybe we are lost and he won't admit it.*

By afternoon, when the sun had crossed its zenith high in the sky and had descended far down toward the other horizon, Joseph was very tired. His skin was sunburned and he was terribly hungry and thirsty; he wished that Napu would wake up and open some more coconuts. And, more than that, he worried that maybe he did not have the Spirit of the Voyage inside him after all and he was sailing in the wrong direction. How would he know? How would Napu know? He had done what Napu had told him to do — kept the wind on the back of his left shoulder and the seas coming under the boat from the same direction. But all around him the ocean looked the same, the seabirds looked the same, the sky looked the same.

Just as he was about to call out to wake Napu, the fishing line went taut and, with a snap, the old rubber tire tube was pulled out of the boat and stretched out across the water until Joseph was sure it would break. A moment later, a large fish leaped out of the water far behind the boat. In an iridescent blue shimmer it danced across the waves on the tip of its tail before disappearing again beneath the surface.

Joseph yelped.

Napu sat up. "What is it?" he asked, rubbing his eyes.

"A fish!" Joseph yelled. "We've caught a fish! He's jumping out of the water!"

"Good," Napu said, his voice calm, and he moved to the seat next to Joseph. He grabbed the line in both hands and began to pull it in and as he did so, the fish jumped again. "A mahi-mahi," he said, "a big one." Hand over hand he pulled it in, wrapping the line back around the fishing stick until the fish was right next to the side of the boat. Then, with a heave, he pulled it on board.

Joseph had never seen such a thing. The fish was almost as long as Napu, and Napu had to use all his strength to get it on board. They fell into the bottom of the boat together and as the fish flapped, Napu struggled to keep it from jumping back out into the ocean. He wrapped his arms and legs around it and tried to hug it to him but the fish slipped from his grasp and got its head back up on the gunwale and almost went overboard taking Napu with it. But the hook was still in its mouth and Napu had a grip on the line. He pulled hard and the fish came back down on top of him and again he wrapped his arms around it. This time he managed to get on top of it and he sat on the fish, his hands gripping its head.

Napu had won. Slowly the fish stopped struggling and as it died, its wonderful, radiant blue color faded away to a dull yellow-gray. Napu sat on it for a long time until he was certain it was dead and all that time, Joseph had remained on the seat holding onto the tiller and trying to keep the boat on course while he watched the battle. Finally, Napu sat up. He was covered with fish slime and blood, but for the first time since Joseph had met him, he smiled.

"Now we can eat," he said.

Chapter 9

Napu pulled the knife from the sheath at his hip. Its blade was long and thin and when he stuck it into the fish, Joseph saw that it was very sharp. With a few quick strokes, he cut off a thick slice of the pinkish-colored meat and without hesitating, shoved it into his mouth and began chewing. He cut off another slice and reached out to hand it to Joseph.

Instead of taking it, Joseph gagged and said, "It's—it's not cooked."

Talking with his mouth full of raw fish, Napu said, "Of course not. How could we do that? Build a fire in the boat? Take it. It is very good. It won't hurt you, believe me."

When Joseph hesitated again, Napu shrugged and stuffed the meat into his own mouth and went back to work on the fish.

Joseph watched Napu eat, waiting for him to throw it up. When Napu had swallowed his third big mouthful without difficulty, Joseph's hunger overcame his disgust. "All right. Give me some."

Napu cut a large piece of meat from the fish and handed it up to Joseph. Keeping one hand on the tiller, Joseph reached out and took it. It felt cool and wet, but it had a fresh smell that was not unpleasant. He held his breath and did what Napu had done; he stuffed the fish into his mouth and started chewing, chewing hard so he would not be able to spit it out.

At first he thought he would gag again, but the taste was the same as the smell—not unpleasant. He chewed as quickly as possible and then swallowed it. He waited for something to happen but nothing did. The fish stayed in his stomach. Napu handed him another piece and, without hesitating, he stuffed it into his mouth, chewed it quickly, and swallowed it. They did this until half the fish was gone and then Napu reached over the side of the boat and rinsed his hands. Next, he used the machete to open another coconut and again they shared the cool, sweet water inside it.

When they were finished eating, the sun was getting low in the sky and the clouds on the horizon were turning pink. The sky in the east was a deep blue that was almost black. Napu studied this, thought for a moment, and said, "I will steer now. It's time for you to rest."

"A great sailor must be able to steer for many days without rest," Joseph said. "That's what you said. I want to be a great sailor, too."

"It will be dark soon," Napu said. "You don't know how to steer by the stars yet."

"I can learn," Joseph said, "just like I learned how to do this. You can show me."

"You can steer a little while longer," Napu said, "but remember to wake me when the first star comes out. It's very important." He looked at Joseph closely and said, "You have a bad sunburn; your skin is red." He lay down again on the canvas and closed his eyes and fell asleep almost immediately.

Joseph felt his face. His skin felt sore and hot and his arms and legs were raw-looking. Still, there was nothing he could do about the sun, so to take his mind off it, he concentrated on steering the boat and watching Napu sleeping, waiting for the Spirit of the Voyage to come back out of his mouth.

Beyond Napu's head, the ocean was turning darker and darker as the sun went down and its multi-colored rays glittered off the backs of the waves. Joseph kept both hands on the tiller and kept the wind and the waves on the back of his left shoulder as he had done all day, as he waited for the first star to appear.

After what seemed like a long time, when the sun had already gone below the horizon and the sky, off to his right in the west, was nearly a blood red, he still had not seen a star. He began to think that the Spirit of the Voyage had worked some more magic and the stars were not going to come out that night and then how would they steer? But then, something made him look over his left shoulder, toward the east, from where the night was coming over them, and here he saw an ink-black sky that was filling with stars.

He felt panic rise inside him. He was supposed to have woken Napu when the first star came out. What now? Maybe it was too late. Maybe they were lost and would never find their way to the islands where there were no soldiers and no war.

"Napu, wake up," he said. "I see—I see stars."

At first Napu did not stir, but then his eyes opened and he sat up. He was looking back toward the stern of the boat, past where Joseph sat, toward the east. "You should have woken me sooner," he said.

"I didn't see them because I was looking that way, toward the sun."

Joseph was relieved when Napu did not seem to be angry and did not scold him. "Let me steer now," he said and he moved back to the stern of the boat and sat beside Joseph.

Joseph relinquished the tiller and moved down to the tarp where Napu had been. He lay down and felt the pain of the rough canvas on his sunburned back. He looked straight up. Now there were stars there, too, directly above them, and more appeared even as he watched. There were so many, how did Napu know which one would guide them to the right islands? He thought of asking him, but stopped himself; for some reason Napu did not like it when he asked him questions about such things and Joseph did not want to admit to himself that maybe Napu really did not know how to steer using the stars. What would happen to them then?

Joseph picked up the Spirit of the Voyage and studied it for a long time. He ran his hands over the sleeping face and touched the raw wound where the bullet had struck it. Before he fell asleep, he cradled the stick in his arms just below his mouth. *Maybe,* he thought, *while I'm asleep, the Spirit of the Voyage will come out of Napu's mouth and into mine and I will be a great navigator, too.*

Chapter 10

Joseph was awakened by a loud roar. He sat up. It was morning; he had slept all night without dreaming, without once waking up. The Spirit of the Voyage was still lying across his chest and now it clattered into the bottom of the boat. Napu was looking up into the sky at a plane that was circling the boat, flying just above the tops of the waves. It was a fighter plane, the kind that Joseph had seen strafing the village. As it banked around them, they could see the pilot huddled in the cockpit and could see him turning his head as he looked down on them.

"Will he shoot us?" Joseph asked.

"I don't know."

"Is he the enemy?"

"I don't know."

"What does he want?"

Napu was trying to stay calm, but his voice had been high pitched with fear and he did not answer this last question. As they watched, the plane rose higher in the sky and then banked over hard and dove straight at them. There was nothing to do but wait for what would happen next. Joseph had seen what a plane like this could do to a village. Bullets would come from the wings and rip them and the boat into pieces and the sea would swallow them.

It seemed to take forever for the pilot to decide what to do, whether the boys would live or die. The plane was a roaring black shadow as it descended on them, diving nearly straight down at them. At the last moment, when there was no time left to change his mind, the pilot pulled the plane up. The roar from the engine became a scream as it passed just over their heads. A moment later, it was climbing back up into the puffy white clouds.

For an instant, Napu and Joseph's eyes met and then they again watched the plane as it continued its steady climb until it rose above the clouds. Soon the sound of its engine was diminishing as it flew toward the horizon.

"Do you think he'll come back and kill us?" Joseph asked.

"I don't know."

"Maybe—maybe he will send a boat to come and get us?" Joseph asked.

"No, he will not do that."

"Why not? Maybe they are looking for us."

"No one is looking for us."

"How do you know that?"

"Because we don't have anyone who wants to look for us."

Joseph thought about this. Was Napu right? Was there no one who would want to come to look for them? He stared out past Napu, out toward where the plane was just now disappearing into the blue haze. At first he had been terrified because he thought the pilot was going to kill them, and now he was terrified because the pilot was leaving them. Then, out of these thoughts, the face of his uncle came into his mind and he felt tears begin to well up. He turned away and pretended to be studying the horizon so that Napu would not see that he was crying.

*****

As the day wore on, it blended into the day that had come before it and it seemed like they had been at sea forever. They never seemed to reach that far place where the sky met the ocean and there was never any end to the waves, no end to the sunlight glaring from the surface of the sea, no end to the lifting and plunging of the boat. Joseph's skin was raw and sore and his stomach rose up inside him with each wave.

Napu again trailed the fishing line from the stern, bailed the water from the bottom of the boat, and used the machete to open some coconuts to drink. Then they ate the rest of the fish that he had put under the tarp, out of the sun. Before he lay down on the tarp, Napu tied the machetes to a cleat on the inside of the boat. "We don't want them to fall overboard," he said. "Wake me when you get tired."

It was then that they noticed birds diving and flying around the boat, different birds than the large, oceanic birds that had occasionally visited them during the day. These birds were busy diving and fishing and then, as if on some silent signal, they all took off in the same direction toward the southern horizon. But Napu only glanced at them before he lay down and a few moments later, he was asleep.

*****

Napu had told Joseph to wake him when he got tired, but as Joseph watched Napu fall asleep, he was already tired. Though he had slept all night, his body ached and it was hard to sit up straight. His sunburned skin was blistered and his eyes burned and he had to fight to keep them open. Still, he did not want to admit this to

Napu. If Napu got tired, he never complained about it. If he was hungry, he never admitted it; if he was frightened, he never showed his fear. *I can never be strong and tough like Napu,* Joseph thought.

But this time when Napu fell asleep, he did not lie still and quiet as he had before. Now he began whimpering as if he was having a bad dream. Sitting up on the stern of the boat with the tiller in his hands, Joseph tried not to watch, tried not to listen. He concentrated on what he saw out across Napu's sleeping body, across the bow of the boat and out across the blueness of the sea, trying to ignore the sounds Napu was now making. It was then, when the boat was on top of a wave, that Joseph saw something strange etched against the far horizon. Were they trees? The birds had flown in this direction, but there could not be trees in the middle of the ocean. He rubbed his eyes and looked again but the boat was down in the trough of a wave and before it came back up on the back of another one, Napu's whimpering changed.

He started crying and calling out in his sleep. He called out the name of his grandmother and then seemed to be begging her for something in a language Joseph had never heard before, a language that did not sound like the one the people on Guahan spoke.

It went on for a long time. Joseph did not know what to do. He forgot about the birds and the trees in the middle of the ocean and remembered that when he was a little boy and had a bad dream, his mother would hold him and comfort him. He could not do this to Napu. Napu would be embarrassed and would get angry. Still, Napu seemed to be very frightened. He began to writhe on the tarp, twisting this way and that as he called out.

After a while, though, he stopped crying and lay still, breathing deeply. The sun beat down on them and the waves lifted the boat and dropped it again and again and again and Joseph had to work hard at the tiller to keep the wind on his left shoulder. Every time the boat rose to the top of a wave, Joseph again thought he saw the faint outline of trees far out beyond the tops of the seas but he knew this was not possible; he thought it must be a mirage like he had read about in *A Boy's Picture History of the World in One Volume*.

He got sleepier and sleepier until he was struggling to stay awake and, finally, it seemed like he was dreaming with his eyes open. He found himself full of envy for the seabirds soaring around the boat so easily on their broad wings and then disappearing into the blue sky. And then he was flying with the seabirds, flying to a place where there was a house and a bed with clean sheets. He was just going to step into a bathtub full of cool water when, through his dreaming, he saw tall coconut trees and heard a great roaring sound and then something hit him hard on the side of his head.

He opened his eyes and found he was lying in the bottom of the boat, lying at Napu's feet. He had fallen asleep and fallen off the helmsman's seat and now above him he saw the tiller, swinging wildly from side to side. Then he felt the boat rise up on the top of a wave and a moment later it turned hard on its side.

Chapter 11

Then he was in the sea. It was roaring all around him and the water was coming over his head as the seas lifted him up and dropped him down. When he rose on the top of a wave, he could see the boat near him, see it lying on its side, the sail gone, the mast nearly in the water. But he could not see Napu.

He swam hard toward the boat and tried to grab it but as he clutched at it, it turned completely over and now the bottom of it was pointing toward the sky and there was nothing to hang onto. The seas lifted them up and dropped them together, Joseph and the boat, and he called out for Napu. Then he heard Napu's voice coming from inside the overturned boat; he was trapped underneath it.

Joseph hammered on the hull with his fist and called back to him. "I'm out here, Napu! I'm out here! The boat turned over!"

There was no answer and Joseph was now too tired to hit the hull again or even to call out. But a moment later, Napu's head popped up next to Joseph. They both grabbed at the boat and found places on the gunwales to hang onto.

"What happened?" Napu sputtered. He spat seawater as the waves washed over his face.

"I don't know," Joseph gasped, trying to keep his head above water. "I was steering—and then—I—I fell into the bottom of the boat—and the boat turned over."

But Napu did not respond. He seemed to be thinking and then, with a quick heave, he tried to pull himself up on the bottom of the boat. But the bottom was slick with a green slime and sharp with barnacles and he fell back into the water and disappeared below the surface. When he came up again, he said, "It's an island."

"What?" Joseph yelled.

"Look!" Napu said.

But Joseph was behind the overturned boat and could not see what Napu was talking about.

"We're on the reef," Napu said. "Don't let go of the boat. There are bad currents here."

Then Joseph felt his foot hit something hard, something that stung. He kicked away from it and when he did, his head came up out of the water so he could see over the bottom of the boat. Then he saw them: trees, tall palm trees and white sand.

"Let's swim for it," Joseph said.

"No, the currents might carry you out to sea again. Stay with the boat."

"But it's right there!"

"No!" Napu said, "Hang onto the boat!"

They clung to the overturned boat and the seas breaking on the reef foamed and roared around them. But gradually the waves pushed them closer and closer to the island and then Joseph felt his feet touch sand.

"I can touch bottom!" he yelled and a moment later he had both feet down and he was standing, holding onto the boat and balancing himself against the tug of the currents.

Napu, shorter than Joseph, was still treading water. Joseph pushed the boat toward the shore until Napu, too, could walk on the bottom and then they both worked at pulling the overturned boat closer to the beach.

As they did this, they studied the island. It was very small, just an atoll, with a long beach fringed with palm trees. There were no houses, no thatched huts, no canoes—no sign of anyone living.

In the end, with the currents against them, they could only get the boat just inside the reef line, just past the breaking surf, before, exhausted, they let go of it and slowly waded the rest of the way up to the beach and lay down next to each other on the sand.

When he closed his eyes, Joseph felt as if the island itself was moving like the sea and he could still see the small, white clouds rushing through the endless blue sky and the sun was hot and brilliant through the tops of the coconut trees. Now, though, there were different sounds than there had been at sea. Now he could hear the surf pounding on the reef and hear the wind rustling in the palm fronds. The air was filled with the smell of vegetation and the perfume of flowers and these were the last things he remembered until he heard Napu's voice. It sounded hard and cold: "Wake up, Joseph."

Joseph opened his eyes. The sky was different. It had turned to a deep blue and the trees cast long shadows down the beach. Napu stood above him holding the machetes, one in each hand.

"It is low tide. I got the machetes from the boat. It's there. The sea washed it back out on the reef."

Joseph looked where Napu was pointing. He could see the surf breaking on the reef's edge where the water got shallow. There, with the surf breaking over it, was the boat. The waves had turned it over again so that the broken mast poked up into the sky.

"You got the machetes?"

"Yes. I'm glad I tied them to the boat. Otherwise they would have sunk to the bottom of the ocean when…" He did not finish, but he did not need to. The anger in his voice said enough.

"Did you get anything else? What about the Spirit of the Voyage?"

"You mean that carved stick? No. It must have floated away. Believe me, we need the machete more than a stick with a bullet hole in it. He hesitated for a moment and said, "Everything else is gone. All the food, all my fish hooks and line—everything." And he turned on his heel and went back into the trees.

Joseph did not watch him go. Instead, he stared down the beach past where he had been standing and he thought, *I'm the one who lost everything. I'm the one who couldn't get anything right. I wrecked the boat because I couldn't steer it. The fishing hooks are gone, the Spirit of the Voyage is gone, all because I fell asleep, because I'm so stupid.* Then he could not see the beach anymore because it was blurred by his tears and he put his face in his hands and cried.

Chapter 12

But he had seen something. Before the tears came hard and he could see nothing, he had seen something. It was black against the bright water and it was not rounded or shaped like a coconut. When the tears had almost stopped, Joseph stood up and walked down the beach toward it. It was the book—*A Boy's Picture History of the World in One Volume*—floating just beneath the surface, its pages opened and undulating with the waves as if the book had become a fish, the pages its many fins.

For a moment Joseph stared down at it in wonder, for he thought he saw his uncle's dead face staring at him from inside the book. But it was not his uncle; it was a picture of Charles Darwin, the great scientist with his great, gray beard, gazed up at him with his penetrating eyes. A moment later, Joseph had picked the book up and held it in his arms. He glanced around as if his uncle might, in fact, be standing next to him but saw only water, the white sand beach, the coconut trees, and the empty sky.

He clutched the sodden book to his chest and walked back to the shore and then back from the beach into the edge of the trees. Here the earth was covered with ground-crawling vines, dried coconuts, and big brown palm fronds that had died and fallen from the trees. He picked out a spot and set the book down carefully on its spine. He slowly opened the pages, letting them riffle in the breeze so they would dry without sticking together.

As he did this, he saw all the things he had grown up with, all the familiar people and places that he had seen in books all his life, but had never seen in person. There was a Bedouin riding a camel across a desert with the great pyramids of Egypt in the background, and there were George Washington and Abraham Lincoln, Julius Caesar and Socrates, Queen Elizabeth I and Keiser Wilhelm with his silly helmet with the spike sticking up from the top.

Though they were just pictures in a book and had been dead long before he had been born, they seemed wonderful, like long-lost family—the only family he had now. Again he felt tears well up and he wiped them away. It was okay to cry, he told himself. Hadn't Napu himself cried for his grandmother in his sleep? Yes, and Napu, he now knew, was a master navigator and seaman who had found this tiny island in the middle of the ocean and who was afraid of nothing and knew how to do everything—and still, he had cried. And then he thought, *He said I would be nothing but trouble and I have been and now he hates me—Napu hates me.*

He did not know what to do. He sat next to the book, watching the pages dry and looking again and again at all the pictures of the wonderful, familiar things in the world until the ocean had turned pink with the sunset and then darkened to black and the only thing he could see was the white of the foaming surf and it roared on and on forever. When he looked back down at the book it was almost too dark to see the pictures, but the last one he saw was of Africans sitting around a fire roasting a piece of meat.

Fire—we need fire. He thought this at the same moment he heard Napu's voice. Turning his gaze, he saw Napu's dark, shadowed figure standing over him.

"You found the book," he said. "Good. Give it to me. I'll use it to burn in the fire."

"No," Joseph said. "It's my book. We're not going to burn it."

"Give it to me," Napu said and he took a step closer, his feet kicking up sand that hit Joseph in the face.

"No," Joseph said and he picked up the book and held it away from Napu.

Then Napu kicked at Joseph and Joseph felt his foot hit him in the face and there was a hot, burning pain in his nose and then Napu was on top of him in the dark and Joseph could feel Napu's fists hitting him on the head.

"You wrecked my boat! You lost my fishing hooks and my good fishing line and my throw net is gone!" he yelled as he pounded on Joseph with his fists. "I would be better off without you. I should have left you on Guahan! I should have let the soldiers cut your head off! I'm going to burn your book!"

Joseph rolled away from Napu and covered the book with his body. He felt Napu's fists on him, on his back and on his ribs and the sand was in his mouth and he tasted blood, sweet and sticky blood, mixed with the sand.

Then Napu was sitting on Joseph's back and he grabbed Joseph's hair. "I'm going to smash your face!" he yelled. "Give me the book!"

Joseph let go of the book and, for a moment, Napu relaxed his grip. Joseph twisted around hard and in the dark he felt Napu fall away from him. Joseph got to his feet and began screaming and kicking at the shadow that he knew was Napu lying on the sand and then he fell on top of him and their fists found each other in the darkness and there was no more yelling, just the sound of their fists hitting each other's bodies.

They fought for a long time, rolling in the sand, falling against the exposed roots of the coconut trees, scrabbling in the dried vines and palm fronds. Sometimes, by sheer luck, a fist would find a mark, but mostly they missed, neither able to land a blow hard enough to really hurt the other. And then it was over. For no reason other than exhaustion, it was finished.

They found themselves lying together at the very edge of the sea and the moon was coming up and the stars were very bright in the black sky. The sound of the surf on the reef was a steady, distant roar. Breathing heavily and crying, Napu stood up and walked into the water and lay down in it and Joseph followed him. They lay near each other sobbing and panting and the water was cool on their bodies and burned where they had hurt each other and they lay there a long time and felt the small waves lap at them. Gradually their breathing slowed and their sobs diminished to nothing.

Joseph was the first to speak and he was surprised to hear his voice join the night sounds without disturbing them, as if they came from the same place: "Do you know how to build a fire?"

"Yes," Napu said, "I know how to build a fire. But we don't have any matches."

"I mean without matches. There's a picture in the book that shows how to do it," Joseph said. "It's the same way we learned in Boy Scouts."

"Good," Napu said. "We'll do it in the morning."

*****

They slept next to each other on the beach, and in the morning, Joseph was the first to wake. Quietly he picked up his machete and stood over Napu, looking down on him for a long moment without understanding what he was thinking. Then he moved away back into the trees. When Napu awoke, he found half a dozen green drinking coconuts at his feet and Joseph sitting among them smiling. The nuts had all been cut open, their tops gone, ready for drinking.

"You got some blood on your face," Napu said, "under your nose."

Joseph washed his face with seawater and they drank the nuts. When they couldn't hold any more coconut water and had eaten the coconut meat, they went out to the boat lying on her side. During the night, the tide had brought it in closer to the beach and though the tide was still high, it was easy for them to dive down to it.

All the food was gone, but they retrieved what was left inside. the bailing bucket tied to a cleat; the canvas tarp that had covered the food; the lines that had held the sail up; the sail itself, tangled in the broken mast; and, best of all, something big and white that had gotten wrapped around a thwart and was billowing out in the current.

When Napu saw it, he became very excited. "There it is! My throw net! Now we don't need the fishing hooks," he said, sputtering water as he surfaced.

"What is it?" Joseph asked.

"My fishing net. Now we can catch fish. As many as we need."

Back on the beach, they took inventory: the machetes, the bailing bucket, Napu's knife, the rags they were wearing as clothes, a throw net with lead weights attached, sixty feet of line, and the big sail.

Joseph studied the trees around them. "And there are enough coconuts to last for a long time."

"We won't need them for a long time," Napu said. "I don't think the boat is damaged too much. We can get it floating again. We'll sail away from here."

"Isn't this the island we were sailing for?"

"No. Grandmother said there is an island with people. There are no people here."

Joseph picked up *A Boy's Picture History of the World in One Volume.* Its cover was broken and wet and filthy, the pages wrinkled and thickened by water, some of them torn away from the spine. He sat down on the sail and began leafing through it. Finally, he found what he was looking for and read it out loud. "'Learning to use fire was mankind's most important early invention. Early man may have first learned to use fire after lightning started forest fires.'" "Look," Joseph said, holding the book out, "There's a picture of a cave man starting a fire just like we learned in Boy Scouts."

"Boy Scouts?" Napu asked.

"Yeah. They teach you great stuff like first aid and starting fires. You go hiking and camping and at night you tell stories around the campfire. I was a Scout once—for a little while."

"Did you go camping?"

"No. My dad was gone and Mom didn't have time to help me get all the stuff I needed—like a backpack and a sleeping bag. But we did learn to make fires at the meetings we had every week. We used to practice for the campouts."

Joseph showed Napu the picture. In it, a man dressed in an animal's hide was squatting down and holding a stick between his hands. Smoke was coming from where the stick met the ground.

"You know how to do that?" Napu asked.

Joseph stood up. He took in a breath. Now he knew something Napu didn't—he could teach him something. "It's friction that starts the fire," he explained. "You spin the stick between your hands and the end of the stick is in something called tinder—like a bird's nest or something small and dry that will catch on fire easily. We didn't do it that way though. We didn't spin the stick with our hands. We made a bow with a string and used it to spin the stick. It was easier."

What Joseph kept to himself was that he had never actually started a fire that way—none of the other Scouts had been able to do it either. They could get smoke, but they couldn't get the fire to start. In the end, they had always used a match. But instead of divulging this, he said, "Let's find something that will work as a bow. There's lots of dry stuff around here to use as tinder."

They set off together and walked into the forest of tall coconut palms. They followed a sandy track that led them deeper and deeper into the trees and then the trees stopped and they were on another beach on the other side of the atoll.

"Look," Napu said, "a lagoon."

The water in the lagoon was very different from the water that had washed them up onto the island. No surf crashed on a nearby reef; no windrows of flotsam lined the beach. Instead, it looked like a broad, calm lake. Only in the distance could they see waves breaking on an outer fringe of reef.

"I've seen pictures of a lagoon in my book," Joseph said. "Captain James Cook sailed into them. There were natives in canoes all around his ship."

But Napu did not appear to be listening. He was lost in his own thoughts. "Lagoons are full of fish," he said. "I'll get my net."

"But what about the fire?"

Napu stopped and thought for a moment. "You build the fire, I'll catch the fish. And I saw a breadfruit tree full of fruit. We can cook some on the fire." Then he turned again and ran off into the trees.

Chapter 13

They moved their salvaged treasures to the beach on the lagoon-side of the atoll and set up camp. Here the trees blocked the trade winds and provided deep, cool shade. Napu worked on untangling the throw net and then waded out into the lagoon with it hanging over his shoulder.

For a while, Joseph watched him. When Napu was out far enough, he studied the water as he folded the net on his arm until it was just so. Then, with a broad, sweeping motion, he cast it out. It opened up like a big, white wing, hung in the air for a moment, and then landed gently on the surface. He let it sink and then began to haul it in.

When Joseph saw that the net contained several shiny, flapping fish, he yelled out, "That's great!"

Napu, though, did not smile. He carried the net to shore and solemnly emptied the small fish onto the sand, where they struggled in the sun. "The lagoon has lots of fish," he said, and now, finally, he smiled. "Get the fire built and we won't have to eat them raw anymore."

Joseph knew it was now up to him. Napu had done his job, had caught fish, had again proven himself. Now it was his turn. He must build a fire. He wanted to tell Napu that he had never really made one before, but instead, he picked up his machete and walked off into the trees.

He knew what he was looking for, though: something from which to make a small bow. Any stick wouldn't do—it had to be perfect. He walked again through the small forest of tall coconut palms until he had crossed the atoll and came out onto the beach they had been washed up on the day before. Out near the reef with its endless foaming seas, he could see the sunken boat, just the top of it with its broken mast sticking up from the water. Again, a feeling of guilt and regret swept over him and he started to turn away.

But then he spied something on the beach. He recognized it as the branch of an ironwood tree that must have come from some other island and been washed ashore because he had seen no ironwood trees growing on the atoll. He picked it up and examined it;

it would make a perfect bow and it was long enough to break off a piece to use as the spinning stick. That was it. He had it all pictured in his mind.

He went back to the lagoon. Napu now had a small pile of fish set out on coconut leaves, and he was standing out in the water up to his waist getting ready to cast the net again. Joseph watched him as he fussed with getting it folded just right on his arm and then looked down into the water, watching for fish. Then, again, with one practiced motion, he flung the net outwards. When he pulled it up on shore, it had several fish struggling in its folds.

I've got to build a fire, Joseph thought. *I can't let him down.* He searched among their possessions for an appropriate string. This, too, had to be just right—not too big, not too small—and strong enough to spin the stick. He found it attached to the bailing bucket. It was a good string—strong and easy to tie. He untied it from the handle of the bucket, tied one end to the ironwood branch, bent the branch into a bow shape, and tied the string to the other end. There it was—a perfect bow.

He needed a stick. He had been concentrating so hard on the bow that he had forgotten this necessity. He untied the string from one end of the bow, broke a piece of the stick off, and then bent the longer piece back into a bow shape and retied the string. Then he took the shorter piece he had broken off and carved both ends into points.

He found a dead palm branch with a broad base where it had broken away from the tree. In this he cut a notch shaped like a V, then he set everything down near the pile of fish. Now he needed tinder—something very dry and very small—something like a bird's nest. There were a lot of birds on the atoll but they built their nests of small sticks. He needed something even smaller.

Napu approached. "Are you almost ready?"

"Yeah. You see, this is the bow. You twist the string around the stick like this." Joseph showed Napu how to wrap the string in the bow around the stick. "And then you put the stick in the notch I made in this palm stalk and push down on the top of the stick and you move the bow back and forth and the string spins the stick."

He tried to move the bow and make the stick turn, but he could not put enough pressure on the top of the stick to keep the bottom of the stick from slipping out of the notch. "I need something to put on top of the stick that I can push down on with my hand—and I need something for tinder. Something that will catch fire quickly."

"I used to burn coconut husks. Maybe they will work," Napu said and he walked away and came back with an old dried-out coconut. He hacked at it with the machete until it was broken apart and then he began pulling out the fibers inside the husk. They were like coarse, brown hair and pretty soon he had a pile of it. "How about some dried leaves?" Napu said.

They spent some time gathering these things and soon had what they thought would be enough. But Joseph was not satisfied. "My scoutmaster used to say, 'When you think you have enough, get twice as much.'" And so they gathered more old coconut husks and more dried leaves, dead branches, and driftwood until the pile was a couple of feet high.

"I guess that's plenty," Joseph finally said. "But I still need something to hold in my hand to push down on the stick."

He began looking up and down the beach and then he saw it: a big conch shell. He ran to the edge of the water, grabbed it, and held it up in triumph. "This is it! It should be just right!"

He was careful to set everything up perfectly. He set the palm frond with the notch cut into it on a solid piece of coral and he put the chopped-up leaves and dried coconut husks under it so that when he put the stick into the notch of the V it would rub against them. Then he twisted the stick into the bowstring, put the bottom point of the stick into the notch, and rested the shell on the top point. He leaned over the stick and pushed down on the shell with one hand and started to push and pull the bow with the other.

On his first few tries, the stick started spinning, but the bottom of it came out of the notch and sent the palm frond and tinder flying off into the sand. After a while, he learned exactly how hard he had to push down on the shell to keep the bottom of the stick in the notch and how hard to push and pull on the bow to keep the stick spinning.

At first, though, nothing happened. No smoke, no fire—nothing. After awhile, he found his arm was getting too tired to work the bow more than a few seconds. Finally, he dropped the bow and the stick, sat back, and rested his head on his arms. He thought, *This is never going to work. It has to work but it's not going to.*

"Let me try," Napu said, and he picked up the bow, twisted the stick in the bowstring, put the bottom of the stick in the notch and began bowing. As it had with Joseph, on the first few tries, the bottom of the stick came out of the notch and knocked the tinder and the palm frond off the coral and into the sand. But on the third try, he got the bow moving smoothly and the stick spinning fast. In a few moments, the smell of smoke reached Joseph's nostrils.

"You got it!" he yelled and he leaned in close to watch.

In another few moments, more and more smoke began coming up from where the bottom tip of the stick was spinning in the notch.

"Okay," Joseph said, "pull the stick out."

Napu stopped bowing and lifted the stick out of the notch. In the middle of the V they could see the orange glow of a tiny ember.

Joseph bent over it, put his face close, and gently blew. The ember glowed brighter and then, with a puff of smoke, went out.

But Joseph was jubilant. "We're going to do it," he said, "we're going to make fire. You're really good at the bowing, Napu. Really good."

Napu sat back and rested and Joseph took another turn. He rearranged the tinder, fitted the stick in the notch, and began bowing. This time he was more careful, starting slowly until the bow was just moving and the bottom tip of the stick was spinning smoothly in the notch. Then he began moving the bow back and forth faster and faster until he again began to smell smoke and then saw a delicate tendril of it rising from the notch.

But he did not stop. He worked steadily for another minute and then, when his arm was too tired to move anymore, he lifted the tip of the stick from the notch and dropped the bow. A small ember was again glowing in the tinder. He bent over it and blew gently. The ember glowed brighter. He picked the tinder up and held it in his hand and kept blowing. The glowing ember grew larger and larger and he blew harder. He turned the tinder a little more and then, with a suddenness that made him pull his head back, a small flame burst into life.

Chapter 14

When the sun had touched the horizon in the west, the shadows from the trees crept out over the beach and embraced the still water of the lagoon. Napu and Joseph tied the sail to the trunks of three coconut trees that leaned out over the sand and so had a shelter. Then they moved the fire close to the shelter, where its flickering light played against their faces until they were haunted by their own shadows dancing against the whiteness of the sail.

Joseph opened some coconuts and they roasted the fish by putting sticks down the fishes' throats and holding them over the fire. When there were enough hot coals, Napu laid a breadfruit on them and when it was cooked, they cut it open with the machete and feasted on the soft meat. Afterwards, they rinsed themselves off in the dark water at the edge of the lagoon and then sat by the fire.

After a long silence, Joseph said, "We did pretty good today, you know? I mean, I think we did. We got a real camp set up, and fire too, and you caught fish. We have enough to eat and drink with the fish and the breadfruit, and the coconuts and all that."

Napu did not answer him and again there was silence except for the crackling of the fire and wind in the tops of the palms and, always, the sea pounding on the distant reef.

To fill the silence, Joseph said, "And I didn't mess up again. I'm real sorry about all the trouble I caused. I feel really stupid. But you got us here—to this island. There aren't any soldiers or planes. We're safe. You really are a great navigator—like your ancestors."

Napu was playing with a stick, drawing circles in the sand between his feet. "We need to be careful about sharks in the lagoon," he said. "I saw them today—reef sharks. And we can't let the fire go out tonight." He looked up into the flames. "We need to load it up with driftwood before we go to sleep."

Then he threw the stick into the fire and hesitated for a moment as if getting up courage to say something. Then he said, "I'm not a great navigator. I never said I was. It takes a long time to become one—many years. Only a man can be one, not a boy. "

"But you found this island," Joseph said. "If I hadn't fallen asleep and messed everything up, you could have sailed us right into the lagoon."

Napu stood up and disappeared into the darkness, his feet kicking sand into the fire as he left. He was gone a long time but when he returned, he was carrying a piece of wood. At first he said nothing. He poked at the coals with the wood and sparks rose up into the darkness and the breeze carried them out over the water. Then he carefully placed the wood into the flames. "I will tell you the truth," he said, and Joseph thought he saw a great sadness in Napu's eyes. "We must, from now on, tell each other the truth. I am not a great navigator. I don't know how to steer by the stars. Until this voyage, I had never sailed that boat out on the ocean—only in the cove."

"But you are a good sailor," Joseph said, "A really good sailor. I saw you."

"Yes, I can sail the boat and I have been out on the sea before with the men from my village. But never by myself."

"But, your grandmother—you said…."

"My grandmother taught me many things, but she did not know how to use the stars to navigate a canoe across an ocean. She could not teach me that."

"But how did you get us here—to this island? You yourself told me how to steer by keeping the wind and the seas on my back and at night, to watch for the stars. You said it was in your blood."

Napu brushed the sand off his hands and, looking into the fire, said, "I thought it *was* in my blood. I thought that once I was out on the ocean and the stars were over me, I would know how to steer by them. But now I know the truth. Such things are not in one's blood. One needs to learn such things and I only know what grandmother told me—and what some of the men in the village remembered about it. But none of them could do it. That knowledge has been lost to the people of my island. It is gone from our blood. I didn't find this island—somehow this island found us."

Joseph had watched Napu's face as he spoke but now he looked away, into the fire and said, "That's what the old man—the spirit of our voyage—told me that night in the forest. The night after the war came to the island. He said I must help you find the ancient knowledge and bring it back to the island. He even knew your name." But as soon as Joseph said those words, he regretted it. Now Napu would get angry and hate him all over again.

But Napu's expression did not change. He just kept staring into the fire. Finally he said, "Tell me what the *taotaomo'na* said. My grandmother used to say that when you tell the truth, people will listen. Tell me the truth. I will listen."

Joseph watched Napu's face. The firelight created flickering shadows that moved across it and his black eyes were moist and gleaming. He thought for a moment, choosing his words, and then spoke carefully: "I already told you what happened. How I got the stick with the face carved in it. I know it's hard to believe, and maybe I was just dreaming. But that's how I remember it.

"I was in the jungle when the war came and I was really scared. I hid inside the roots of a nunu tree and after a long time, when it was getting dark, I got pretty tired and I guess I fell asleep. When I woke up, it was still dark and I saw lights and—and then people. But they weren't real people. They were ghost people—walking in the forest right in front of me. They were carrying torches and it was like a procession and the old man was in the front of it. He took a root from the nunu tree and pulled on it and it broke off. And then the root changed into a face and a body and the old ghost said that every sea voyage has a spirit and that he was the spirit of our voyage. He said I had to find you—and he said your name, he said 'Napu'—and I had to go to sea with you and together we had to learn the way the old people navigated by the stars and bring that knowledge back to this island. He said he would help us."

Napu listened quietly and then said, "I found it today."

"You found it? What?"

"The root from the nunu tree—the Spirit of the Voyage."

"You did? Where was it?"

"On the beach. On the other side. I went out to the boat again. I remembered that I had put out the fishing line before we—before we hit the reef. I thought it might still be tied to the boat and it was, but I couldn't get it back. It had sunk down and the hook had gotten stuck on the reef. It was too deep for me to dive."

"Where is the Spirit of the Voyage?"

"I threw it into the bushes. It's there somewhere. I'm sorry. I thought it was all just a story. We can get it in the morning."

"No," Joseph said, and he was surprised at the determination he heard in his own voice. "We can't leave it out there alone. Let's get it now. We'll make a torch. Let's go."

Chapter 15

They made five torches by bending dried palm leaves over on themselves so that the fronds formed a clump at the end of the stalk. They lit one and Napu carried it, leading the way back across the atoll, while Joseph followed carrying the others. Before one burned down completely, they used it to light the next one.

Now familiar with the trails they had made through the trees, they moved easily to the other side of the island. The torches, though, burned quickly. Only two were left by the time they reached the place where Napu remembered throwing the Spirit of the Voyage.

"Somewhere here," he said and he held the torch out in front of him and their eyes searched the foliage in the flickering, uneven light.

"I don't see it," Joseph said as Napu cast the torch around in half circles. "Maybe it got caught up in a tree."

"No, I didn't throw it up high. I just tossed it."

"Okay, let's look down lower."

They lit another torch from the one Napu was holding and Joseph got down on his hands and knees while Napu held the fire close.

"Here it is! I found it!" Joseph yelled over his shoulder.

There it lay in the sand at the base of a coconut tree. They saw the smooth body of the carved figure and the ragged place where the bullet had struck it. The face was peaceful, the mouth unsmiling, the eyes shut tight.

"Grab it, quick," Napu said. "The torch is burning me."

Joseph reached for it just as Napu dropped the torch into the sand and then the flames were gone; the night closed in around them.

At first, the darkness seemed to be complete. The moon had not yet risen and they were back from the beach, deep in the trees and undergrowth.

"Did you get it?" Napu asked.

"No. When I grabbed for it, it was gone. It just disappeared," Joseph said, his voice coming from the dark.

"It's got to be there," Napu said, "It can't just fly away."

Napu could hear Joseph scrabbling in the bushes, searching for the stick with his hands. And then there was a shriek from the darkness ahead of them and the bushes began snapping and breaking as if a large animal was struggling to escape. The sound rose up, higher and higher into the air, but Napu could see nothing, and still it rose until it was in the tops of the trees, like a great bird trying to fly with a broken wing.

"Joseph," Napu called, "what was that? Are you alright?"

For a moment there was no answer and then Joseph's voice again came out of the darkness. "I—I'm okay. I don't know what happened. It was a big bird, I think. It must have been sleeping. I've got sand in my eyes."

Napu felt Joseph's feet against his legs as Joseph backed out of the bushes and stood up. He held Joseph's arm and helped steady him.

"So do you have the stick?" he asked.

"No. I don't know where it went. It was there and I was reaching for it and then the torch went out and—and it was gone."

"Maybe the bird took it," Napu said.

"Maybe it was a man o' war bird," Joseph said. "They must be pretty strong. Where did it go? Could you see it?"

"It was too dark to see anything. I just heard it going up, higher and higher into the tops of the trees."

Joseph's heart was racing and he felt the now-familiar tug of fear knotting up his stomach. "Let's get back out to the beach."

This time Joseph led them. They went back through the trees holding their hands out in front of them to protect themselves from branches and stepping carefully to avoid tripping. For the first two hundred feet there was nothing to guide him but lucky guessing. Then he saw the familiar loom of the surf breaking on the reef and a moment later they were on the beach.

The stars were brilliant in the inky blackness of the night sky. The broad swath of the Milky Way arched above them from horizon to horizon and Joseph again saw the great constellations he had learned as a Boy Scout: Orion with his sword hanging from his belt, and his great hunting dog that held the brightest star, Sirius. And here he could see both the North Star and the great Southern Cross. Yet their familiarity gave him little comfort. They seemed cold and distant and he shuddered.

Then he heard Napu's hard whisper: "Look! Look there!"

Joseph pulled his eyes away from the heavens and looked at Napu to see where he was pointing. In the darkness, just the shadow of his silhouette was visible. But it was not Napu that caught his eye; it was what Napu was pointing at. In the trees where they had just been, there was a glowing light and as they watched, it moved as if someone was walking among the trees carrying a dimly glowing torch.

"What is it?" Joseph whispered back.

But Napu was speechless; he could not answer. They both watched as the light moved past them and then moved away out across the atoll toward where they had built their camp. A moment later it was gone, lost among the trees.

"It was a *taotaomo'na*! It went to our camp! What do we do now?" Napu asked, and Joseph heard real fear in his voice.

"I think it's him, the old man—the Spirit of the Voyage," Joseph said, matter-of-factly. "Maybe he'll be there when we get back to camp." He was working hard to sound unfazed by the ghostly light, but his throat was so dry it was difficult to swallow.

"I don't want to go back to camp now," Napu said. "Let's stay here for the night. It'll be okay. It's not going to rain. We can sleep out here on the beach."

"The fire will go out," Joseph reminded him, "and we might not get it started again. We might have been lucky the first time. Let's go. We have to."

But it was Napu who took the first step back toward camp and Joseph regretted that he had been so convincing. He took in a deep breath and followed him. They walked up the small incline of the beach and then were in among the tall palm trees whose tops whispered in the wind far above them. All their senses were alert as they stopped every few feet to listen and watch.

Once away from the beach, the darkness took them in again. They walked blindly through the trees and vines holding onto each other with one hand and keeping a free hand out in front of them. But the atoll was small and in a few minutes they saw the flickering of their fire through the foliage.

They stopped and watched for a long time but saw nothing—no old ghost stood within the small circle of light cast by the flames. They moved closer, stepping carefully so as not to make a sound, and in a few moments were back in camp. The sail was still stretched between the coconut trees, their small pile of possessions lay undisturbed next to the fire, and the fire itself still burned with a strong flame.

"There's nobody here," Joseph said, but still he stayed close to Napu and for several minutes they did not sit down at the fire, but stood together, their eyes searching the darkness beyond the firelight.

"It was nothing," Napu finally said. "Probably just the reflection of a star off the water."

In his heart, Joseph did not believe this but he said, "Yeah, that's probably right." Then he said, "Let's build the fire up so it doesn't go out while we're sleeping."

Staying close together, they moved off into the darkness. Each carried back an armful of sticks and dried coconut husks, which they stacked next to the fire and then began to add to the flames, piece by piece, until the blaze rose high into the night sky.

They had worked quietly, without speaking, but then Napu asked, "Do you think that someone living on those stars can see our fire?" He threw one last piece on the blaze.

"I don't think so," Joseph said. "In *A Boy's Picture History of the World in One Volume* it says that when scientists first figured out how fast light traveled, they realized it took a real long time for the light to get to Earth from the stars. Maybe hundreds or even millions of years. Anyway, no one can live on a star. It's too hot."

Napu sat down in the sand and stared into the roaring flames. "Can I look at it?"

"Look at what?"

"At the book?"

When Joseph hesitated, Napu said, "I won't throw it in the fire. I promise."

Joseph ducked under the sail-shelter and retrieved the book from the base of a tree. He handed it to Napu and sat down beside him. Napu opened the water-wrinkled pages and began to slowly leaf through them.

When he came to a picture of a dinosaur, he stopped. For a long time he said nothing and then said, "I saw a picture of one of those before."

"That's a brontosaurus," Joseph said. "It was the biggest dinosaur."

On the next page were two more dinosaurs. "That's a tyrannosaurus rex fighting with a stegosaurus."

Napu studied the page carefully and Joseph moved closer and read aloud what was written under the picture. *This large carnivorous dinosaur lived 65 million years ago in what is now western North America.*

"Do you think there are any still alive?" Napu asked.

"No. They're all extinct."

"They're what?"

"They're all dead."

"Yes, that is right," Napu said, nodding.

He flipped through the pages until he came to the drawing of the cave man starting the fire with a stick. He pointed to it and said, "That's how we did it. Well, kind of how we did it."

Napu nodded again and handed the book back to Joseph. "I'm going to sleep," he said, and he crawled underneath the shelter and lay down on the sand. "Tomorrow we will weave some sleeping mats."

Before he lay down, Joseph said, "I think it was just a bird—or a star."

"What was?"

"What we saw tonight—over there on the other side of the island."

Napu nodded. "Yes, I think so, too."

"I'll check the fire during the night," Joseph said. "We've got to make sure it doesn't go out."

If Napu heard Joseph, he did not acknowledge it, and when Joseph looked at him, his eyes were closed as if he had already fallen asleep. Joseph lay down in the sand near him and put *A Boy's Picture History of the World in One Volume* under his own head for a pillow. He watched the fire and then stared up at the sail that was stretched over them and then he tried to look out past the fire into the darkness but he could see nothing, and all he could hear was the low, endless roar of the surf on the distant reef.

Chapter 16

Something woke him—a whisper or a fluttering or something moving over him without touching him. It was still dark. The fire still blazed as high as it had when they had fallen asleep. *Napu*, he thought, *must have gotten up and put more wood on it*. He seemed to be sleeping soundly enough. Joseph started to say something, but stopped himself. He lay back down and closed his eyes.

When he woke again, he knew he had been sleeping for a long time because he was stiff and his head had slipped off the book and sand was stuck to his cheek and the sunburned skin on his side was sore from lying on the coarse sand. He sat up, wiped his cheek clean, and looked at the fire. The flames were still burning high as if someone had just put more wood on it. He glanced at Napu, who had rolled over on his side, facing away from Joseph.

He still heard only the ocean, but now the moon was up, a thick, yellow crescent that sent a path of light over the lagoon, right to their resting spot. He watched this for awhile and thought about his uncle and his mother and how they all seemed far away in some distant past. He did not cry now, but instead closed his eyes and drifted away again into a deep sleep.

*****

Waking, Joseph heard Napu talking to someone, telling them about the throw net. He kept his eyes closed and listened.

"It is a very expensive net," Napu was saying. "It belonged to my uncle. My uncle is dead, but he showed me how to use it. I can catch a lot of fish with it."

Joseph sat up. It was early morning. The sun had just risen from the sea and the lagoon stretched out before him, rippling with the morning breeze, sparkling a bright, cool blue. At its far edge, the surf on the reef sent up small explosions of foam. Joseph felt damp and he was covered with sand. He could not see whom Napu was talking to. He was folding the net carefully on his arm, getting ready to go fishing, but no one else was there.

Joseph sat up and rubbed his eyes. The fire was burning high, the flames reaching into the air. "Who are you talking to?" he asked.

Napu kept fussing with his net. He did not look at Joseph. "The Spirit of the Voyage," he said.

Joseph came out from under the sail and stood up. "What?" he asked.

But then he saw what Napu meant. The root of the nunu tree with its sleeping face was there, standing upright, stuck in the sand near the fire.

"Where did you find it?"

"What do you mean?" Napu said. "You must have found it. It was there when I woke up this morning."

"No," Joseph said, and he pulled the stick from the sand and turned it over in his hands, examining it. "It wasn't me. I was asleep all night."

Now Napu stopped fiddling with the net and stared at Joseph, stared at him long and hard and said, "I don't believe you." He turned and waded out into the lagoon to fish.

Still holding the Spirit of the Voyage, Joseph ran out after him, his legs splashing the clear water. But he stopped before he got too close. He did not want Napu yelling at him for scaring the fish away. "I'm not lying. We said we weren't going to lie to each other anymore, remember? And I'm not. But now you have to tell me the truth. Why didn't you get me up to help with the fire during the night. You shouldn't have done it all by yourself."

Napu turned and their eyes met across the water. "I never got up. Not once. Whenever I woke up, the fire didn't need any wood. That's why I thought you had found the Spirit of the Voyage—while you were out getting firewood."

"That can't be," Joseph said. "I didn't put wood on it either. I thought…."

He felt the smoothness of the Spirit of the Voyage in his hands. It was heavy and solid and the expression on the sleeping face gave away nothing. He watched Napu cast the net and then turned and waded back to shore. He stuck the stick back into the sand near the fire where they had found it.

Napu carried the first net full of fish up onto the sand. The fish were small and their bodies fluttered in the sun. When Napu dumped the net out, Joseph gathered the fish up, rinsed them off one by one, and placed them carefully on palm fronds they had spread on the sand near the fire.

"That's enough, I guess," Joseph said.

"No," Napu answered as he began folding the net over his arm again. "We can smoke them and eat them later—when we leave here in the boat."

Joseph felt his heart sink in his chest as it always did when he thought about the boat. Even at low tide, the water around it was chest deep. He did not think it would be possible to move it up to the beach or to get it floating again. *But Napu must know,* he thought, *Napu is a sailor.*

"I'm going to get some more coconuts," Joseph said and he picked up his machete and walked back into the trees.

He usually enjoyed going back into the small jungle of vines and bushes that grew in the middle of the atoll. It was shady and cool and the sound of the wind in the palms was somehow comforting. But now, this morning, after the night by the endless fire and the mysterious appearance of the Spirit of the Voyage, it was all different; today the jungle felt haunted by spirits.

In the whispering of the wind through the tops of the palm trees, he heard something he had not heard before—was it a threat? A warning? Was it the *taotaomo'na?* In the shadows cast by the trees he now saw shapes that he did not recognize, movements that startled him and made his heart race. Even the machete felt different, as if it had an energy that he could not completely control—as if it were alive. He tried to push these thoughts away. He told himself that Napu was fooling with him. He must have found the Spirit of the Voyage and he must have gotten up during the night and put wood on the fire.

He found a low-growing coconut tree with big, green, drinking nuts close enough to the ground that he only had to climb up the trunk a few feet and then swing the machete over his head to cut them down. But before he started, he hesitated. The wind moving through the tree sounded like voices. It reminded him that he should ask permission from the tree before he took its coconuts. Maybe the spirits of the ancestors were here, too, and would not be happy about his taking what belonged to them. "Please forgive me," he said out loud to the tree, "but I must ask you to share your coconuts."

Still, the wind in the palm leaves did not sound happy. He heard voices that sounded like warnings, but saw nothing. He picked out a low-hanging nut, shinnied up the trunk a few feet, and swung the machete at its stalk. The blade dug in deep and stuck there. Joseph's legs lost their grip in the trunk and he started to slide back down to the ground. He tried to hang onto the machete's handle, but his hand slipped off and he fell down hard on his side. When he looked up, he saw the machete falling down towards him.

He rolled to his side and put out his hands to protect himself, but the blade struck him in the back of his leg, just below his knee. He felt the edge of it cut into him, felt the sting, and saw the blood. The weight of the machete pulled the blade from the wound. A moment later it lay in the sand with dead palm leaves next to him.

He stared at the bloody blade of the machete and at his wound. The blade had cut him deeply and the blood welled up and began dripping on the dried leaves that lay around him. He yelled out, "Napu! Come here! Help me!"

As soon as he said the words though, he knew that Napu would never hear him. By now he was standing out in the lagoon casting his net and would not be able to hear him over the sounds of the wind and the waves on the reef.

At first he did not know what to do. The blood was flowing freely and watching it made him feel dizzy. He tried to remember what he had read in his Boy Scout manual about first aid training— *stop the bleeding, treat for shock*—what else? How would he stop the bleeding? What did the book say about that? It came to him. He could see the words: *Apply pressure.* He had nothing to put on the wound except his shorts and they were filthy. In desperation, he put his right hand over it and pressed. The blood oozed out from under his palm but he held it and pushed harder.

He would have to get back to camp and get Napu to help him. He would have to stand up, have to walk. He tried to get up but fell back and found himself looking up into the trees. He was dizzy and weak and there were spots dancing in front of his eyes. Then the trees and the sky faded away and there was nothing.

*****

He heard the wind first. It rustled the palm fronds far above his head, and he again saw the blue sky through the fronds and the low-scudding white clouds and the brilliant sun coming down through the shadows. Then he remembered. He looked at his leg. The bleeding had stopped but there was a large, wet, black-red place in the sand where the blood had soaked in.

He wanted to jump up and run back to camp and to Napu but he still felt weak and dizzy. Maybe he had lost a lot of blood. Maybe he was dying. He felt scared and his heart was pounding hard. He lay back down and waited. *Do not panic. Do not panic.* He repeated the words over and over again, whispering them through his dry lips. After awhile his head stopped spinning and he tried to get up again, this time more slowly.

He was able to get to his feet by pushing himself up against the coconut tree. He saw the machete lying on the ground near the blood-soaked sand, but he knew he could not bend over to pick it up. He took a step away from the tree and found he was able to walk. He moved slowly, step by step, placing one foot in front of the other. His leg started bleeding again, but it was just an oozing now, sending a trickle down his calf.

When he started to feel dizzy, he pulled his eyes up away from the wound and watched the trees around him. He limped from tree to tree, stopping at each one to rest, leaning against it until he felt strong enough to move on. Finally, he saw the white sail tied between the trees and the smoking fire. In the lagoon beyond it he saw Napu standing out, far from shore, his body a dark silhouette against the bright water.

Joseph stumbled into camp and lay down under the sail. He had remembered something else from the Boy Scout manual—elevate the wound. He placed his leg on an empty coconut shell. The cut was oozing freely now and drops of blood were being soaked up by the sand under it. He wanted to call out to Napu but felt too weak. He would come back in soon, anyway. He lay his head back and closed his eyes.

Chapter 17

He heard Napu calling for him excitedly. "Come see what I've got. I got a big trigger fish." Then a pause. "What happened to you? What's wrong?" and he felt Napu at his side.

Joseph opened his eyes. "My machete—it fell out of a coconut I was trying to cut down. It cut my leg. Bad."

But Napu was already looking at the wound and the bloody stain on the tarp under it. "You're right, that's pretty bad," he said, and then he just stared at it.

"I think I lost some blood."

"Yeah, maybe you did. How do you feel?"

"I feel kinda weak—and I get dizzy when I try to get up."

Napu did not take his eyes from the wound. "My uncle cut himself once—with a machete. It was like this one. Pretty deep. They took him to the doctor and got it sewed up."

The boys looked at each other. There was no doctor here. Joseph felt his eyes fill with tears. "What are we going to do?"

Napu was thinking. "When I cut myself, my grandmother always took care of me. We never went to the doctor. She always cleaned it up. Poured medicine on it and put a bandage on it. You'll be okay. I can fix it up."

"How? We don't have any medicine. We don't have anything."

Napu moved out from under the sail and stood up. "I know I can fix it up. I know I can. I just have to think."

Joseph closed his eyes and tried to listen to the sounds of the island—the wind in the palm trees, the sea breaking on the reef. But then he started crying and there was nothing he could do to stop himself and he wondered what Napu would think of him, crying like a little kid.

But Napu did not seem to notice. He was busy. He took the rusty, dented bailing bucket and filled it with seawater and brought it back to the camp. He set the bucket down in the sand and began to poke at the fire with a stick until he'd made an open space among the glowing coals, into which he set the bucket of water.

Then, hearing Joseph crying, Napu came in under the sail and sat beside him. He put his hand on his shoulder and said, "You're going to be okay. I'm going to boil some water and we'll pour it on the cut and that will clean it out and then we'll put some coconut water on it. My grandmother said coconut water was good for just about everything."

Joseph opened his eyes. "I'm real thirsty."

"Yeah, okay. I'll get you some coconuts. I'll be right back."

"Napu, I don't want to die."

"What? That's crazy, Joseph. You got a cut. Lots of people get cuts. Maybe later you can die, when you're old or something, but not now. I need you here to help me. I'm going to take care of it."

When Napu came back with the coconuts, he had Joseph's machete. "I found the tree you were going to cut the coconuts from and I saw your blood in the sand. I got your machete."

Joseph, almost asleep, made no answer but watched as Napu lopped the top off a coconut. When Napu put an arm around his shoulder and helped him sit up, Joseph gulped at the sweet, cool water, a lot of which dribbled down his chin.

"Hey, drink slow," Napu said, "we got plenty."

When Joseph had drunk all he could, he lay back down and closed his eyes. In a short time, he was asleep.

*****

For the next three days, Napu took care of Joseph. He cooked fish, breadfruit, and papaya and presented them to Joseph on small mats he wove from palm leaves. He kept a supply of open coconuts nearby so Joseph could reach them easily, and always he kept the fire built up. At night, he sat next to Joseph and together they watched the flames and Napu told stories of big fish he had caught. When the flames were high enough, Joseph read aloud from *A Boy's Picture History of the World in One Volume.*

But by the evening of the third day, the wound did not seem to be healing. It had turned red and swollen and was beginning to ache and by the next night, Joseph had a fever. He was shaking with chills but there was nothing to cover him with and Napu sat next to him and comforted him as best he could by singing old island songs that his grandmother had sung to him when he was sick.

"I hurt pretty bad," Joseph said. "I need a doctor or maybe I'm going to die. Maybe there's a ship out there somewhere. If we build the fire up, they might see us and come and help me."

Then he said, "Look, out there, Napu. There's a ship. It's coming this way."

Napu looked out from under the shelter, out toward the ocean, but it was dark now and the sea was an impenetrable blackness.

*****

Joseph's fever rose higher and higher and he began to hear voices as if people were talking to him. He fell asleep watching the flames of the fire dancing across the sail stretched over his head and listening to Napu's soft voice singing in his strange language. He felt himself floating up from the ground and then he was looking down on himself and he could see everything perfectly—the fire, the sail stretched out between the coconut trees, Napu's small, brown body sitting next to his own still form.

He wondered at it all, wondered how he could be flying above the earth, and wondered at how good it felt to be free to drift on the breeze like a seabird. Far beyond him, he saw the stars in their now-familiar patterns and they no longer seemed cold and far away. Instead they seemed to be calling to him to come up with them and be one of them, to shine forever in the night sky and guide sailors across the vast oceans. He tried calling out to them but his voice was weak and when he tried to fly up to them, his arms were not strong enough and he felt very tired.

But then he saw something else below him; someone was standing next to the fire. It was the figure of a man, a man with no head who wore only a loincloth around his hips. He carried a long stick covered with blood. And even though he had no head, Joseph could hear him laughing and then he raised the bloody stick over his head and from the hole in his neck where there was no head, Joseph heard a shriek that filled the darkness. It came up to where Joseph hung in the air and rushed past him like a strong wind and as Joseph watched, it moved the stars in the heavens, scattering them and putting their lights out, one by one.

Joseph heard his own voice calling out to the stars, begging them to come back, to help him and Napu find their way home. But his small voice was lost in the emptiness of space and as he watched, the headless man stepped under the sail where Joseph's body lay sleeping. He lifted the bloody stick and began to swing it down on him to stab him through his heart.

Then Joseph saw something coming from the darkness, from the black, still water of the lagoon itself. It was the ghost of the old man—the Spirit of the Voyage—and it stepped into the circle of firelight. He, too, wore only a cloth around his hips and he was dripping wet. In his hands, he, too, carried a long, sharp stick and now he called a challenge to the headless man and the headless man turned away from Joseph's sleeping body. He came out into the firelight and screamed through the hole in his neck and swung his stick at the Spirit of the Voyage. And so they fought, back and forth across the fire, sending cascades of sparks up into the night air, screaming and swinging their sticks until the darkness was filled with sounds of their battle.

Floating above this, Joseph watched and wondered how Napu could sit so quietly under the sail, staring into the fire and singing in his low voice as if he could not hear the fighters' shrieks or see them lunging at each other.

Nor did Joseph's sleeping self wake up and watch the struggle. Yet the fight was a great one, and for a long time neither the headless man nor the Spirit of the Voyage could gain the advantage until, with a wild cry, the Spirit of the Voyage came straight at the headless man, his stick held out before him, his bulging eyes filled with the firelight. His stick struck the headless man full in his chest, knocking him backwards into the fire, and the fire raged upwards around him until Joseph thought the blaze would set the world on fire. A moment later, with a screech of rage and pain, the headless man was gone, consumed by the flames.

Then, in a thunderous voice, the Spirit of the Voyage called up to Joseph, "Come back now. The Spirit of Death is gone."

Joseph looked at himself sleeping under the sail and he floated back down and went back into his body.

*****

Then it was morning. In the bright sunlight, shadows of the palm trees played across the sail. For a long time Joseph lay watching them until he realized he was awake and Napu was not there next to him.

The fever and the pain were gone. The wound was wrapped in something that looked like wet bark and leaves tied on with string made from coconut husk fibers. It was no longer throbbing. His head felt clear and good and he wanted to laugh. Then he remembered his dream. The fire was still burning brightly and next to it, still stuck deep in the sand, was the root of the nunu tree—the Spirit of the Voyage. Its eyes were now closed, its face serene.

He sat up and looked out beyond the fire toward the lagoon. He smiled when he saw Napu's dark figure standing waist deep in the water, his fishing net slung over his arm. The water was a bright blue and the sunlight sparkled from its surface, sending millions of beams of light back out toward the sky, and Joseph wondered if the stars would catch this light and be strong again and some day guide them away from this island.

*****

When Napu came in from fishing, he dumped a net full of fish on the mat he had woven from pandanus leaves and came under the shelter. "How are you, Joseph? You look better."

Joseph was sitting up against the trunk of a coconut tree. He smiled. "I think my fever's gone. Thanks for putting that—that thing on my leg last night. I think it really helped."

Napu examined Joseph's leg and shook his head. "I did not do that. I saw it this morning when I got up. I thought you had done it."

"Come on, you're kidding with me," Joseph said.

"No, I'm not. I'm telling you the truth. I did not do it."

"Do you think the *taotaomo'na* did it?"

"I don't know."

"Did you see them last night?" Joseph asked.

"No."

"They had a fight here, right over the fire. At first I thought it was a dream because of my fever, but—but they were here. The Spirit of the Voyage beat the bad *taotaomo'na*. He pushed him in the fire and then he was gone."

Napu looked at the Spirit of the Voyage, still stuck in the sand near the fire, its eyes closed. It did not appear to have moved.

"When they were fighting," Joseph went on, "I left my body and was floating above the fire—up there. I could see us down here—you and me. And when the fight was over, the Spirit of the Voyage told me I could come down, that it was safe. Then I came down and went back into my body and woke up and that stuff was on my leg and you were out fishing."

Napu shrugged. "Maybe it was a dream, maybe it wasn't, I don't know. There is no way to tell. I didn't see anything, but I know this: My grandmother said the *taotaomo'na* are powerful. You are lucky the good one won the fight. If the bad spirit had won— who knows." He turned to leave the shelter.

"You know about *taotaomo'nas*, right, Napu?"

"Yes, I know about them. My grandmother told me about them."

"I want to thank him." He pointed at the Spirit of the Voyage. "He saved me, you know? And put this stuff on my leg and made me get better."

Napu was watching the Spirit of the Voyage, waiting for it to move or to breath—to do something. "That's a good idea."

"How can we do it?" Joseph asked.

Napu thought for a moment and said, "I think we can have a ceremony." And then he sat down and looked at the fire and at the stick and at the shiny fish lying on the pandanus mat. He turned to Joseph and said, "Yes. It will be a fire ceremony. We can thank the *taotaomo'na* by putting things in the fire. It will burn up and go to the spirits." His voice began to sound excited.

Joseph said, "We'll do it tonight. We'll build the fire way up and throw stuff on it for the Spirit of the Voyage. It'll be stuff that helped keep us alive. Stuff like coconuts and fish. Stuff like that."

"Coconuts are too big," Napu said. "But we can throw small pieces of coconut meat on the fire."

"Offerings!" Joseph said, and now he heard the excitement in his own voice. "Things the Spirit of the Voyage would like to eat, or things he could use—like pieces of rope." Joseph gazed down at his leg, touched it, and said, "Napu, did you ever have a brother?"

"No, I had a sister, but she died when she was a baby."

"I never had a brother either, and so, I was thinking. In America, two Indians, if they saved each other or something, would make themselves brothers—blood brothers. They'd make a small cut on their arms and then tie them together so their blood mixed together and then they were blood brothers forever."

Napu frowned. "I don't think it's such a good idea to cut ourselves." He glanced at Joseph's leg.

"We don't need to actually cut ourselves. We could just tie our arms together with something and—and…."

"And hold our arms over the fire—just for a second," Napu said. "Would that make us brothers?"

"Sure. We'd be fire brothers!" Joseph said.

*****

They spent the afternoon preparing for the ceremony. Napu smoked the fish over the fire and gathered more firewood. Joseph sat in the shade of a coconut tree and made the offerings. He cut open a coconut and dug out some of the white meat and put it on a banana leaf. He chopped up pieces of the shell and then made a small piece of coconut fiber rope the way Napu had shown him, by rolling pieces of the coconut husk on his thigh until they braided themselves together to form a string. Then he borrowed Napu's knife and carved an effigy of the headless *taotaomo'na* out of the stalk of a palm frond. They lay all this next to the fire on a pandanus mat that Napu wove for the ceremony.

*****

When night came, it came quickly. The breeze died and the darkness spread out from the sky and then from the trees and over the lagoon. Joseph found that, if he was careful, he could walk, and they went down to the beach and watched as the sea closed around the sun, and the sun sent tendrils of red and orange light up from the water into the gathering blackness.

When the sun was gone and the lagoon lay flat and the surf on the reef seemed to fall quietly back into itself, they went back to the fire. First, they each picked a piece of burnt wood from the ashes and painted each other's faces with soot, putting dark smudges under their eyes and black lines across their cheeks. Then they piled driftwood on the fire and waited until the flames were leaping high in the air.

Joseph rolled up the pandanus mat on which they had placed the offerings—the coconut meat, the shells, the string, and some hair from each of their heads—and each taking an end, they lifted it over their heads.

Napu began to sing a song in Chamorro, the ancient language of his people, and when he was finished, Joseph stared into the flames and then up into the sky at the stars and said, "Thank you, Spirit of the Voyage, for helping us get away from the soldiers, for helping us cross the sea, for helping us catch fish, for bringing us to this island, for not letting us drown on the reef, and for killing the bad spirit and fixing my leg." Then they tossed the mat into the flames and watched as the fire consumed it.

Without thinking about it, they began moving slowly around the fire and as they moved Napu began to chant in his own language, repeating the same words over and over. When Joseph had heard them enough times, he began chanting the words, too, and they walked around and around the flames.

When the fire had died down, they reached across it and gripped each other's forearms. Joseph took a long piece of rope he had woven from coconut husks and with their other hands they took turns wrapping the rope tightly around their arms, tying them together.

Joseph said, "Napu, you taught me a lot of things. Without you I would be—I think maybe I would be dead."

Napu hesitated for a moment and then said, "Thank you, Joseph. I am sorry if I lied to you and sorry that I got mad at you because you did not know how to fish or sail a boat. You taught me how to make fire and the *taotaomo'na*, the spirits of my ancestors, gave you the Spirit of the Voyage and told you to come and help me learn to navigate by the stars. At first I did not believe you, but now I see that I need you just as you need me—we need each other. So now, because it is what the *taotaomo'na* and the Spirit of the Voyage want, we are brothers—fire brothers."

The smoke from the fire reached up into the sky and was carried away on the breeze, and Joseph's eyes followed it. "Hey," he said, "there's that big red star that looks like it's on fire. It's the only thing I remember about my father. When I was little, he used to take me out and look at the stars and there was one he used to call the fire star. Maybe that's it. We can be brothers of both the fire and the stars—brothers of the fire star."

They looked at the fire and then up at the star and they looked at each other across the fire and then at their arms, bound together over the flames.

"Look at your arm," Napu said.

"What do you mean?"

"Look at it. You don't have a sunburn anymore. Your skin is dark brown from the sun. It's almost as dark as mine."

For a long moment they stared at their arms and then Joseph said, "There's not much difference between us now. Maybe we really are brothers."

Chapter 18

Joseph's leg healed quickly and he never again saw the spirits fighting by the fire. Soon he was able to join Napu in collecting firewood and coconuts, papaya and breadfruit, and they settled into a routine. The days seemed to blend together, day into night, night into day, and there was no need to keep track of weeks or months. Instead, they ate and slept and woke up according to the natural cycles of the sun as every day it rose from behind the distant edge of the water, traveled through its great arc, and then slid once more into a dark red sea. And by turns, the moon grew full and then slowly disappeared and then grew again and Napu and Joseph found that the success of his fishing depended on these cycles and that they could live by them as did the creatures around them.

When the wet season came, the sudden, furious downpours filled the stretched sail with fresh water and from it they drank, filled empty coconut shells, and washed the salt and sand from their bodies.

Every night, they lay awake and watched the fire burn down and the stars emerge from the many-colored heavens and they wondered at their numbers and made up their own stories about the constellations.

Some of stars they knew. Joseph knew the planet Venus and could pick out the Big Dipper and the North Star. Napu, who had grown up under more southern skies, showed Joseph the great Southern Cross that each evening rose and moved serenely across the bottom of the world. But their favorite constellations were Orion the Hunter and his hunting dogs and the terrible and beautiful Scorpion with its glowing red heart—the fire star—that began rising in the east as the dry season grew older.

Joseph found it was true what Napu had said about his grandmother. He had learned many things from her and now he taught them to Joseph. He showed Joseph how to weave a mat from pandanus leaves and a hat from palm fronds, how to eat the tender shoots of the young coconut tree, and how to eat a coconut at any stage of its growth. He taught him how to choose a good drinking nut, how to climb a coconut tree and get the nuts without having

to use a machine. He showed him how to soak the fibers of the coconut husk in salt water and weave them into rope by rolling them
on his thigh, and how to catch and cook the coconut crabs whose
burrows were scattered everywhere around the atoll. And best of
all, how to cook the fish, crabs, and breadfruit in coconut milk for
a special treat.

When the moon was full and the tide was high, Joseph liked
to walk along the edge of the far side of the lagoon. One night, he
saw a great creature struggling from the water and onto the beach.
It was a big sea turtle and in the bright moonlight, he could see the
trail its body left in the sand, like a message from the sea written in
a strange language.

He came up next to her and watched her make her ponder-
ous way up from the water. She—and he knew it must be a female
come to lay her eggs—did not seem to notice him, or at least she
ignored him. Once above the reach of the tides, she stopped and
rested and then began digging in the sand with her front flippers.
The sand flew away in small cascades and as soon she had dug a
hole deep enough for her body, she used her back flippers to dig a
smaller hole under her. And then the eggs began to tumble out into
the smaller hole.

Joseph lay in the sand next to her so he could watch closely,
and still she seemed to ignore him. The eggs poured out into the
moonlight, glistening wet and glowing, until she had nearly filled
the smaller hole. Without a glance back at them, she covered them
and then turned and began her struggle to reach the sea.

Later, when Joseph told Napu what he had seen, Napu said,
"What? You should have come and gotten me. We could have
turned her over on her back so she couldn't get away."

"Why? What would we want to do that for?"

"We could eat her. Turtles have good meat. My uncles used to
catch them sometimes."

Joseph felt a real horror rise up and clutch at his heart. "No! I
could never kill a turtle."

"Why not? They live in the sea like a fish. We can eat them like
a fish."

"But they're not fish. They're turtles. I had a pet turtle once. A
little green one."

Napu was sitting by the fire weaving a hat from palm leaves.
He laughed at this. "A pet turtle?"

"Yeah. His name was Simon. He got pretty big, too."

"What did you do with him when he got big?"

Joseph hesitated and said, "Well, he wasn't as big as a sea turtle,
but he got pretty big—and then my teacher said I should let him go
in a pond, so I did."

"You see," Napu said, "you should have eaten him after he got big. Too bad."

Joseph felt the blood rise into his face. "No. I wouldn't eat Simon and I would never eat a turtle."

Napu was carefully weaving the palm leaves and then pulling them tight until he had the shape of the hat just right. It had a broad brim and a conical top. "Here," he said, "try this on. I made it for you because your nose is always red from the sun."

Joseph took the hat and turned it over in his hands a few times and then put it on his head. "It's a little tight."

"That's okay," Napu said, and he reached up and pressed it down farther on Joseph's head until it touched his ears. "Just wear it that way for a while. The coconut leaves are still green. It will stretch out, and then, when it dries, it will fit perfectly. Anyway, we could eat the eggs."

"What?"

"The turtle eggs. They taste good."

"No, I want to watch them hatch and then keep one for a pet. Like Simon."

"Joseph, I don't think you can keep a sea turtle for a pet. They're not the same as that turtle you had. They need to be out in the ocean. That's where they live. You keep a sea turtle for a pet and it will die pretty soon, I think."

"Well, I'll just keep him for a little while. Then I'll let him go."

"Okay, keep one. But we can eat the other eggs."

Joseph thought for a moment. He could not imagine eating any eggs except chicken eggs. "I don't know. Just one turtle might get lonely. When it hatches, you know?"

"I don't think turtles get lonely. They live all alone way out in the ocean all their lives," Napu said. "Come on, show me where the nest is. We can eat some and leave some there. You got to learn to eat anything we can if we're going to live on this island forever."

"Forever?" Joseph had never thought of that. It already seemed as if they had been there forever. "You don't think we're ever going to get off this island?"

Napu shrugged. "I don't know. Maybe someday somebody will find us. But I don't care anymore. Come on. Let's go get some of the eggs."

Joseph led Napu around the atoll and out to the beach where the turtle had laid her eggs. It was easy to find the spot and in a few minutes, while Joseph watched, Napu had dug down into the sand and uncovered them.

"Hey, there must be more than a hundred eggs in here. Look."

Joseph knelt down in the sand and looked into the hole. The eggs were clustered in a pile just as he had seen them before the turtle covered them over. Napu brushed the sand off them, then picked one up and handed it to Joseph. It was white and about the size of a ping pong ball and had a soft, leathery skin.

"We can take some of these," Napu said. "There are plenty. I don't think one of them will get lonely."

He reached in again and this time scooped up a handful and set them in the sand next to him.

"How are we going to cook them?" Joseph asked.

"Cook them? No, just eat them raw, like the fish."

Joseph made a face. "I don't want to eat a raw egg."

"Okay, then. We can put them in the fire. I think they will cook pretty fast."

*****

They each carried a handful and went back to camp. Napu cleared a place in the fire so there was a bed of hot coals but no flames. He set the eggs on them.

"There. Just give them a few minutes."

When he thought they were done, he took two sticks and lifted one out of the fire. "Here," he said, "try this one."

Joseph held out a flat piece of broken seashell and Napu set the egg on it. When Joseph hesitated, Napu said, "Go on. Try it. It's good."

"How do I open it?"

"Here, watch."

Napu lifted another egg out of the fire and put it on a piece of seashell. He waited a minute to let it cool, and then picked it up with his fingers and bit a hole in the shell and tore it open with his teeth. The egg was partially cooked and it oozed out into the palm of his hand. He licked it off with his tongue and said, "There. Tastes pretty good." He reached for another one.

Joseph looked closely at his egg and then watched as Napu repeated the process with a second one. This one was cooked more and, when he squeezed it out onto his hand, it was a little like the soft-boiled eggs his mother used to make for him.

"You want to try this one?" Napu asked.

"No, you eat it. I'll eat this one."

He did what Napu had done, picking the egg up and biting it open, tearing at the soft shell. A gelatinous glob with a dark yellow yoke plopped out into his hand. He held his breath and put it in his mouth.

It had a strong taste and the gooey feel of it made him want to gag. But Napu was watching him and he did not dare spit it out. He held it in his mouth for a moment and then forced himself to swallow it.

Napu laughed. "You did it. Here. Try another one. They're cooked more now."

Joseph waved his hand in front of his mouth and said, "I think I'm just going to eat fish."

*****

Napu agreed not to eat any more of the eggs as long as they had enough fish, and every day Joseph visited the turtle's nest. The tides came up but did not reach it and it was well hidden from the seabirds. Some days, after collecting coconuts, he would sit on the beach near the nest and watch and wait. Finally he asked Napu if he knew how long it took for the eggs to hatch.

"I don't know," Napu said, "but it's maybe like a chicken. My grandmother's chickens always took three weeks to hatch their eggs. And the turtles usually hatch at night, you know? So the birds don't get them. Anyway, that's what my uncle said."

Joseph tried to remember how many days it had been since he'd witnessed the turtle laying her eggs. He had lost track of time, but he knew it was not three weeks. Then he remembered the moon. It had been full when she had crawled up onto the beach to lay them and it would take twenty-eight days until it was full again.

So then every night he went to the nest and watched the moon come up and waited. After a while, he felt that he and the moon were partners, watching together, and the stars, too, were there with them, and they were all together in the darkness, waiting, waiting, waiting.

*****

It happened when the moon was halfway through its next cycle, when it was bright and lopsided and the moon-bright clouds passing across its crooked face were rimmed with silver. He had fallen asleep in the sand, his head resting on his palm frond hat, his face looking straight up into the night sky. He could not remember what woke him—the moonlight on his face, or the cracking sound when the wind broke a palm frond off a tree, or the wind itself teasing his bare skin.

When he reached the nest, the texture of the sand had changed. Over the passing weeks, the wind and the rain had smoothed it, hiding the secrets that lay beneath its surface. But now the fickle, cloud-scattered moonlight revealed something. The sand began to pucker, to fall in on itself, and then to heave upwards in little mounds.

Joseph rolled over and put his face next to the top of the nest. He held his breath. Something emerged, tiny and dark: it was a head. Then the front flippers came up, struggling, digging, pulling at the dry sand that collapsed around it. It was a silent struggle; not a sound was made, not a whisper.

Then other heads began to appear and soon the sand over the whole nest was moving, churning, the sand falling in as the small bodies came out. And the baby turtles knew where the water was, in which direction lay the sea. There did not seem to be any hesitation; once free of the nest, they scurried down the beach toward the surf.

Joseph watched them go, first one by one, and then two and three together, and then more, five or six at a time, tiny shadows racing each other toward the sea. At first, he stayed back, keeping a distance. But after a while, he drew closer, and then, when it seemed the last one of them had left the nest and was heading for the water, he reached down and picked it up.

The tiny creature's flippers flailed in the air and its shell was surprisingly soft. Joseph studied it closely and then spoke to it. "I could name you Simon, too, but I won't. I'll call you Moonlight." He carried him back to camp and as he walked around the lagoon he saw the sky brightening in the east—it was morning already.

When he arrived at the shelter, Napu was sitting at the fire eating smoked fish and drinking from a coconut. "You been out there all night?" he asked.

"Yeah. I fell asleep by the nest." He held out the turtle. "Look. They hatched. There were lots of them. I caught one."

He held the turtle out and Napu took it from him, turning it over in his hands. "What are you going to do with it?"

"I think I'll build a pool for it—in the lagoon. I can use rocks. That way it will be safe. You want to help me?"

Napu's face lit up for a moment and then he caught himself. "Yeah, sure," he said in a serious voice. "In my language it's called a *gigao*. We can make it a big one, too." He thought for a moment and said, "And then we can use it as a place to keep some of the fish I catch."

*****

They built a small cage for the turtle out of sticks and coconuts and left him in the shade of a coconut tree that leaned out over the lagoon. Then they spent the rest of the morning carrying chunks of broken coral rock from the bottom of the lagoon and walling in a large pool. They built the wall up high enough so that it would keep the fish and the turtle in at high tide.

When they were finished, Joseph brought the turtle down to the lagoon and, before releasing it, held it in his hands so they could look at it again. "What do sea turtles eat?" he asked.

"I don't know. I guess fish, maybe."

"I don't see how they could catch a fish," Joseph said. "They're pretty slow and he's pretty small. I used to feed my turtle a special food we got at the pet store. I don't know what it was."

"Anyway, you're right," Napu said, "he's too small to catch a fish."

Joseph held the turtle up and watched its flippers moving helplessly in the air. "Maybe he eats seaweed and stuff like that. I think I'll get all sorts of stuff and put it in the pool with him."

He stepped into the pool and leaned over, holding the turtle just above the water. "Well, here goes," he said and he dropped it in.

The turtle swam frantically for a moment and then dove under a piece of coral that formed a small, shaded shelter.

"Look," Napu said, "he wants to hide under something."

"Good," Joseph said, "You watch him for a minute so he doesn't get out. I'm going to use your net to get some stuff to put in the pool for him to eat."

Part II:
Instruction, War, and Deliverance

Chapter 19

At first Napu had been reluctant to teach Joseph how to throw his *talaya*, the fishing net, explaining that it was made of pineapple fibers and was very delicate and if it got torn, there would be no way to fix it. But finally he had relented. It had taken several days for him to master it, but soon Joseph was able to walk out into the lagoon and come back with a net full of flapping, silvery catch.

And then one day, as Joseph was standing up to his waist in the lagoon about to cast the net, everything changed. He had searched the water for fish and then begun the process of throwing the net outwards. He lifted his arm and took a corner of the net in his free hand. With a twist of his body he swung the net out and away so that it spread out over the water.

When the net had been cast, when the whiteness of it had dropped and disappeared onto the surface of the water, it revealed another whiteness that caught Joseph's eye. Far out beyond the edge of the lagoon, out past where the reef ended and the deep blue ocean began, shone the wing of a great bird—but this wing did not disappear below the surface; it stood up straight, holding steady in the wind and catching the bright sunlight. It took a long moment for Joseph to understand what it was and then he started yelling for Napu.

Napu was still standing in the pool watching the turtle. He yelled out across the lagoon at Joseph. "Are you all right?"

"Look!" Joseph said, pointing out beyond where Napu stood. "Look! A sail!"

Napu turned and stared out onto the sea where Joseph was pointing and when he was certain that what they saw was not a sea-bird or the crest of a breaking wave on the reef, he began running out into the lagoon toward where Joseph stood holding the net.

Long before he reached Joseph's side, Joseph was calling out to him. "It's a sail, isn't it? Really? It *is* a sail. Who do you think it is?"

As usual, Napu worked hard to hide his excitement; his face showed little emotion and when he was standing next to Joseph, he pretended to concentrate on what Joseph had caught. A few small reef fish struggled against the netting, their shiny bodies fluttering in the clear water, bright against the darker sand beneath them.

Joseph repeated his question. "Who do you think it is? It's not the soldiers, I don't think. They wouldn't be in a sailboat."

"No," Napu said, "They're not soldiers. It's a canoe—a *proa*—probably from an island south of here."

With sudden, studied nonchalance, he took the net from Joseph and lifted it from the water. He slung it over his shoulder, and, with Joseph right behind him, walked back to the beach. He put the net down on the sand and surveyed the fish. Then, finally, he looked back out toward the sail that now loomed larger on the near horizon.

"A canoe." Joseph repeated the words. His eyes followed Napu's gaze out toward the sea. In his mind, he pictured the kind of canoe used by the American Indians, but he wondered how there could be a sail on it. "Do you think they're coming here? Should we build the fire up and send them a smoke signal or something?"

Napu was watching as the sail made its slow progress along the outer edge of the reef. "They're going to come into the lagoon," he said, his voice serious, "through that narrow entrance over there. The tide and the wind will be with them."

Joseph admired Napu's ability to understand the sea and the wind and how they affected sailboats. He had watched the sky and had seen in which direction the clouds were moving and then studied the still water that marked the entrance of the lagoon. He was right; the wind was blowing in across it with the incoming tide. Joseph decided he must not say anything else; he must try to be more serious, like Napu. He must stay calm and figure things out by quietly watching and waiting before speaking.

It was another hour before the canoe reached the lagoon entrance. The boys stood on the beach near the fire and watched and waited. When the canoe was lined up with the entrance it turned hard and the wind filled the sail from the back. Then it seemed to fly into the lagoon, skimming across the water like a huge waterbug.

Now Joseph realized that he had seen such a canoe before. He ran to the shelter and got *A Boy's Picture History of the World in One Volume* and started leafing through it until he found what he was looking for. Despite his determination not to talk and sound foolish, he said, "Look, Napu. Here is a picture of the same kind of canoe. The islanders had them back when Captain Cook was exploring the Pacific. They're call 'outriggers.' That's what the long thing is out on one side."

Napu did not look at the picture. He kept his eyes on the lagoon where the canoe was now quickly approaching the beach and

Joseph then realized that he must have seen canoes like this many times. He felt foolish again—he had opened his mouth and shown his ignorance. But then, a moment later, he had to bite his tongue to keep himself from saying, "You're right, they're not soldiers. They're not wearing uniforms."

Like the men in Joseph's spirit dreams, the men in the canoe were wearing only small cloths around their waists. Their muscles bulged under their deep brown skin and their hair was shiny black. They were watching the boys as curiously as the boys were watching them.

The canoe, with its long outrigger and outstretched sail, was quickly closing the distance to the shore and now the boys could see that it was painted a shiny red and black and had high pointed prows at either end.

A moment before the canoe touched the sand, the men turned it into the wind. The sail was furled on its spars and dropped onto the side of the canoe's hull. A moment after that, three of the crew jumped into the shallow water and guided the *proa* to a gentle stop and together they pulled and pushed the canoe far enough up onto the sand so that it would not float away.

Chapter 20

Then the men were on the beach, all four of them. They stood at the edge of the water with the canoe and the sparkling lagoon behind them. They stared at the boys and at the boy's fire and at the sail shelter tied among the coconut trees.

The boys did not know enough to welcome them with a raised hand and a smile. Instead they simply stared back until the eldest of the men raised his hand and spoke in a language Joseph did not understand. He looked at Napu. "What did he say?"

Instead of answering Joseph, Napu spoke back to the man in Chamorro, the language of Guahan. When he had finished, the men were smiling. Had they understood him?

The oldest man stepped forward and reached a hand out toward Napu and Napu took it but stared down at the ground as he did so. Then the man pointed at his own chest with his finger and said, "Raumwele."

Joseph thought it must have been his name but because it was so foreign to his ears, a moment later he could not remember it. Napu, though, now did what the man had done; he pointed at his own chest and said, "Napu."

Then the man looked at Joseph and Joseph felt himself blushing but he knew what was expected of him. He pointed at his chest and said, "Joseph."

When he said this, all the men smiled again and one of them made the sign of a cross on his chest and pointed at the sky, and said in English, "Joseph, Mary, Jesus."

"He spoke English," Joseph said.

"It sounded like it. They don't speak Chamorro. But they know about my island. I think so, anyway. I think they understood the name."

The man who called himself Raumwele studied Joseph closely and pointed at his hair that had been bleached a bright yellow-brown by the sun. "America?" he said.

Joseph nodded.

"Speak English?" Raumwele asked.

Again, Joseph nodded and hesitated and said, "Yes."

Raumwele again pointed at himself and said, "I speak English. A little."

Then the men all started talking to each other at once in their language and they walked up the beach past the boys and went into the camp. They examined the sail shelter and nodded approval and then Raumwele spoke to Joseph, too, but this time he pointed at the sail and made gestures in the air with his hands and said, "Boat?"

At the same moment, both boys pointed across the island and the men all began walking in that direction. Joseph and Napu led them through the palm trees and the low vines and bushes, following the path through the sand and dead palm fronds and brown coconut husks until they came out on the other side.

They all looked out across the reef and because the tide was coming in but was still low enough, they could see the top of the hull of the sunken boat outlined black against the bright water. Joseph pointed and said, "There it is. That's our boat. It sunk on the reef and we can't get it to shore."

The men spoke among themselves, and after a moment two of them walked out into the water and went out to the boat. When they reached it, they began diving around it. Again and again they went under and stayed under for a long time and each time they came up, they spoke to each other, their voices carrying clearly across the water.

Then they came back to shore and walked up on the beach. The two swimmers spoke quickly and softly to the other two and then they all turned to Joseph and Napu. Raumwele shook his head and then he seemed to have an idea. He walked back into the palm trees and found a stick and began drawing a picture in the sand.

Carefully he drew a picture of the hull of a boat and then made a round, jagged-edged hole in the side of it. He looked up at Joseph and Napu and shook his head and said, "The boat is broke."

Joseph glanced at Napu, whose eyes were downcast, and the men saw this, too. Raumwele put his hand on Napu's shoulder and said, "You can come with us," and again gestured with his hands. He pointed at Joseph and then at Napu and then at the other men and made a circle in the air. Again his intent was clear—you are now one of us. We can sail together if you wish.

"Okay," Napu said, "We've been here a pretty long time."

Joseph and Napu's eyes met and then Joseph nodded and he looked at Raumwele. "Yeah. We'll go with you."

They went back to the camp and the men, talking among themselves, got machetes from the canoe and they all went into the middle of the island and caught coconut crabs, and harvested coconuts and breadfruit and a small, sour fruit they called *nen*, until they had a large pile on the beach near the canoe. They built the fire up and lay breadfruit and crabs in among the coals and skewered and roasted some of the fish the boys had caught. Then they sat around the fire and talked and ate and drank coconuts and each of the men pointed to himself and said his name and Raumwele explained what each name meant. He said Raumwele meant "a whale that stands alone." Pianwai meant "sand bar of voyaging." Orhanmwar meant "reef," and Buguwairhew, "a reef in the ocean."

Then Raumwele said, "my island—Puluwat," and he pointed in the direction where it lay far over the horizon.

*****

That night, they all sat on the beach and studied the stars. Joseph told them the names of the constellations he knew, saying them in English and the men would repeat the words carefully and then discuss it among themselves. They then pointed to stars and named them in their own language while Joseph and Napu listened and tried their best to remember.

Then Joseph pointed at the stars and then at the canoe and said one word: "Navigate."

"Ah," Raumwele said, "navigate!" and he pointed to himself and pointed up at the sky.

"Wait," Joseph said, and he regretted that once again his voice betrayed his excitement. "I have to show you something."

He got up and walked to the fire and came back with the carved stick. He handed it to Raumwele and as Raumwele turned it over in his hands, studying it in the moonlight, Joseph told the story of how the old ghost, the spirit of the ancestors, had appeared to him and given him the root of the nunu tree and had turned it into this, something he called the Spirit of the Voyage.

Raumwele listened carefully and then spoke to the others in their language and they all nodded at Joseph and Napu and Raumwele said, "Yes. Good. Then it must be done."

Then Napu said, "Japanese soldiers," and he pointed at Joseph and said, "Maybe they kill him because he is a white American." He ran his hand across his throat.

There was a long silence and Joseph could hear the familiar sound of the surf on the distant reef and the beating of his heart in his ears.

Raumwele frowned and said, "Japanese come to Puluwat." He shook his head.

Joseph felt the old fear well up inside him. "I can't go with you then, Napu. I'll have to stay here."

Napu said, "We are fire star brothers now. Don't forget that. If you can't go to Puluwat, I can't go either. We will stay here together." And he looked across the fire at Raumwele and said, "We will stay here then. If the Japanese soldiers are on Puluwat, we will stay here. This is a good place. We have enough food and there are no soldiers."

Raumwele frowned again. "Yes," he said, "soldiers come here, too—someday."

Joseph and Napu glanced at each other and then at Raumwele.

"We haven't seen any soldiers here," Napu said.

"They will come here," Raumwele said again and the look on his face said he was not to be argued with.

Joseph's heart sank. There was nothing to do then. They could not go with the men on the canoe to Puluwat and eventually the Japanese would come to this island and find them. There would be no place to hide.

But then Raumwele said, "Listen, Joseph. Listen, Napu. There is another island. An island called Pikelot that we call Pik." He turned and pointed out across the lagoon. "Soldiers come there sometimes but don't stay there. Only one man lives there—an old man called Retawasiol—he is a navigator—a *pwo*—a master navigator."

Joseph and Napu waited. What did Raumwele mean? They could go there, to this island?

Raumwele went on: "You come, tomorrow, with us. We take you there—to Pik." Then he smiled and said, "It's okay. No soldiers. Only Retawasiol lives there. Retawasiol means 'a bird in the ocean.'" Then he laughed softly and said, "He is tough old man. Just a little sick and a little mean, but…." His voice trailed off and he laughed again.

*****

The next morning they loaded the coconuts, *nen*, and breadfruit onto the canoe and they helped Joseph and Napu fold up the sail and the tarp they had been using as a shelter and they took the rusty, dented bucket, too, and the fishing net and their machetes. While they did all this, they cooked more fish, wrapping them carefully in banana leaves and putting them into the canoe.

The Spirit of the Voyage stood in its place of honor, close to the fire. Joseph pulled it from the sand and held it out to Raumwele. "The old ghost told me every voyage has a spirit and that I should always take this with me. He said it would protect us and bring us luck."

Raumwele took the Spirit of the Voyage from Joseph's hands and again examined it. "The old spirits are wise," he said. He carried it to the canoe and handed it up to Pianwai and said something in a soft voice. Orhanmwar took it from Pianwai and moved to the end of the canoe and tied it there so that it was facing out to sea.

Then, while the men finished tying down everything on the canoe underneath pandanus mats, Joseph and Napu found themselves standing together looking down at the still-burning fire.

"Should we put it out?" Joseph said. "I know this sounds stupid, but I wish we could take it with us."

Napu was quiet for a moment, and then said, "I know. It is a sacred fire. It's full of spirits."

"Yeah," Joseph said, "I think it is. The spirits made us brothers. I don't want to just kill them—well, you know what I mean."

Napu said, "Let's put it out with coconut water. We can thank the fire spirits that way. We can make them an offering."

He seemed pleased with that idea and without waiting for Joseph to agree, he got his machete from the canoe and set off to find a green drinking coconut. When he came back, he opened the nut and he and Joseph stepped up to the fire together.

Without hesitating, Napu said, "Thank you, spirits of the fire, for looking after us, for cooking our food, and for giving us light— and for making us brothers." Then he poured the water from the coconut onto the flames and there was a loud hissing noise and smoke and a fragrant steam billowed upward around their heads.

The men had pushed the canoe off the beach and they waited for Joseph and Napu to finish what they were doing. Joseph held *A Boy's Picture History of the World in One Volume* up above his head and followed Napu out into the water.

Before he could climb on board, though, he stopped and yelled, "Moonlight!"

The others looked at him.

"My turtle. I have a baby turtle. I have to bring him with me."

"No, you can't do that. He'll die here on the canoe," Napu said. "You have to let him go."

Joseph stared at Napu for a moment and then said, "Yeah, okay."

He handed the book up to Napu and waded back to the edge of the lagoon. It took him a moment to find the turtle in the pool they had built for it. When he did, he grabbed him and held him up and put his nose to the turtle's face. "I've got to let you go now, boy—or girl. Whatever you are," he said. "It might be pretty lonely for you after I'm gone, but I got no choice. I've got to let you go. I think maybe you'll be safe in the lagoon. But watch out for the sharks. And don't go out into the ocean yet. It's scary out there, so wait until you're bigger. That's what I had to do."

He bent down and set the turtle in the water outside the pool and it swam quickly toward a brown coconut frond floating close by and went under it. Joseph watched for a moment and then walked back out to the *proa.*

The men helped him onto the canoe and then, while two of them raised the sail and the others began paddling, they made their way across the lagoon to the open place in the reef where the outgoing tide swept them out to sea.

Chapter 21

There were six of them on the canoe and Napu and Joseph soon learned who was responsible for what jobs. Pianwai sat in the bottom and bailed water with a wooden scoop. Orhanmwar sat high in the very back and steered by keeping his feet and his hands on a big rudder. Buguwairhew and Raumwele took places on platforms that hung out over the water on either side of the canoe, Raumwele next to the mast where he could control the set of the sail. They showed Napu and Joseph where to sit so the canoe was balanced and rode through the water just right.

From their positions, the boys could watch the men handle the sail by adjusting the lines attached to the spars and see the helmsman steer from his perch. Raumwele, from his seat on a bench next to the mast, watched the island as it fell away behind them and he watched the wake the canoe was leaving in the water and spoke to the helmsman in a quiet voice. He then watched the water and kept the canoe at an angle to the ocean swell so that it always lifted the canoe from the same direction.

They sailed this way through the day and, when Raumwele gave them permission, they opened coconuts with a machete and drank the water and scraped out the white meat or cut open a baked breadfruit. As the day wore on, Joseph noticed that the men did not seem to tire. Sometimes they all changed positions, the bailer becoming the helmsman, the helmsman resting on the platform, the man who had been resting getting into the bottom of the canoe and bailing out the water that was constantly splashing in. Only Raumwele did not change positions. He stayed at his post in the middle of the canoe, his hand on a line that controlled the sail, and sometimes gave commands to the helmsman in a quiet voice.

So it was Raumwele the boys watched the most. He was the navigator, the captain. The other men deferred to him, for it was his skill they all depended on to get them to the next island. Yet there was not much to watch. He sat placidly, never raising his voice, always watching the sea, and making small adjustments in the set of the sail. His skin had been burned black by the sun, but his eyes were bright and alert and he had a quick smile and a gentle way.

*****

When darkness approached, the men seemed to grow restless. As the sun moved closer and closer to the western horizon, they watched the darkening sky to the east, until one of them called out and pointed; it was a star, the first star, and they spoke its name. Raumwele spoke to the helmsman and the course was adjusted so this star was fine on the windward bow.

As other stars appeared, the men spoke their names, each in turn, but the heading was held until the first star they had seen was too high in the sky to be useful for navigating and then another rose above the horizon behind it and took its place just off the bow of the canoe.

And so they steered through the night. Raumwele did not sleep, but kept watch on the sea and the stars as they wheeled overhead. Napu and Joseph, though, were free to sleep when they wanted to, so Joseph found himself lying on his back staring up at a sky filled with stars from horizon to horizon, great bright clusters of them, and dim, milky clouds of them. And as the stars moved overhead, the sea moved under them and the canoe was lifted and dropped by the big ocean swells, and time passed over them as though it, too, were part of the wind. And that was his last thought as sleep overtook him that first night of the voyage—that time and the wind were the same thing, and the stars too, were all part of the wind and sea and time, and so was the canoe and everyone in it.

*****

As with their own voyage in Napu's boat, the hours on the canoe blended into each other until Napu and Joseph lost track of them. Both the days and the nights became times of wakefulness and sleep. Sometimes the men talked and laughed among themselves, and they looked at the pictures in *A Boy's Picture History of the World in One Volume.* Sometimes Raumwele told long stories the boys could not understand but which the other men listened to with great interest. When they caught a fish, usually a big mahi-mahi, it was divided up among everyone equally and eaten raw.

And so the boys did not know how much time had passed, how many days, how many miles of ocean had been crossed when, one day when the sun was near its zenith, Raumwele stood up and studied the horizon and then smiled.

The others followed his gaze and then, by standing up themselves, they saw what the navigator had seen: a small, low, gray line emerging from the ocean dead ahead of them. Soon they were looking at what Joseph had seen that last day of the voyage in Napu's boat—trees growing up in the middle of the bright, blue sea. But now Joseph understood what the others knew. It was not a mirage, not part of the sea—it was a low island, an atoll. The voyage was nearly over.

Now Raumwele gave the boys special instructions. "You must remember something when we come close to Pik," he said. "This island is the home of many spirits, good ones and bad ones. And many birds. To disturb the spirits or the birds will bring bad luck. You must be very quiet when you are on Pik."

It took the rest of the day before they reached the tiny island of Pikelot. There was no lagoon here and the water seemed deep enough, but still, Raumwele seemed intent on finding a certain spot to approach it. They tacked back and forth and then sailed up to the beach next to where another canoe had been pulled up on the sand. Here they were greeted by half a dozen young men who spoke softly but excitedly. But when the greeters realized that there were strangers on the arriving canoe, they became shy and simply stared at Napu and Joseph, while Napu and Joseph stared back.

When the canoe touched the sand everyone jumped off and, with many hands helping, it was brought up onto the beach next to the first canoe. Then Joseph remembered something; he untied the Spirit of the Voyage from its place of honor and took it and *A Boy's Picture History of the World in One Volume* off the canoe and carried them with him.

For a long time Joseph and Napu stood apart from the gathered men. Though the boys could not understand what they were saying, the others kept looking at them and they knew that Raumwele was explaining where they had found them and what had happened. Finally, Raumwele motioned to Joseph and Napu to follow him.

He led them away from the beach back among the coconut trees and then along a sandy path until they came to a large hut with a thatched roof that drooped almost to the ground. Just before they reached it, Raumwele lifted his hand and stopped walking. He held his hand out to indicate they should wait and then he thought for a moment and whispered, "Let me have this." He touched the Spirit of the Voyage and Joseph handed it to him, and then he bent low and disappeared under the edge of the roof.

He was gone for a long time, and all that while the boys were watched by the young men who had followed them from the beach. They seemed especially curious about Joseph, whose yellow-brown hair had grown down below his shoulders. Finally, one stepped forward and reached up and touched Joseph's head. When the others saw that Joseph just smiled and did not seem to mind, they all came up, one by one, and did the same.

When Raumwele came out from the hut he did not have the Spirit of the Voyage and his face was serious. "Retawasiol will talk to you now. But you must be careful what you say. Treat him with great respect and maybe he will agree to save your lives. But remember, if he hides you from the Japanese soldiers, he is putting himself in great danger." Napu and Joseph looked at each other and then nodded at Raumwele, and he motioned for them to go inside.

It was dark and cool under the thick roof of thatch. Until their eyes adjusted to the dim light, they could see only shadows. But soon objects began to emerge from the gloom. There were carved paddles and sleeping mats on the sandy floor, and spars and poles lay up in the cross beams, but most of the space was filled with a large outrigger canoe. Like the others, it was painted a shiny black and red and had high, pointed ends each adorned with a V-shaped carving.

Joseph was looking at one of these carvings when they heard a voice from the shadows. Deep and rasping, it said, "They are called 'eyes.'"

It took a moment for the boys to realize the voice had spoken in English. Then they saw the speaker: an old man sitting cross-legged in a corner on a woven mat. He was thin and his brown skin hung loosely on his bones and his figure blended with the dim light as if he were a part of it, as if he were a shadow. The boys stared, waiting for him to say more.

"Every canoe must have eyes so the spirit that guides the voyages can see. Even spirits need to see where they are going. They help the navigator follow the star paths across the water."

Getting slowly to his feet as if he were stiff or in some pain, he walked past the boys to the canoe. He touched the part he had called the "eye," and then ran his hand along the sides. "A canoe is a sacred thing," he said. "It must be treated with great respect." He walked down along the length of it, never taking his hands from it. "Before we leave on a voyage, we must pray to *anunwaii*, the spirit of navigation. We must receive forgiveness for our bad deeds on land. We must pray for the sea to open for us."

He stopped when he reached the end of the canoe and he touched the carved eye at that end, too. "My name is Retawasiol. I am an old man who has made many voyages, followed many star paths, trusted my life and the lives of my crew to the spirit of the voyage many times."

It was at that moment that the boys understood something about the old navigator who called himself Retawasiol. There was something wrong with his eyes. They were opaque with clouds that made them as gray as a stormy sky.

"Yes," the old man said, as if he had read their thoughts. "Like the others, you think I am blind. All the more reason for me to treat the spirit of navigation with great respect, don't you think? I need its eyes." Then he said, "But am I really blind? How then do I see you? Come here with me to my mat. Sit with me and we'll talk story. You are young so you must be hungry. Young men are always hungry. We'll eat some fish and some breadfruit cooked in coconut milk."

Retawasiol led the boys back to his mat in the corner of the hut. He sat down and invited them to sit before him. "So," he said, "Raumwele has told me about your voyage from the atoll. Now you tell me how you arrived on the atoll in the first place."

Joseph started to talk, but stopped himself and sat silently waiting for Napu. When Napu glanced at him, he shrugged and Napu started. He spoke very slowly, his voice low and serious. He told about the soldiers and planes coming to his island and how he and Joseph left in his boat and how they sailed for many days eating fish and drinking coconuts and were finally shipwrecked on the atoll where Raumwele and his crew had found them. To Joseph's relief, he did not tell Retawasiol why they had become shipwrecked, how Joseph had fallen asleep on his watch, how he did not know what an atoll looked like coming up out of the sea.

When Napu was finished, Retawasiol nodded and said, "Now you, Joseph, you talk your story."

Joseph felt his face redden and was grateful for the dim light. *Still,* he thought, *he knows I am blushing—somehow he knows. He cannot see but he sees everything.* He cleared his throat. "I am not from the islands," he began. "I am from a place called Massachusetts in the United States. My father left my mother and me alone and then my mother got sick and then she died and so I was sent to live with my uncle who worked at the cable station on Guahan."

He told about how he was out in the jungle when the war came to the island and how he had hidden in the nunu tree, and how, at night, he had seen the ghosts walking through the trees. He told how one of the ghosts—one that looked like an old man—had taken a root from the tree and changed it into the Spirit of the Voyage and how the old ghost told him he must help bring the ancient skill of navigation back to the island because it had been lost, and then the old ghost had gone into the root, had become a part of it.

When Joseph said those last words, Retawasiol picked up the carved stick that had been lying beside him. "Yes, here it is," he said, "the Spirit of the Voyage."

Retawasiol held it at arm's length for a moment, as if was too hot to hold, and then he felt it carefully, moving his hands over it as if he was listening to it, as if the stick was talking story, too.

Then he handed it back to Joseph and said, "You must already understand that this wood is filled with spirits. It has much power.

It is what has guided you and kept you safe. You must treat it with the greatest respect. What happened to it? I felt a terrible wound in its side."

Joseph told how the soldier in the truck had shot at him as he fell down the side of the hill and how the bullet had struck the stick.

Now Retawasiol shook his head. "You see," he said, "the spirit in the wood is very strong to have protected you like that—to have deflected a bullet," he said. "Keep it with you at all times and you will be safe."

Then he lowered his voice and, nearly whispering, said, "There are many spirits here, too. They are in the sea that surrounds this island—and on the island. They live in anything that floats on the water—in pieces of bamboo and wood, even coconuts. And they live in the forests here. You must take care when you walk through the trees at night, especially when there is no moon. The bad spirits will eat you and make you sick."

"Now," he said, raising his voice again, "we must eat before the spirits eat us, and I will talk story as you have. I have asked Raum-wele to leave food for us outside the hut next to the big coconut tree. Please bring it in."

Joseph and Napu both jumped up quickly and, stepping outside the hut, found the food wrapped in banana leaves just as Retawasiol had said. They carried it in and set it down in front of the old man. They were very hungry, but they waited until Retawasiol said impatiently, "Come, come. Eat."

There was baked fish, some kind of meat, papaya, and breadfruit cooked in coconut milk, and coconuts opened and ready to drink. When Joseph had his mouth full of the meat, Retawasiol asked him how it tasted.

"It tastes good," Joseph said.

"Yes," the old man said, "The turtle is fresh. They caught a big one last night."

Joseph stopped chewing but he dared not look at Napu or be thought impolite. He swallowed the meat.

The boys ate quickly while Retawasiol picked at his food and while he ate he told them his own story. He was born on Pulu-wat, an atoll south of Pik. He was the son and grandson and great-grandson of navigators. He had started learning the ways of the star paths from his grandfather when he was just five years old. When he was thirteen, he had made his first long ocean voyage to Truk and when he was twenty-five years old, he had gone through the *pwo* ceremony and was ordained a master navigator. Since then he had made many voyages and visited many islands. He said he had lived for a time on Guahan, Napu's island, and there had learned to speak English. He said he had even lived in California, where he had worked as a cowboy.

But then the Japanese had come to Puluwat. They brought the disease of smallpox that had killed many, and then they had taken his sons away to work on the island of Yap and they had forbidden voyaging. He had grown bitter and angry and decided to leave the island of his birth. He and his wife and daughters had lived here on Pikelot, but then his daughters had left to find husbands and now, not long ago, his wife had died. So now he was alone and it is not a good island for an old man to live on alone, and sometimes he was sick and sometimes his mind did not work right and he became forgetful and confused and he no longer went to sea.

When the young men of Puluwat came here to hunt turtles — as they are now — he had visitors and ate well. But mostly he was here alone and he spent his days scrabbling about for food and harvesting wild taro and his *tuba*, the alcoholic drink islanders made from the sap of the coconut tree. Or he sat in the shade and thought about the old days, the days when he was young and before the soldiers had come.

When Joseph heard this, he felt his heart sink. Soldiers? They were here, on this island, too?

But it was Napu who asked the question. "Retawasiol," he said, and Joseph could tell he was trying to keep his voice low and calm, "are there soldiers here? We haven't seen any."

The old man shrugged, and said, "Oh, they are not here all the time. They come and go. Some mornings I see a ship outside the reef and sometimes they come in on a smaller boat. They look around, they ask me questions. But there is nothing here but an old man and his old canoe and some sea birds and coconuts and breadfruit. There is no lagoon and no place to land planes. So they don't stay very long."

He laughed when he said this but then he seemed suddenly tired. He sat back and sighed. "Now," he said, "I must sleep for a while. I have decided that, as visiting bachelors, you will live here, with me, in this sacred *utt*, this canoe house. You will put your sleeping mats over there, under the canoe. The spirits of the ancestors have given you a great responsibility. Joseph, although you are not one of us, not an islander, you as well as Napu have been chosen by the Old Ones to learn the great secrets of following the star paths. It is a great honor.

"But you both have a great deal to learn and you are no longer little boys. Soon you will be men. I will keep you safe from the soldiers and be your instructor, but in return, you must help me. You will gather and prepare my food and keep me company. And we will repair my old canoe so it can once again sail the star paths."

He stopped talking and looked at the boys for a long time and then said, "I believe that the spirits have sent you to me because, before I die, I will sail away from here and go to the island where the spirits live in the earth and spit fire from the tops of the mountains. The spirits have sent you to take me there." Retawasiol finished his food and said, "Go now, out with the others. I will sleep for a while."

Then, without saying another word, he lay down on his sleeping mat and closed his eyes. Napu and Joseph did not know what to do. For a while they sat and watched the old man sleep and then Napu nodded toward the beach and they stood up and went out into the sun.

Chapter 22

The men had covered what Retawasiol had called the "eyes" of the canoe with palm fronds and they were now sitting around a fire eating roasted turtle and fish and drinking something from a cup made from a coconut shell. It was getting late in the day; the trees behind Retawasiol's hut sent long shadows over the beach. The men were talking and laughing quietly.

When the boys approached, Raumwele invited them to sit at the fire and eat. The men kept talking in their language and passing a coconut shell cup and Raumwele motioned for them to eat from the common bowl filled with turtle meat that sat by the fire.

"We ate with Retawasiol," Napu said, but he took the cup that was filled with a whitish liquid, put it to his lips, and drank a little. He passed it to Joseph, who studied it for a moment, smelled it, and then sipped. It had a sweet flavor and burned in the back of his throat but he did not ask what it was. He passed it to the man sitting next to him.

They sat this way until dark and the stars began to fill the sky. The cup was passed around and around and when it was empty, it was refilled from a rusty metal can. The men were laughing louder now and by the third time the cup was passed to him, Joseph felt strange and his head was beginning to spin. When he looked up at the stars, they, too, were spinning and he put his hands down on the sand to keep from falling over.

He glanced at Napu and saw that his eyes were half closed and looking at nothing. He wanted to ask him what was in the cup but he found his tongue was thick and heavy and no longer worked right. Then Napu fell against him and rolled backwards and lay looking up at the stars.

"Napu," Joseph said, slowly, "what—what—is—in—the—cup?"

But Napu did not answer, even though his eyes were open. He continued to lie still and stare up at the stars. Joseph pushed himself to his feet, took a step backwards and then a step forward, and fell headlong into the sand next to the fire. The men all laughed, but then two of them picked him up and lay him next to Napu.

*****

When he woke, the fire was out and he could see the outlines of the men sleeping on the beach around him. He felt very thirsty and his head was pounding. Napu was still sleeping next to him.

"Napu," he whispered and he pushed him on the shoulder. "Napu, wake up. I feel sick."

Napu groaned and pushed himself up on his elbows. "What?" he asked and then he fell back down and rubbed his face with his hands.

"How do you feel?" Joseph asked again.

"Bad. I feel bad," Napu answered, and his voice sounded clogged and hoarse.

"What was that stuff we drank?" Joseph asked.

"*Tuba.*"

"It's bad stuff," Joseph said. "It made me sick."

Napu laughed softly. "It made you drunk. You're right. It's bad stuff. I had it before. My uncles used to make it from coconut tree sap."

"We should go back to Retawasiol's hut to sleep," Joseph said. "He told us we were supposed to sleep there." When he stood up, he staggered for a moment and then got his footing. "Come on, let's go."

He reached down and took Napu's hand and pulled and Napu stood up and they helped each other walk up the beach to the dark shadow of the canoe house.

Inside, it was too dark to see anything and they had to feel their way along the outrigger of the canoe and around the end of it to the place where Retawasiol had said they would sleep. They would not be able to find their sleeping mats in the darkness, so they felt around for enough space to lie down next to each other on the sand.

As they lay in the pitch blackness, Joseph felt wide awake. His head ached and he wanted to talk, to ask Napu about the soldiers; what would happen when they came? They might want to try to kill him again, but where could he run to this time? There was no place to go on this tiny atoll. But he did not dare take the chance of waking Retawasiol, and so he lay quietly and listened to sounds that came from the night. There were the whisperings of the breeze and the sounds of insects and the faint rustling of the thatched roof and the creaking of the beams that held the roof. Joseph finally drifted off to the sound of the old navigator sleeping: his quiet inhalations, the sigh of his dreams.

*****

Something woke Joseph from a sound sleep. Though it was dark, he had a sense that there was light coming from somewhere. He listened. He could hear Napu sleeping and he could hear the ocean. But there was more. There was the sound of low voices and that was where he knew the light was coming from, from the sound itself, from the spoken words he could barely hear. He sat up and looked outside the canoe house under the low edges of the thatched roof. He could see the bottoms of the palm trees and the breadfruit trees and the moon shadows that played among them.

But there was more than just the moonlight and shadows; there was the light from a fire glowing in a clearing among the trees. Joseph could only see part of it so he moved carefully away from Napu and out from under the side of the canoe house, out into the night air. It felt cool and good on his bare skin and he breathed it in. It tasted of the sea and the moon and the smoke from the fire and he stood very quietly and breathed and listened and watched.

Four figures sat at the fire; he knew them all. One was the ghost of the powerful old man who had defeated the *taotaomo'na* the night of Joseph's fever—it was the Spirit of the Voyage. He had come out of the root of the nunu tree again. He looked across the flames at a man Joseph knew was Retawasiol. But it was not the same old man who had fallen asleep in his corner of the *utt*, it was not the half-blind old navigator who had sat with them that evening and talked story. The man who sat across from the Spirit of the Voyage was young. His hair was thick and black and his eyes shone clear and bright in the flames. His arms were knotted with muscles and as he talked, he stared upwards and swayed back and forth, as if he were dancing with the night.

But when Joseph realized who the other two figures were, he had to bite his tongue to keep from crying out. One of the figures was Napu and the other was himself. He glanced down at his arms and legs to be sure he was where he was, inside his own body, and then he looked again at the people sitting around the fire. It could not be—but it was; he was there, by the fire, sitting cross-legged, and next to him Napu sat quietly. They were both listening to the young Retawasiol, who was showing them something.

Joseph moved closer until he could hear Retawasiol's voice, but the words were incomprehensible. The syllables he spoke were more like music than spoken language, rising and falling in pitch and intonation, floating on the air like a song. Yet he and Napu seemed to understand everything he was saying. Their eyes were on his face and then they moved down to what Retawasiol was showing them in the dirt. He had made a circle out of small stones and he was pointing to each of the stones in turn and speaking a name.

Joseph did not know how long he watched and listened. Time was part of the song and the song seemed to be without beginning and promised no end. But then the song did stop and the night sounds hushed themselves until there was utter silence and Joseph could hear only his own breathing and the beating of his heart and he knew the people sitting at the fire must be able to hear it, too. Then they turned their eyes toward him and in their gazes there was no reproach, but no invitation either. He tried to speak, to apologize for his intrusion, but he could not form the words; they stuck in his mouth, nearly choking him. Nor could he raise his hands or lift his feet and when he tried to turn and run, the ground under him became like thick mud.

*****

Then it was morning. Joseph was lying on his mat next to Napu and Napu was still sleeping. He sat up and looked across the *utt*, past the canoe to Retawasiol's bed; the old man was gone, his mat empty. Sunlight was coming in through open places in the thatch and the morning air was warm and moist. He could hear the voices of men talking.

Napu stirred next to him and opened his eyes. He stared up at Joseph and then up at the roof and Joseph knew that he was remembering what had happened to them and where they were. "Is Retawasiol there?" Napu whispered.

"No. He's gone already. We should get up. He will not approve of us sleeping so late." He stopped for a moment and then said, "Napu, do you remember anything from last night? Did you go anywhere after we fell asleep?"

Napu looked into Joseph's eyes for a long moment, and said, "What do you mean. Where would I go? I had too much *tuba*."

Joseph turned away and stood up and said, half to himself, "It was just a dream. All of it was just a dream."

They had slept under one end of the canoe and now Joseph took a big drink from the water pail and then leaned his forehead against the cool wood of the canoe's hull. He held it there, as if that would stop his head from throbbing and help him understand the memory.

"I had a dream," he said, "I dreamed that we were sitting by a fire—all of us, you too, out there, outside the canoe house—and Retawasiol—Retawasiol was not old. He was young and he was teaching us something in a strange language that sounded like music and we could understand him. He made a circle in the sand with small stones and he was telling us something about them. But—but I was still myself like I am now—and I was watching them and watching myself by the fire—there were two of me."

Napu laughed quietly and shook his head. "That's a good one. It was a *tuba* dream. *Tuba* makes you a little crazy. Then what happened?"

"Then they heard my heart beating and they all looked at me watching them. You looked at me and Retawasiol looked at me—and I looked at myself. And the Spirit of the Voyage was there, too. He came out of the wood and was sitting with us by the fire."

Napu shrugged and said, "Like I said, it was just a *tuba* dream. You're okay. Come on, let's go. I'm hungry."

But before Napu could stand up, Joseph asked, "What will the soldiers do when they find me here?"

"I don't know," Napu said. "You're just a kid. They probably won't do anything."

"But they might—they might do something. That soldier tried to shoot me. I'm white—I'm not an islander. I don't look like you."

Then Napu stood up, pointed at Joseph, and said, "Look at you. You're not so white anymore. Anyway, come on, let's go. We can ask Retawasiol about it. He'll know what to do."

"Napu," Joseph said, "I don't think we should drink *tuba* anymore."

Napu laughed again and pressed his hands against his head. "Yeah, you're right, brother. No more of that stuff."

Chapter 23

When they left the *utt* they did not see Retawasiol, but as they walked down the path to the beach they met Orhanmwar, one of the men who had sailed up from Puluwat on the other canoe to hunt turtles. He smiled at them and began talking to them in his language and motioned for them to follow him.

At the edge of the beach was a small canoe, an outrigger like the others, but without a sail. Orhanmwar motioned for them to help him push it from the beach and a moment later they were all sitting in it as he showed them how to paddle. They went out to the edge of the reef where the shallow water was a light turquoise and then, as it got deeper, a darker blue.

When they reached what Orhanmwar seemed to think was the right spot, they started fishing with hand lines. Soon they started pulling up small reef fish and dropping them into the bottom of the canoe, where they struggled and flapped in a pile of many bright colors. This seemed to make Orhanmwar very happy. He talked to Napu and Joseph constantly as if they could understand him, as if the fishing itself was the language and the words were not important. When they had caught enough, they paddled back to the beach and unloaded the fish.

Now Orhanmwar said something and among the unfamiliar words Joseph and Napu heard Retawasiol's name. Orhanmwar pointed up the beach toward the canoe house.

"We better go find Retawasiol," Napu said, and they nodded goodbye to Orhanmwar.

Entering the dark coolness of the canoe house, they found the old navigator resting on his sleeping mat. But he was not asleep. When he heard them come in his eyes opened and he sat up. Again he stood up slowly as if he was in pain. "I've been waiting for you. Where have you been? It's time to start. Come with me," he said and he walked past them and went out under the side of the *utt*.

Joseph and Napu followed Retawasiol outside to a small clearing from where they could see the blue water of the sea and where the coconut trees arched overhead, providing shade. The old man sat down on the ground and crossed his legs. Napu hesitated for a moment but then understood that they were to do the same. They sat down facing the old navigator.

Retawasiol used the Spirit of the Voyage to make a perfect circle in the sand. Joseph observed that he had not even glanced down while he drew it. His eyes stared out past the boys. When he was finished, he stuck the Spirit of the Voyage in the sand next to him.

And then the memory of the night before came back to Joseph and he felt the skin on the back of his neck prickle. He realized he was sitting in the same place he had watched himself sitting in his dream and Spirit of the Voyage was there, and the old navigator was in his place and Napu was there, too, right where he had been.

Joseph knew what would come next. Retawasiol carefully set out pieces of coral pebbles around the edge of the circle and Joseph waited for him to start singing the strange song, but instead he spoke, first in the language of his island, and then he repeated it in English: "This is the star compass. It is called *paafu*. And these are the stars whose paths we follow across the ocean."

He started at the top of the circle, the part nearest his crossed legs, and lay down pieces of shell, one after the other around the edge of it. As he set each piece he spoke the name of the star it represented in his language and sometimes he said something about the star in English: "This is *Wenewenen Fuhemwakut*—the Pole star, the *star-that-does-not-move,* and next to it, *Mailap Anefang,* the star that controls the Universe of the North. Here is *Ukunik,* the tail of the fish, and *Moll,* the star that is in the month of big waves, strong currents, and high tides. Then *Mwerikar,* the star of rainy weather when you don't climb trees." He looked at Joseph and said, "Your people call this star the constellation Pleiades—The Seven Sisters."

He said the name of one more star, *Un*—the star of no bad weather—and then he stopped and put down a big, unbroken shell and said, "And this is *Mailap,* the star that controls the Universe, north and south and the Earth, too. It is called the Big Bird. Joseph, your people call it Altair."

He went on, until he reached the bottom of the circle. "The last star's name is *Wenenewenen Up*—the Trigger Fish, straight up." Again he turned to Joseph and said, "Your people call this the Southern Cross, because in your religion, it looks like a cross. To us, it looks like a trigger fish standing on its tail. Like the Pleiades, it is not one star, but a constellation."

While he said all this, while Joseph and Napu watched him in silence, he did not sing, but his voice was low and he spoke with a lilting rhythm. When he had finished, he asked them to repeat the names after him. He said them all again and he listened as Napu and Joseph spoke their names, first together, and then by himself.

Joseph and Napu struggled with the more difficult ones but Reta-wasiol patiently repeated them until they said them correctly.

This drill went on for a long time until Retawasiol finally stopped and closed his eyes. He took a few deep breaths and sat very still for a few moments. When he opened his eyes again, he looked upwards. Then he turned to the boys as though he could see them and he said, "The small paddling canoe that you used to go fishing this morning is what you will use to catch our fish. Orhanmwar was teaching you what to do. Those men from Puluwat are leaving today to go home. You will now have to catch our fish. Do you understand?"

"Yes, sir," Joseph said and Napu nodded and murmured, "Yes."

"That is all then," the old man said. "You will come back here at dusk and we will practice the stars again. Now go."

They walked down to the beach and saw the men from Puluwat launching their canoe. They had loaded it with the turtles they had caught, laying the animals on their backs so they could not move, and with seabirds, too, and now, together, they pushed the canoe back into the water on its road of palm fronds and climbed on board. The sail was quickly set and, with the wind behind them, they sailed out through the opening in the reef. After they were back out at sea, they turned and waved and Joseph and Napu waved back.

Chapter 24

Then started the routine of their days. The boys fished and collected turtle eggs, breadfruit, *nen*, and coconuts in the morning and, afterwards, they met Retawasiol at the circle near his *utt*, and he instructed them in navigation. But they learned about more than the stars. The old navigator talked about birds and when he did, his voice took on a soft, happy tone as if he loved seabirds almost as much as he loved the heavens.

It was the magic *kuling* bird, he said, that first taught people how to navigate and it was women who were the first navigators. The kuling bird, a kind of sandpiper, was not just a bird, but also a ghost. It flew from island to island eating all the people, but when it came to Pulap, the daughter of the chief gave it coconuts and taro to eat and so it did not eat the people there. It taught the chief's daughter the secrets of steering by the star paths and when she had learned all these secrets, her father told her that they must kill this bird. So they gave it a lot of food, that it flew off with, but it fell into the sea and turned into an octopus and now navigators must protect themselves from this octopus.

But, still, he said, birds are very important for finding your way at sea. Once, he said, he was coming back to Puluwat from a long voyage to the Marianas. He needed to stop here, at Pikelot, but the sky had clouded over. It was getting late, getting dark, soon it would be night. They had been at sea for five days steering only by stars and waves. How to find this little atoll?

Then he saw birds—brown noddies and terns—birds that fish the ocean during the day and fly back to their homes on the islands at night. He watched them hunting the water, diving and catching fish and then flying up again and diving again. But then one of the birds broke away from the others. It flew low across the top of the water, off towards where *Wenenewenen Up*, the Southern Cross, would rise that night.

Soon after that, another bird did the same and then another and another until there were only a few birds left feeding. So, he knew that was where Pik lay. It was where the birds flew back to every night to sleep.

He stopped talking for a moment and he let the silence bring the boys' eyes and ears back to him. Then he said, "We must use everything that the Earth and the sky provide us, everything in nature, to help us find our way across the sea. You must remember what most men have forgotten. We are a part of the Universe, just like the stars and the birds, and the Universe provides for us if we are clever and pay attention."

*****

One day, though, after the boys had fished the reef in the paddling canoe and had climbed coconut trees to get some drinking nuts and then had gone to have their lesson, the old man was not at the circle. Joseph and Napu went looking for him and found him on the windward side of the island, sitting on the beach, staring out to sea. They did not approach him, but stayed back, not wanting to disturb him, but not knowing what to do.

But then he spoke as if he knew it was Napu and Joseph behind him. "The Japanese soldiers are coming. They will be here this evening. Before they get here, Joseph, you must go to my *utt* and get into the canoe. Napu will cover you with mats. Take the Spirit of the Voyage with you. It will protect you."

The boys looked out to sea. Far in the distance they could barely see the low, gray outline of a ship. But how had Retawasiol seen it?

The old man stood up. "I know. You think I'm blind. You must remember, there is more than one way to see. Let's go back to the canoe house. We must prepare ourselves for the soldiers."

They followed Retawasiol across the beach and then into the trees. While he walked, he again talked story. "Let me tell you something else," he said. "The stars and the waves and the birds sing to us of the Earth and help us find our way across the endless sea. And so, too, the sky. The clouds and the many winds that carry the clouds are messengers, bringing us news. We must only learn their song and they will tell us what is important."

"I once was the navigator on a canoe that was driven before a storm for many days. In truth, I did not know where we were. We were very tired and very thirsty and we thought, perhaps, we would not live. But then, far off, I saw a cloud. I watched it closely for a long time. I saw that it did not move and did not change shape. I thought, there must be an island underneath that cloud. We sailed toward it and as we got closer, the bottom of the cloud brightened and changed colors, and I knew, yes, we had found land. We were saved. I say this because a ship is not a cloud though it hangs on the horizon like a cloud over an island."

Napu and Joseph followed Retawasiol to the *utt*. They went inside and Retawasiol told them what to do. "When we hear the boat is coming, Joseph, you must lie down in the bottom of the canoe. Napu will cover you with mats and put the paddles over them. You must stay very quiet until they leave. They will meet with me here and then look around for awhile. They will not suspect anything and will not look in the canoe. Just lie quietly until it is safe to come out."

Napu said, "I am going to hide in the canoe with Joseph."

"It is not necessary for you to do this," Retawasiol said. "I will tell them you are my grandson."

"Joseph needs me," Napu said and in his voice Joseph heard the old determination he had heard when they were sailing together on Napu's boat. "He is my brother. We take care of each other."

"No," Retawasiol said, and now his voice had hardened. "I will tell them that you have come from Puluwat to help me—to take care of me. They will believe that. A sick old man cannot live alone on this island. Now, Joseph, get into the canoe."

They knew better than to argue any more. Joseph found the Spirit of the Voyage and he and Napu climbed up onto the outrigger and then into the canoe. Joseph lowered himself into the bottom where it narrowed into a sharp V. Napu lay mats over him and then, following Retawasiol's instructions, lay three paddles and coils of coconut husk rope over the mats.

When he was covered, Joseph could see that the small points of light coming through the mats looked like constellations of stars and he could smell the old wood of the canoe's hull that carried the salt of many voyages. He held the root of the nunu tree, the Spirit of the Voyage, close to his chest. Then, when Napu and Retawasiol stopped talking, he could hear nothing except the sound of his own breathing.

After what seemed like a long time, he remembered the book— he had left it lying out somewhere in the *utt*. He called out to Napu, "Are you there?"

"Shssh!" Napu whispered. "No talking now. Be quiet."

"I left the book out there," Joseph said.

"What?"

"My book. It's out there near the corner of the *utt*. If they find it, we'll both get caught. They'll chop your head off, too."

Before Napu could respond, Joseph started to push his way up through the mats and the paddles and the coils of line. He was wedged into the bottom of the canoe and it was difficult to get himself up. He grunted with the effort as he shoved away the mats with one arm.

Then he heard voices and someone came into the canoe house. He dropped back down into the bottom of the canoe and glanced up to see if the mats had fallen back down on him and were still covering him. He could see more light coming through now but there was nothing he could do. He lay quietly, barely breathing.

They heard Retawasiol speak English to someone. "No," he was saying, "I have not sailed my canoe in many months. I cannot sail it alone. It is still here."

Another voice spoke English with a heavy accent Joseph had never heard before: "I see. And will you sail it again?"

"I am old and sick," Retawasiol said. "But someday I will get help and I will sail it again. A canoe must be sailed or it is not happy. The spirit of the canoe becomes hungry for the sea."

"And who is this boy?"

"This is Lewalmwanger. He is a grandson. He is staying with me to help me fish and get breadfruit and coconuts."

There was silence for a moment and then someone touched the outside of canoe near Joseph's head. He could hear something scraping lightly against it right next to his ear.

"He is here to help you, heh? Well, okay. He's a strong looking boy. And your canoe, it is still very beautiful," the voice with the accent said. "I should like to sail it. Someday, perhaps, you will take me out on the water in it."

Retawasiol did not answer him. There was silence and then the voice said, "What is this? A book?"

Again there was silence and then the sound of pages ruffling and the voice said, "Hmm. It is written in English." He read the title out loud: *A Boy's Picture History of the World in One Volume*—very interesting. Where did you get this?"

Without hesitating, Retawasiol said, "I suppose a missionary left it on Puluwat. Lewalmwanger brought it with him as a gift for me."

"Are you reading it?" the voice asked.

"Lewalmwanger is trying to read it to me but I think he is only pretending to."

"I see, yes. But it is mostly photographs, so if the boy has a good imagination, as most of them do, he could easily make things up— as most of history is made up."

There was silence again and then the voice said, "This book is not very old. It was just published two years ago. There have not been missionaries on Puluwat for a long time."

"Perhaps," Retawasiol said, "it washed up on the beach and the boy found it."

"Ah, that must be true. It looks like it has been floating in the sea for a while. It's filthy and its pages are ruined from being in water."

Joseph again heard the sound of pages being turned. Then the voice said, "Ah, here's a picture of a Samurai. Very good. Very good indeed. The Samurai were once the military aristocracy of Japan—professional warriors, like myself."

There was silence and then the voice said, "We don't want to take a chance of this getting wet again. I'll put it in the canoe where it will be safe."

A moment later, Joseph heard the sound of the book hitting the inside of the canoe and then he felt it land on the mat that covered his face. He held his breath.

Then the voice said, "We are just making a short inspection this time. I must get back to the ship. Goodbye."

Then the silence overtook everything again and Joseph waited for what seemed an endless time. Finally, he heard Napu's voice and Retawasiol answering him and then saying, "Come out now. The soldiers are gone."

Joseph pushed the mats aside, took the book up in his arms, and climbed out of the canoe. "Who was that?" he asked.

Retawasiol's face was grim. "A Japanese naval officer," he said. "He speaks English because he thinks I don't speak Japanese—and he's proud of his English. But he is a dangerous man. We must be careful. There's no telling when he could change his mind and cause trouble. He always carries a sword and pistol and it is said he enjoys using them."

Chapter 25

By that evening, the soldiers had been forgotten and Retawasiol continued his instruction. He had been teaching them about a special part of navigation called *etak*, which meant breaking a voyage up into segments using stars, islands, or birds. One was required to imagine the canoe sitting still in the water while the world moved past it, but it was difficult to understand. How could the canoe sit still on the water while the islands moved around it? Yet Retawasiol told the boys as they sat around the circle drawn in the sand that they could not be true navigators unless they mastered the art of *etak*.

Today he had his usual pieces of shells representing the stars set out in the circle. But now, instead of two pebbles representing the island they were sailing from and the island they were sailing to, he had two more pebbles off to one side.

"These are the *etak* islands," he said, speaking in his usual slow rhythmic way. "You must learn them all if you are to always know where you are at sea. Each island can be an *etak* island for any other island and you must always know in which direction every other island lies from whichever island you are on."

For some reason, this confusing idea seemed very simple to Joseph and he nodded understanding. Napu murmured that he, too, knew what the old navigator was saying. Each voyage was broken up into parts as each *etak* island moved from under one star to the next. You always knew the direction of the island you had sailed from and the direction of the island you were sailing to. With *etak*, you also always knew the star path to all the other islands as they passed and so you always knew where you were.

But the lesson was long and the concentration tiring and when Retawasiol sighed and looked up towards the sky, the boys knew they were finished. During the lesson, Retawasiol had seemed more tired than usual. He had stopped several times and just sat while he took in deep breaths. The boys had waited in silence until the spell had passed.

"You understood the *etak*?" he now asked.

"Yes." Both boys said the word together.

But rather than being pleased, the old man was angry. "So, what is it then? Why do you stay here when you could be off fishing? Do you want us to starve?"

They hesitated a moment and then both stood up, backed away from the circle, and turned and began running toward the beach. They pushed the small paddling canoe into the water and paddled out toward the reef. Coiled in the bottom of the canoe, the men from Puluwat had left fishing lines and lures made from hooks and bright pieces of metal. Now the boys unwound the line and dropped the lures overboard and began trolling as they paddled along the surf line.

While they paddled, they left their lines touching their legs so they would feel it when a fish struck. Within a few minutes Napu yelled out that he had something. They stopped paddling while Napu pulled in a fat fish with big teeth that he called a *chudel*. As he pulled it into the canoe, the hook came out of its mouth and the *chudel* fell into the bottom, flapping wildly.

Napu put his line back out and they started paddling again. Soon they both had fish on their lines and, laughing and yelling at each other, they pulled them in and dropped them into the canoe.

Then something caught Joseph's eye, something swimming on the surface just ahead of them. "Look," he called out, "what's that?"

"It's a turtle!" Napu yelled back. "Let's see if we can catch it."

The turtle lay quietly on the surface and as the canoe approached, it began to swim. But instead of diving below the surface, it only swam in circles.

In a few minutes the boys were nearly on top of it and still it did not dive.

"What's wrong with it?" Joseph asked.

"Sharks!" Napu answered.

"Where?"

"They attacked the turtle and bit his flippers off. He can't swim."

Then their canoe reached the turtle. It was a big one and it kept its head under the water pointing down as it struggled to dive.

"What should we do?" Joseph yelled, his voice rising with excitement.

Napu brought in his fishing line and coiled it in the bottom of the canoe. "It still has two flippers on one side. I'm going to try to grab it and get a line around one of them."

Joseph could see that Napu was right; the shark had bitten off both of the flippers on its right side.

"Hold the canoe here," Napu yelled. He dropped his paddle into the canoe and reached into the water. He held a loop of his fishing line and now, with the turtle banging into the side of the canoe

116

as it tried to swim, Napu grabbed the front flipper, slipped the loop over it, and pulled hard.

The loop tightened and Napu jerked backwards. Feeling the line on its leg, the turtle fought harder and started to go under water. Napu held onto the line and leaned over the side of the canoe.

At that moment Joseph saw a dark outline of a big fish swimming just below the turtle. "There it is!" he yelled, "Look!"

"What?" Napu yelled back. He was trying to hold onto the line but the turtle was big and, despite his injuries, still very strong.

"The shark! He's just below the turtle! See it?"

As Napu leaned farther out over the water to look where Joseph was pointing, the turtle began to thrash, jerking hard on the line. Napu lost his balance and, with a sharp cry, fell into the water.

For a moment, Joseph could only watch as Napu disappeared below the surface and then came up gasping and swimming for the canoe. He grasped the side of the canoe and tried to get one leg up on it, but his leg slipped off and he fell back into the water.

"Let go of the turtle!" Joseph yelled, "The shark's just below you!"

But Joseph could see that the line holding the turtle had gotten wrapped around Napu's hand and he was gripping it tightly as he again tried to pull himself up onto the canoe. This time Joseph moved back to the middle of canoe and, when Napu pulled himself up, he tried to grab his shoulder and pull him in. But Napu's skin was wet and slippery and, when the turtle struggled again, it pulled him back down into the water and he slipped below the surface.

Joseph reached down, grabbed Napu's hair, and pulled hard. Napu's head came up out of the water and Joseph pulled him back to the side of the canoe. Napu had freed himself from the line holding the turtle and now he put both hands on the gunwale, heaved himself up, and rolled into the canoe.

Joseph heard a loud thrashing sound coming from the water and when he glanced back at the turtle, he saw the gray body of a shark slam into the turtle's side with its jaws open. It bit into the turtle's front flipper, twisted its body, and rolled away. Now, though, the turtle seemed too exhausted to struggle; it floated on top of the water, head down.

Napu sat up and looked over the side of the outrigger at the turtle. "Where's your fishing line? Let me have it."

Joseph found his coil of line in the bottom of the canoe and handed it to Napu, who again leaned over the side and grabbed the turtle by its only remaining flipper. Still the turtle did not struggle. It lay quietly as Napu slipped a loop over it and pulled it tight.

"We've got it," Napu said, "Let's paddle to shore."

*****

When they got the turtle to the beach, it was not necessary to turn it on its back to keep it from escaping; the animal could not move. The boys determined that it must have been a female come from the sea to lay eggs in the warm sand of the atoll's beach. They sat and watched her for a long time. She seemed to stare at Joseph and Napu accusingly with her dark, moist eyes.

"What are we going to do with her?" Joseph asked.

"We'll have to eat her," Napu said.

Joseph's heart jumped. He couldn't imagine eating turtle meat, but all the men from Puluwat had eaten it, and Retawasiol, the great, wise navigator had eaten it too. He had even unknowingly eaten it himself the night he drank the *tuba*. Now, though, as he watched her lying helpless in the sand, it seemed impossible to do such a thing.

But then the turtle lowered her head and they heard a long, slow breath come out of her nose. After that, she lay still.

"I think she's dead," Joseph said.

"Let's get the fire built up," Napu said. "We'll cook her in her shell and surprise Retawasiol with turtle meat that we caught ourselves.

Chapter 26

And so time passed on the atoll, time measured not in months and years, but by the birth and growing and dying of the moon, and by the passage of dry seasons and wet seasons, one after the other, and by Joseph's and Napu's own slow passages from boys into young men.

They grew tall without realizing it, their voices deepened, and one day Napu said, "Joseph, I wish we had a mirror. Look, you got a beard now."

Joseph felt his face and tugged at the fine, blond whiskers that grew from his chin. He studied Napu's face and said, "You do too, you know. You got one. Except it's black. And you got a moustache, too. A little one."

Napu laughed and said, "Maybe we'll both look like Santa Claus pretty soon."

*****

The routines of life on the atoll were endless and pleasant. Joseph and Napu fished and gathered food and prepared Retawasiol's meals and kept the canoe house clean. When the men from Puluwat came in their canoe to hunt turtles, they took the boys out to sea where they practiced sailing the *proa*. Sometimes Retawasiol accompanied them when they went out at night for short voyages and they practiced steering by the stars.

The men showed the boys how to weave the coconut fiber rope big and strong enough to use in repairing Retawasiol's *proa*, and then later, under Retawasiol's supervision, they gradually replaced all the old lashings that held the canoe together, making it ready to go to sea again.

And for hours every day, too, they sat around the circle while the old man continued the lessons in navigation. They mastered *etak*, and learned the star paths to many islands. They continued to learn about the birds and clouds and how the great ocean swell was bent and changed by islands and how to use that change to steer between islands. Retawasiol told them how to handle the *proa* in a storm, how to stay with the canoe if it was swamped by big waves, and how to bail water again once the storm had passed.

But there was so much more to learn—too much, Joseph thought, and he said so to Napu. "I will never be able to learn all this. It's crazy. I'm not smart enough. Every time I learn one thing, I forget something else."

They had just finished a long lesson on *etak*, watching while the old man moved his shells and pebbles around the inside of the circle and asked his difficult questions. Though he did not seem to be looking at them, he moved the shells and stones around to precise points, many different points for sailing between many different islands.

Finally, Joseph stopped him. "I don't understand how you can know all this. I can't remember any of it. What good is it all, anyway? On ships now they have compasses and radios and stuff like that."

The expression on Retawasiol's face did not change, nor did he look in the direction of Joseph's voice. He sat quietly for a long minute and then said, "Yes, the ships have compasses. But you don't. The ships have radios, but you don't. You only have the stars and the sea and the birds, and you cannot leave this island until you know how to use them to navigate. I want to leave this island so I can die. You need to leave this island so you can live because someday, when the Japanese come back, they will find you here and they will kill you."

Then his voice softened. "I know this is difficult. There is much to learn. So you must take the knowledge into your heart first. You must learn to love it. When you love the song the stars sing with the Earth and the sea, when you love the music of the Universe, then the knowledge will move into your head and there it will grow into a blossom with many petals. Always remember that when you are watching a flower grow, it takes great patience. Without great patience you can never be a great navigator." And then he stopped, looked at both boys, and smiled his small, rare smile and said, "You know much more than you think you do."

Later, sitting in the shade of the canoe house, Napu said, "I have always loved the sea. I have been sailing and fishing since I was a little boy. I think that the flower Retawasiol told us about is growing in my head."

Joseph had absentmindedly drawn a circle in the sand with a piece of shell and now he set his ragged book, *A Boy's Picture History of the World in One Volume*, in the middle of it. The book was falling apart, finally. Its cover was gone and its pages were ripped and filthy and swollen from getting wet.

"You have a flower growing in your head," he said, "I still have this book inside mine. I can't get it out. It won't go away. How can stuff you know be in a flower? All the stuff I know was in books."

Napu did not answer him. Instead, he got up and went inside the canoe house. A moment later he came out holding the Spirit of the Voyage. He reached down and took the book out of the circle and stabbed the Spirit of the Voyage into the sand in its place. "This is what you need to do. Take the book away and put this in its place. This is the spirit of our voyages, not that book. The book is only pictures and words. There is no spirit inside it."

Napu dropped the book next to Joseph and it fell open to a picture of William Shakespeare. Joseph had always been told that books were sacred, that they told the many stories of many peoples, stories of the whole world and the whole Universe, too. He studied the face of the great writer and then the face of the Spirit of the Voyage whose closed eyes bulged under their lids and whose mouth was frozen in a grim smile.

"It's hard, though, Napu. Hard for me, anyway. I know a spirit lives in that stick of wood—inside that carved root. You haven't seen it but you still believe it. I believe it because I have seen it—and not just in my dreams, either. It saved my life. But I've always loved books—and now, you know what I think? I think books have spirits in them, too. Just like the root of the nunu tree."

Chapter 27

The soldiers returned early one morning while the boys were rolling up their sleeping mats. As was his habit, Retawasiol had been up before dawn sitting on the beach, his face turned up at the stars. Now he came into the canoe house and said in a soft voice, "Joseph, get into the canoe."

They had done this many times now over the past two years. When they saw a ship on the horizon, Joseph got into the canoe and lay down in the deep V of the bottom while Napu covered him with mats and coconuts and a couple of paddles. And now they always remembered the book, grabbing it from its place of honor on top of Joseph's sleeping mat. Squeezed into the bottom of the canoe, Joseph put the book under his head and used it as a pillow. Then he would lie still and wait.

This morning, nothing happened for a long time, but finally he heard Retawasiol speaking English in the strong, businesslike way he always did with the Japanese captain. It was his way of warning Joseph that they were approaching the canoe house.

The captain's voice was loud, too, and he laughed after everything he said even though nothing he said was funny. "So, you would like to practice your English today. Okay! Let's get down to business as they say in America. There are things I am hearing— rumors, I should say, ha! ha!—about a boy with blond hair living here, on this island—an American boy."

The captain laughed but Retawasiol did not say anything. A moment later, they were in the *utt* and their voices were very close to the canoe.

For a moment, there was more silence. Joseph heard his own breathing, loud and rasping inside the echoing stillness of the canoe hull. He held his breath. Then he heard Retawasiol say, "My grandson does not have blond hair. But maybe the girls would like it if he did."

The captain laughed again and there was a sound of someone leaning up against the side of the canoe and then the captain's voice was very close, as if he was standing right next to Joseph's ear. "Nevertheless, I have ordered my men to search the island."

Joseph let his breath out slowly. He could feel the captain's body scraping against the wood of the hull less than an inch way from his head. "Meanwhile," the captain went on, "I've decided to take your canoe. You are not using it and certainly you will never use it again—you are old, and sick, and nearly blind, after all. When the war is over, I want to put it on a ship and send it home to Japan where its beauty can be appreciated. I would like you to have it dismantled for me when I come the next time."

When Retawasiol spoke, his voice was hard: "This canoe was built by my father. It is sacred, filled with the spirits of my ancestors. I would like to keep it near me until I die even though I am old and cannot sail it."

The captain laughed. "All the more reason I should take it home with me. To honor it and to protect it from typhoons and insects. It will slowly rot away sitting in here with no one caring for it. By the time I return, I want you and your grandson to have it taken apart down to the smallest possible pieces so my men can load it onto my ship."

There was another pause and Joseph again heard the sound of something rubbing against the side of the canoe.

"And where is that book?"

"Book?" Retawasiol asked.

"Yes, that book that you said washed up on shore. The one with the picture of the Samurai in it. I would like to take that with me, too. To show my officers. They have never seen a book written in English."

"My grandson used it to start fires," Retawasiol said.

"Is that true?" the captain asked.

Joseph heard Napu say, "Yes. I burned it."

"Ah, a pity. I wanted to show it to my men." The captain laughed again and said, "That is all now. My men are taking a look around. They will be done shortly. I hope they don't find any American spies here. You know what happened on Guam, don't you? The people there were hiding American soldiers—spies. They were caught and executed. Both the Americans and the people who were hiding them."

Then Joseph recognized a sound he had heard before in Errol Flynn movies—a sword being pulled from its scabbard. "You see this?" the captain said, "It's very sharp, ha! ha!"

Then there was silence, and for a long time Joseph could only hear the sound of his own heart pounding hard, and it sounded like it was making the sides of the canoe beat with it and then, when he knew he could not hold his breath any longer, he heard the sword sliding back into its scabbard and the captain said, "I need to get back to my ship. When this war is over, which will be soon, I'll come for the canoe. Goodbye."

Again there was silence. Joseph heard the captain's feet hard on the ground as he crossed the inside of the *utt*. He waited. He heard Retawasiol sigh as he sat down on his mat. He wanted to speak to him but did not dare—the soldiers might be outside. But where was Napu? When would it be safe to come out?

Another half an hour passed before he heard the sound of running feet. It was Napu. He came into the canoe house and said, "They're gone."

When Joseph climbed out of the canoe, Retawasiol was sitting on his mat, the rusty can of *tuba* next to him. He looked sad and very tired. He motioned for Joseph and Napu to sit near him.

"We must leave this island," he said, and he took a drink of *tuba*, holding the can up to his lips and tipping his head back. "You understood what the captain told me. The story of the American boy with the blond hair has spread in the islands. It would not be possible to stop such rumors. The soldiers will come back and the next time, they might find you. If they do, they will treat you as if you are a spy."

He did not look at Joseph; he let the words hang in the hot, still air before he went on.

"There are three other reasons that we must leave—and we must leave as soon as we can get ready. First, I cannot let him take this canoe. It is sacred to me and the spirit of my father. That I know you understand because you understand the power of the spirits of ancestors. They are not to be denied and it is not a good thing to make them angry. Who knows what they would do to me in the next life."

He lifted the rusty tin to his lips again and drank and then said, "And the next reason we must leave this island is a secret I have kept for many years. There is an island far north of here. Its star path is under *Wenewenen Fuhemwakut*—the *star-that-does-not-move*. It is where I believe our ancestor's spirits came out of Earth when the world was born and where I wish to die."

He was sitting up straight, his hands resting on his lap. For Joseph, the deep, cool shadows of the *utt* made him look like one of the long-ago pictures of great wise men in *A Boy's Picture History of the World in One Volume*. Joseph and Napu waited for what he would say next—what they must do now.

"The third reason we must leave soon is very simple. I will die soon."

Retawasiol shrugged as he said this and quickly went on: "It is true. Each day I am weaker. Each day my eyes tell me less and my heart tells me more. Soon I will become one of the spirits, too, and this is as it is supposed to be.

"So. You are strong and very nearly men and have learned much about following the star paths. To become true navigators, though, you have to do more than sail out around this atoll for a few hours and then come back. You must make a successful voyage—a long one. You must stop sitting in the circle and memorizing star paths. Now you must go far out to sea and test what you have learned. You have learned to sail the canoe from Puluwat, but now that the repairs to my *proa* are finished, you must learn to sail it, too. You do not have long to do these things. You will start today." He sighed. His face appeared strange, pale somehow, and he was sweating. "Now I must rest. You go and fish."

*****

Several hours later, after they had returned from fishing and while they were pulling the small paddling canoe up on the beach, the boys saw Retawasiol standing at the edge of the thicket of coconut and ironwood trees that hid the canoe house. He watched them for a moment and then turned and, using a piece of driftwood as a cane, walked back into the *utt*.

The boys finished dragging the paddling canoe up onto the dry sand. Napu picked up the knotted palm frond on which he had strung the fish they had caught, and together they walked up and into the trees and into the canoe house. Retawasiol was holding a long pole the boys knew was a spar—one of the two poles onto which the sail was tied.

"We must get the canoe out of the *utt* but it will be difficult with just the three of us," he said. "First, cut some coconut leaves and make a path for the canoe. Then cut some poles to help us push it out."

Joseph and Napu grabbed their machetes and went out into the jungle behind the canoe house. They cut the palm fronds from a low tree and spread them out in front of the canoe. Then they found two small trees, cut them down, and trimmed off the branches.

"Good," Retawasiol said. "Now, let's move the canoe out of the *utt*."

The *proa* was too heavy for them to push out, but using the poles as levers, they were able to slowly move it, foot by foot, into the sunlight. Once it was clear of the canoe house, Retawasiol stopped them.

He had directed them, but he had also helped, pushing on the canoe's hull, and now he sat down in the sand and leaned against a tree. Sweat was pouring from his forehead and he was breathing hard. Joseph got him a cup of water from the water can.

"Now," he said between breaths, "get the spars. You need to practice putting them up. You need to practice this on dry land before we go out to sea."

The boys got the spars from the canoe house and lay them on the canoe. Then Retawasiol stood up and slowly climbed onto the outrigger and moved into the middle of the canoe.

"Come up here," he said. "Let's get the sail up. You have sailed on the canoe when it comes up from Puluwat, and you have learned the names of the lines and the spars, but now you need to learn to handle them together on this canoe. Every canoe is different and you need to be able to handle them quickly. At first, we will just pretend we are at sea. When you can handle everything smoothly, then we can go out."

Napu and Joseph climbed up on the canoe and began. When they sailed with the men from Puluwat, they had learned which line went where and how to tie the foot of the mast into a shallow socket on the bow and how to raise the sail. And they had learned the most important and difficult skill—how to change directions; how to make the canoe go the other way across the wind.

In Napu's sailboat, this had been done by turning the boat so that the wind came over the other side. The sail was then adjusted for this new heading. But with a *proa* it was different. The canoe was not turned. Instead, the mast with its sail was untied from the *honifot*, a heavy piece of wood with a socket carved in it, on one end of the canoe, and moved to an identical socket on the other end; what had been the bow became the stern and the stern became the bow. The outrigger was always kept on the windward side. This process, called "shunting," was not easy to do smoothly.

At first they could not untie the knots quickly enough, for it took both strength and balance to move the mast down the length of the canoe. After the first few tries, it seemed as though they would never learn. Retawasiol taunted them: "You are strong boys. Come on, can't you learn to work together? If you can't do it on dry land, how will you do it out on the sea with waves crashing down on you?"

After three days of practice, they had mastered it, and one afternoon Retawasiol said, "Now you are ready to try it at sea. The stars have stopped fighting so tomorrow will be good weather."

Chapter 28

As he often did, early the next morning just before the faintest hint of dawn, Retawasiol left the *utt* and went down to the beach. This time Joseph was ready. He woke Napu. "He's gone down to look at the stars. Let's go with him."

In the dark, Napu rubbed his eyes and groaned but said, "Okay, that's good. Let's go."

They found the old man sitting on the sand looking up toward the sky. If he heard them coming, he did not react, but he did not appear startled when they sat down next to him. It was dark, but in the starlight, they could see the form of Retawasiol's body as he gazed upwards. They both looked up at the sky, filled from horizon to horizon with stars.

"It is a good time for voyaging," Retawasiol said. "The stars have stopped fighting."

"How do stars fight?" Joseph asked.

Retawasiol sighed and they could see his face drop down from the sky and look out to sea. "I do not know how they do it. No one can know that. But you must learn about the fighting of stars to be a navigator, because you must know about the weather. When the stars are fighting the weather will be bad. Now it is a good time. The stars are at peace with one another."

Joseph looked up at a sky that was the palest white with millions of stars. How would you know which ones were fighting and which ones were not? And how do fighting stars control the weather. He wanted to ask these questions, but he kept silent and they sat that way for a long time looking at the night sky and out across the sea.

Then Retawasiol said, "You are both sailors. You have already sailed across the sea from Guahan on your boat. And you have sailed here, to Pikelot, too, on a canoe. You have seen how men handle a *proa* and you have been learning to do it yourselves. And you have learned much about the star paths and the *etak*. There will only be three of us today when we go out and one of us is a sick old man. But I think we will have no difficulties because you are both young and strong. I'm depending on you. Let's go and eat our breakfast now, so we will be ready when the sun comes up."

They walked back up to the canoe house and, in the half-light, ate roasted breadfruit and smoked fish and some roasted turtle meat and drank water from the water bucket. When they were finished, the dawn was full over them and the sun about to rise from the water on the other side of the island.

"Come on now," Retawasiol said, "we'll get the canoe in the water."

They put their fishing lines, a machete, and a dozen drinking coconuts into the canoe and then, by pushing and using the poles, moved the canoe, slowly, foot by foot, along its path of palm fronds to the edge of the water. With a final effort, the *proa* slid down the last few feet of beach until it floated in the surf.

Retawasiol climbed onto the outrigger and, with painful slowness, moved all the way back to one end, from where he would steer. Then Joseph and Napu pushed the canoe out a little farther and pulled themselves on board. The wind was behind them, coming down off the island, and even before they could get the sail up, the canoe was moving away from the beach. Then all the practice on land paid off; they quickly put up the sail and it filled with the breeze and they swung away towards the reef and the sea.

Retawasiol gave the boys quiet instructions on handling the sail as he steered the canoe out through the narrow passage. In a few minutes they could feel the great ocean swells under them and the water became a deep, pellucid blue.

*****

It was a long day. They sailed away on the wind until the island was just a gray smudge on the horizon and the farther they got from the atoll, the bigger the swells became. Each one lifted the *proa* high on its crest and for a moment they could see far out across the endless ocean and then they plunged down into the valleys between the swells and walls of water towered above them.

But the canoe rode the swells lightly like a great waterbug, and Retawasiol sat on the narrow stern, one foot resting on the rudder almost in the water, while both hands gripped the tiller. And he did not seem so old now, or so sick. While the corners of his mouth were turned down in concentration, his eyes were bright and crinkled with pleasure. How long, Joseph wondered, had it been since he had sailed his own canoe?

They practiced shunting the spars to change direction and soon learned to keep their balance in the seaway as they wrestled the poles into position and tied the knots to keep them there. And they took turns doing the other things necessary to sail a *proa* on the open ocean: adjusting the sail so it caught the wind just right, sitting down in the narrow V of the canoe bottom and bailing water that sloshed in, and finally, they each spent time at the tiller.

Retawasiol motioned to Napu first and when Napu was ready, the old man moved, again with painful slowness, from the end of the canoe to the outrigger platform and Napu took his place at the helm. Then Joseph sat at the base of the mast with the line that ran to the sail in his hand and Retawasiol told him how to adjust the sail so that it was also helping to steer.

After what seemed like just a short time, but with the sun well past its zenith, Napu and Joseph switched positions and Joseph found himself perched on the sharp end of the canoe, his hand on the tiller and his foot down on the rudder. Ahead of him, the canoe seemed to stretch out across the seas, its sail full-bellied with the breeze, its bow plunging and rising and sending small flying fish racing off ahead of them.

They did not stop until the sun was getting low in the sky, until they thought they were too tired to even lift their arms. As they were preparing for a last shunt so they could sail back to the island, Napu called to Joseph and pointed up into the sky at the birds that had been fishing, but now had stopped circling and had begun to fly toward the atoll. Joseph knew what Napu wanted him to understand. It was as Retawasiol had told them; the birds will tell you where land is. *We have learned something,* Joseph thought; *we have learned how to sail a canoe and we have learned to watch for birds.*

Then they did the last shunt of the mast and the spars and for the first time that day, they did it flawlessly. Napu untied the yard from its socket on the bow and together they moved it with the sail and the boom down the length of the canoe. Then the yard seemed to fall into the socket at the other end of the canoe of its own accord and Joseph tied it in with two quick movements. Through all their practice, they had discovered the secret: working together, they had mastered what Retawasiol had meant; it was not so much about strength. It was about timing and balancing themselves against the sea—and getting their hands to work the coconut fiber ropes quickly, and tying the proper knot the first time without hesitation.

When they sailed back through the reef and onto the beach after that first day, they were sunburned and exhausted but they still had to get the canoe high enough up on the beach so the tide would not carry it away. Retawasiol, who seemed too tired to climb off the canoe, just rolled off the outrigger platform and into the water, where he lay, face up, resting.

Joseph and Napu ran up on the sand and got the poles and as many palm fronds as they could carry. They laid out the fronds to make a path for the canoe and with Retawasiol pushing as much as he could, with painful slowness they worked it up onto the steep incline of the lower beach. Then the *mah*, the "eyes" at either end of the canoe, were covered with mats to protect them.

When they were finished, Retawasiol said, "I was right about you—about both of you. You are strong and smart. You did well today and I am proud. You tell me you are brothers because of what you have been through together and maybe you are right; you are brothers more than real brothers can call themselves brothers. And now, I will say, I feel like you are my sons."

Joseph felt his heart rise up. He glanced at Napu and Napu smiled at him. At first he had felt clumsy and hopeless out there on the sea. The spars and lines were difficult to sort out, the ocean had been rough, and Napu seemed to learn more quickly than he did; he seemed more at home on the water. Joseph had envied how fast he learned and he had thought that perhaps it was as Napu had once said. It was in his blood. But by the afternoon, Joseph had begun to feel as if he was learning; he began to do things he did not think he could ever do, and by the time they shunted the sail for the last time to start the run home, he could do everything Napu had done.

The old navigator had been smiling but now his smile disappeared and he said, "You must be ready when the time comes for us to go. Today was just the beginning. You must put all your energy into learning what you must learn. At the next new moon, we will leave. We will need to prepare much food."

He sighed, as he did when he was tired. Slowly, unsteadily, he started to walk up the beach toward the canoe house, but when Joseph offered an arm to support him, he pushed it away. So Joseph and Napu walked beside him and as they walked, Retawasiol said, "I want you to think about something tonight while you are eating and resting. It is an important part of navigation—maybe the most important part.

"Over many seasons, I have told you about the seabirds and how they can help us find an island, and you saw that today. I have told you that there is the phosphorescence deep in the sea, a light sent up to us by the reefs that can tell us if we are near land. I have told you that when the sea strikes an island, the island breaks up the waves and changes their patterns. If we can learn to see these different patterns, we can understand where the land lies. I have spoken to you about clouds. Sometimes clouds will form over an island, or near an island. A good navigator can read these clouds and know what they are telling him.

"You have learned that around each island is a circle of these natural things, the birds and phosphorescence, and clouds and that all these are called *pookof*. These will tell you where the island is.

When islands are close enough together, these circles connect with one another. They form a screen to catch the navigator and his canoe. For the good navigator, it will be difficult to pass through such a screen without understanding where the islands lie."

He stopped walking for a moment and took some breaths and said, "What I want you to think about tonight—to dream about—is this. We learn about these things separately, but we must put them together; the stars paths and the *pookof* must become as a single thing inside our souls if we are to be true navigators."

He sighed again and said, "That is enough. I can see you are very tired from being at sea; I am tired, too. But you must make food for us and we must drink as much water and coconut water as we can hold so we can be strong tomorrow."

He lifted his hands in a sign of dismissal and the boys stopped walking and watched him continue up the beach and disappear into the shadows of the trees.

Chapter 29

That night, Napu and Joseph slept on the beach under the glowing stars, and the next morning when the sun was still below the curve of the Earth but sending soft hints of the daylight to come, they were awake. They rolled up their sleeping mats and got ready for another day of sailing. They prepared a breakfast of fish, turtle eggs, baked breadfruit, and mango and brought it to the canoe house to present to Retawasiol. But they found him still lying on his mat, his eyes closed, his breathing slow and regular. They set the food down beside him and quietly left the *utt*.

The old man slept late into the morning while Joseph and Napu sat in the shade and waited. Joseph finally said what they were both thinking: "He is usually up before us. We had better go and see if he is all right."

Napu pretended to be surprised by this idea. "No," he said, his voice almost indignant. "He is old, but he will not die here on Pikelot. He is going to die on the island where the fire comes from the mountains. He is still strong."

Joseph shook his head. "I'm tired from yesterday—and I'm young. I think Retawasiol..." And now he thought for a moment and remembered what his mother used to say when he was little and was very tired—"I think he overdid it."

*****

When the sun was high overhead the old man was still lying on his mat. The boys hung around the canoe house and checked on him often. Each time they found him with his eyes closed, breathing deeply, and they slowly and quietly left the *utt*. To pass the time, they gathered breadfruit and built up the fire and roasted it and then sat in the sand, opening coconuts with their machetes and talking.

"Did you ever kiss a girl?" Joseph asked.

Napu laughed. "Kiss a girl?"

"Yeah."

"You mean, like really kiss one?"

"Yeah. And grandmothers and mothers and aunties don't count."

Napu stopped smiling and took a strong cut at the coconut he was holding. The top of it came off and the piece flew into the fire. "Yes, sure I have. Lots of times."

"Lots of times?"

"Yeah."

"When? I mean, how?"

Napu raised the open nut to his mouth and drank and kept drinking for a long time. When the nut was empty, he set it down and said, "What do you mean how? You don't know how to kiss a girl?"

"Well, yeah, I know how. I saw them do it in the movies lots of times and I almost kissed one once," Joseph said.

Now Napu turned and smiled at him. "You did? Almost?"

"Yeah. I was with a bunch of kids. I was pretty small. Younger than everyone else. They were spinning this bottle on the floor and when you spun it, if it was pointing to a girl when it stopped, she was the one you had to kiss."

Joseph stopped and watched the fire and Napu was quiet for a moment and then said, "Well? What happened?"

"When it was my turn, I spun the bottle and it pointed at this girl and she got up and ran away."

Napu laughed and picked up another coconut and started chopping at the top with his machete. "That's not almost kissing. She ran away. Did you chase her?"

"No. She ran outside the house."

"Was she crying?"

"No. She just ran. Everyone else was laughing."

"It's good that she wasn't crying," Napu said. "That would have really been bad."

"Why?"

"Why? If you try to kiss a girl and she starts crying and runs away, that means she wasn't just being shy. It means she thinks you're ugly or something."

Joseph thought about this and said, "No, she wasn't crying."

"That's good, anyway. If you ask a girl to marry you and she just starts crying, that's good. If she starts crying and runs away, that's bad."

"How do you know?"

"My uncle told me. He said when he asked my auntie to marry him, she started crying and he knew she wanted to because she didn't run away."

Joseph took a quick chop at the top of the coconut he was holding and a chunk of husk flew off into the sand. He held the nut up to his mouth and drank. When he was finished, he said, "Are you going to get married?"

"Yes," Napu said without hesitating, as if he had been thinking about it, "I am. It's a man's job to have lots of children so they can take care of him when he gets old. And I'm going to teach my sons to be navigators, so—"

They were interrupted by the sound of footsteps in the sand behind them. Before they could turn around, they heard Retawasiol's voice: "What's this? Lots of children? When you can't take care of one old man? When you can't catch enough fish to feed yourselves? Do you know your star paths? What of the star path to Saipan? Have you got that in your brains, or has this talk of kissing and having many babies taken your minds away from the sea?"

His face was grim but he seemed steady enough on his feet and when he got to the fire, he sat down and said, "I've had a good long rest, but we have wasted a day. We have to leave before the soldiers come back." He pointed at the circle. "Napu, tell me the star path to steer for West Fayu."

Napu's face fell. Under the pressure of the old man's gaze, his mind had gone blank. He stared down at the circle in silence.

After long moments, Retawasiol said, "Joseph, you tell me. What is the star to steer for West Fayu?"

Joseph looked at Retawasiol's cloudy eyes and said, "I don't remember."

The old man spat in the sand. "You must remember. All this time we have been practicing, learning. You cannot forget. There is no time left. If the soldiers come and find you, they will cut all our heads off. Mine, too. And what if I die out there at sea? What if I cannot follow the star paths because it is getting hard for me to see? Do you understand that your lives depend on you remembering?"

Then for a long time there was nothing but the sound of the surf on the reef and the rustling of the palm trees in the wind and then Retawasiol said, "The spirits have told me that tomorrow a canoe will come from Puluwat. The spirits said they have news for us." He sighed and said, "Now I am hungry and thirsty. I see you have prepared food. Good."

While Retawasiol ate and drank, no one spoke. When he was finished, he slowly got to his feet and walked back up the beach and disappeared into the canoe house.

*****

The next morning it was Retawasiol who woke them. He seemed full of energy and excitement. "Come on then," he said in a voice that was almost teasing, "let's eat and launch the canoe. Maybe you can learn something about navigation before the canoe arrives from Puluwat."

And it was Retawasiol who directed the slow process of getting the *proa* in the water and it was Retawasiol who climbed onto the canoe first and took his place at the helm.

As the boys hoisted sail, Retawasiol told them what was happening: "Now we are pretending to sail to Saipan. Tell me the star path."

It was one of the first star paths they had learned, but now the boys hesitated. This was the big test. They were heading out to sea in a canoe—there must be no mistakes. Joseph started to speak but then stopped his tongue. Retawasiol waited for an answer.

Joseph was sitting near Napu near the mast, holding the line that controlled the sail. It was his job to ease the line out or pull it in to adjust the sail to the wind to keep the sail full and to help the helmsman keep the heading. Joseph looked at Napu, who shot him a glance. Still neither of them spoke and still Retawasiol waited, staring out over the bright sea. Then Napu said, "Saipan is under *Tolon Welo*—setting *Welo*."

"But it is daylight now," Retawasiol said, "there are no stars."

Now Joseph gave his tongue its freedom. "Even if we can't see the stars, we know in which direction Saipan lies from Pikelot. We can look back at the island and judge our direction from the trees and we can see the trail our canoe is leaving in the water and we can adjust for the current . . . ." He stopped. He had said too much. He scolded himself: *Don't try to be such a know-it-all.* He pretended to study the set of the sail.

There was a long silence. They slid out of the channel into the sea and Retawasiol turned the canoe so that its bow was pointing in the direction of Saipan. Joseph pulled the sail in until it was set properly for the heading Retawasiol had chosen.

Then Napu said, "And now we will line up our course by looking backward at the island and we can hold our course by keeping the seas at the same angle to the canoe. There are three swells we can watch. The one from the east is always there—it is the easiest and biggest to see—but there are also swells from the northeast and southeast."

"Good," Retawasiol, said. "But, as Joseph has said, do not forget the current. The ocean moves and it carries the canoe with it. We must adjust. Saipan is there." He pointed out across the ocean. "But the current and wind come from there." He pointed toward the northeast. "Which way should we steer?"

"We must steer as close to the wind as we can," Napu said quickly, "or the wind and the current will push us away from Saipan."

"Yes," Retawasiol said. "Napu, you will be the navigator first. Tell me how to steer. Joseph, you watch and learn. You will bring us home." He said nothing more and they settled into sailing.

Both boys watched the seas, and until Pikelot disappeared below the horizon behind them, checked its position and the angle the wake of the canoe was leaving. But it was Napu who was the navigator and it was Napu who told Retawasiol and Joseph what adjustments to make in the canoe's heading to keep it sailing toward Saipan. Each time he spoke, he was certain the old navigator would correct him, tell him he was wrong and chastise him for not knowing something. But now, Retawasiol did not scold. When he questioned one of Napu's decisions, he did so with a soft voice, and he encouraged him and explained why he was correcting him.

*****

They sailed northeast all morning and then, when the sun was at its highest point in the sky, Retawasiol said, "Now it is time to return to Pikelot and now we are not pretending. We cannot miss the island. Joseph, your life will depend on it. Mine and Napu's also. Napu, you have done well. Now come back here and steer and Joseph will guide us back."

The old navigator's words rang in Joseph's head—*Your life will depend on it.* Could this be true? He tried to focus on navigation—on the waves and on the sun and on the wake the canoe was leaving behind the canoe—but through it all came the sound of the Japanese captain's harsh voice and empty laugh and the sound of the sword he carried at his side being pulled from its scabbard.

Napu's voice forced the image from Joseph's mind. "Joseph, pay attention. We need to shunt."

Working together, the boys dowsed the sail and moved the spars and soon the sail was full again and the canoe was sailing in the opposite direction, back toward Pikelot. The wind was fair and they maintained a good speed.

Joseph found that he now was acutely aware of the seas and the canoe's relationship to them. He felt any change in the motion of the canoe immediately, any change in the wind on his skin was an alarm. He watched the track the wake of the canoe left in the water and so understood how much they had to adjust for the ocean current that was always trying to pull them off course. But it was the sight of the tall trees of Pik rising up over the horizon that they waited for; seeing them would reveal the skills of the navigator.

As the day wore on, as the sun dropped toward the western horizon, Joseph became more anxious. The more he thought of the sun, the slower it seemed to move through its arc. Yet there was no time to be bored, no time to think about the soldiers, no time to take his attention off the task at hand. There was only time for being at one with the great blue ocean and the sky and the wind.

Late in the day, Retawasiol said, "Joseph, what are you watching for now?"

Joseph felt his heart stop. *What could it be*, he thought, *what am I watching for?* Then he saw three birds. They had been circling the canoe, eyeing the fishing line trailing behind it. Birds—that's what Retawasiol meant. "There," he said, and he pointed at the brown noddies that floated so effortlessly on the wind, "I'm watching them."

"Good," Retawasiol said. No sooner had he spoken than the birds stopped circling the canoe, and at some unseen signal all three of them turned in the same direction and flew off toward the horizon.

"That's where it is," Joseph said, "that's where Pik is."

He knew he was right and his heart was racing as fast as the birds were flying. He needed only to make a small adjustment in their heading to line the canoe up with the path the birds had set through the sky, and when this was done, watch the angle of the seas and keep them on that course.

*****

But they would not arrive before dark. When the edge of the sun touched the edge of the ocean, the dark seemed at first to come slowly and then all at once. The sun glowed reddish-yellow as it approached the edge of the sea and then flashed a sudden and startling green as the last of it dipped below the horizon. Abandoned by the light, the sky changed from light azure to deep blue and then black and the darkness that followed might have been the insides of a great fish that had swallowed them and the world with it.

Just before darkness came, while the western sky was still aglow, the first star appeared in the already black eastern sky. They stared at it in wonder. What star was it? Retawasiol was silent, waiting for the boys to answer their own question. But both Napu and Joseph knew: it was *Aweran Mangar*—the light of the flying fish.

As they were now used to doing when they needed to answer one of Retawasiol's questions, they looked at each other first. If they both knew the answer they nodded and then they took turns saying it. It was Napu's turn. "It's the light of the flying fish," he said, his voice rising with his confidence.

The old man nodded but said nothing. The canoe was sailing well, the *tam*, the balancing weight on the end of the outrigger, skimming through the water, cutting through the tops of the seas and leaving a white wake glowing in its trail. They waited for more stars and in a few minutes, the night sky had blinked full of them. Joseph's heart beat faster as he stared up at them. What had seemed so easy sitting in the circle in front of Retawasiol's *utt*, now was hopelessly confusing. Where was *Mailap Anefang*? And *Ukunik*, the tail of the fish? Which one was *Maharuw*, the darting eyes?

But then he saw what he had so desperately hoped they would see when darkness fell over them: there was *Tan Up*—the rising Southern Cross that the islanders called the Trigger Fish. Impossible to mistake, it was right in front of them. And then, just as he saw this, he saw something else: the faint glow of a light. But it was not a star—it was a fire, a fire on an island rising from the immense darkness of the ocean. While they had been away, the canoe from Puluwat had arrived and now Joseph could picture the men sitting around that fire eating fish and turtle and drinking *tuba* and laughing at each other's stories.

They had done it. He and Napu had navigated all day using the wind and the waves and the canoe's trail in the water and now, at night, the canoe was sailing toward the right star—and right toward Pik. There could be no mistaking this—no mistaking their success.

Still neither Retawasiol nor Napu said anything. Joseph could see Napu's dark form and he knew that he had turned to look at him. In the darkness, with just the light of the stars reflecting on his face, Napu smiled.

Chapter 30

Then, out of the darkness, Retawasiol spoke. "There is another skill you need to learn now," he said. "It is called *fu taur*. It means finding one's way through the reef at night. We don't need to worry about this when approaching Pik because the water is deep enough over the reef. But you need to learn the idea. Napu, where is *Wenewenen Fuhemwakut* — the *star-that-does-not-move*?"

Napu immediately pointed to Polaris, the North Star, where it lay low on the horizon.

"Good," Retawasiol said, "Let's say that to sail into Pik, we must put that on the *tam* and then look for the trees on the north side of the island and the beach on the south side. Line them up so you will sail in the middle of them and we can sail through the hole in the reef. This technique is call *fu taur*."

Once they had sailed around to the western side of Pik, Napu turned the canoe until the North Star was over the tip of the outrigger and then, with just the silhouette of the island rising up behind the glow of the fire, they could just make out the trees and the beach that Retawasiol had spoken of. Napu aligned the canoe perfectly between them.

"Now, Napu, you must hold it there. Do not fail. Someday your life may depend on it. Maybe even today if the water is rough. You can never be certain about the ocean around Pik."

So, now, Joseph thought, *our lives no longer depend on me, but on Napu's skill at steering the proa. It's always the same at sea — your life depends on your skill.*

No one spoke as the canoe approached the atoll. They could hear the crashing surf and see the fire getting bigger as they drew closer and then they could see the small silhouettes of the men sitting around the flames. The sea lifted the canoe up and dropped it down. The surf built until it foamed around them and Napu sat high on the end of the canoe and guided the *proa*, his hands on the tiller, one foot down on the rudder.

The canoe pitched in the confused rush of water and then began to turn sideways. Joseph heard Napu yell out, but he held on and brought the bow back straight again and they were lifted on a wave and carried toward the beach. Napu and Joseph worked quickly together to douse the sail and stow it on the outrigger platform.

The men sitting around the fire heard them and saw the shadow of the canoe where it had come ashore. They jumped up and a moment later were helping bring the canoe farther onto the beach. They gathered the palm fronds and placed them in front of the canoe and then pushed it up away from the water.

Only then did Retawasiol climb down from his place near the mast. He moved slowly, but when hands reached up to help him, he brushed them away. When he was standing on the beach, the others stood away from him, letting him stand on his own.

He walked to the fire and sat down. "Do you have some food? I will eat before I go to sleep."

The men brought him a banana leaf filled with turtle meat and baked taro root and the old man began to eat in silence. After a few moments, the men began talking among themselves and Joseph recognized Raumwele, who had been the navigator on their voyage to Pik. He asked about the day's sail.

When Napu started talking, softly but with a certain pride in his voice, Joseph realized that he was speaking in Puluwatese. And he realized, too, that he understood him as easily as if he were speaking English. Somehow, over the past few seasons—had it been a year? two years?—living with Retawasiol, who spoke English, but repeated everything in Puluwatese, they had learned much of the language of the island.

When Napu fell silent, Joseph spoke. His voice, as it carried out over the flames to the dark-eyed faces of the men, sounded different to him. He no longer sounded like a boy. Like Napu, he now had the voice of a man and he spoke with a man's tongue of things of the sea, of voyaging and navigating using the music of the stars.

The men listened with respect and when Napu and Joseph had finished, they sat awhile saying nothing. The *tuba* was passed around from man to man and when it was Joseph's turn, he took only a small sip and passed the cup to Napu. Napu did the same, just sipped at the cup, and then passed it to Retawasiol.

The old man finished it in a single gulp and said, "What news do you have for us? The spirits of the ancestors told me last night that you were coming."

Again there was silence, and then Raumwele said, "There are stories of a great battle being fought on Saipan. The stories say that the Americans have landed a huge army and that the Japanese are fighting and that many people are dying." He fell silent for a moment, the flames playing on his face. Then the *tuba* cup was passed to him and he drank it and said, "The Japanese thought that the Americans would fight here in the Caroline Islands, but they did

140

not. They surprised the Japanese and attacked Saipan. Now the Japanese here will be cut off from Japan."

"Where did you hear this?" Retawasiol asked. He drank another cup of *tuba* and took a bite of turtle meat.

"From the Japanese captain."

Retawasiol nodded and again there was silence, and the silence allowed the sea to intrude its sounds and the fire spoke, too, and the wind was loud in the tops of the palm trees.

After a long time, Retawasiol said, "We will leave tomorrow night. Maybe before he goes back to Japan, the Japanese commander will come to find the blond American spy and to take my canoe. I will not let him do those things and I will not allow myself to die here." He turned to Napu and Joseph and said, "You cannot allow yourselves to die here either."

Again silence and again the sea came to them with its music and the stars were very bright and filled the sky. There was a feeling of great power in the wind. Not a one of them questioned the old navigator.

Then Raumwele said, "We will provision your *proa* tomorrow and we will make any repairs you need."

"Good," said Retawasiol. "Now, it is time to sleep."

He stood up very slowly but everyone watched the fire as he disappeared into the dark.

Joseph found Napu's eyes across the fire for a moment and each knew what the other was thinking. This was the time they had been waiting for, the time of leaving, the time of voyaging.

*****

Joseph and Napu followed the old man up to the *utt* and fell asleep as soon as they lay down on their mats. But Joseph had not been asleep long when was awakened by a soft chanting—someone speaking in the singsong manner of the islands. He lay still and listened. There were the usual night sounds of the sea and the wind and it was the wind that was carrying the voice to him through the darkness. He could hear Napu's deep-sleep breathing but not Retawasiol's.

He moved carefully, pushing himself up off his mat slowly. He knew the inside of the *utt* well enough to walk through it with his eyes closed, but he chose his footing carefully. When he reached the edge of the low, sloping thatched roof, he again dropped to his hands and knees and crawled out into the night.

The chanting was louder now, though still very soft. Seeing the flames of a fire, he lay down behind a stand of low bushes and watched. After a while, he saw Retawasiol approach the fire and sit down. The flames danced on the old man's face while he chanted in his low, hoarse voice as he looked across the fire. Joseph followed his eyes and saw what he was staring at as he sang: it was the Spirit of the Voyage. The root of the nunu tree with the spirit's image carved into it was stuck deeply into the sand at the fire's edge, the firelight shining on its closed, bulging eyes.

Joseph watched and listened until he began to feel sleepy, and then he rested his head on his hands and closed his eyes—just for a moment or two, not longer—but while his eyes were still closed, he heard another voice and looked up. There was the Spirit of the Voyage itself, the powerful old ghost. It had come out of the wood and now sat cross-legged across from Retawasiol. It watched the old navigator through fierce eyes and answered his questions in a voice that came from the night itself, from the wind, from the shadows of the trees, and from the fire.

They spoke to each other for a long time, each chanting in turn, until Joseph felt himself getting sleepy again and then the chanting changed to the sound of a building wind in the tops of the trees and Joseph woke up to the pearly light of dawn. The fire was gone and Retawasiol and the Spirit of the Voyage, too, and the clearing where the fire had been was filled with the deep, cool shadows of early morning.

Chapter 31

They prepared for the voyage all next day. The men from Puluwat had brought food and supplies for voyaging with them and now this was transferred to Retawasiol's canoe. It included a fermented paste made of pounded taro root, packed in bags made from tightly woven coconut leaves, as well as coconuts and *mwar*, baked and fermented breadfruit. All this was loaded onto the canoe's platforms and covered with pandanus mats. Then they replaced the *proa*'s pandanus-leaf sail with the canvas sail salvaged from Napu's boat. Fishing lines with razor-sharp hooks made from shells, they wound into tight coils and stored on board, and they repaired all worn lashings on the canoe with new coconut fiber rope. Extra spars and coils of rope were lashed together and put down inside the hull.

Napu and Joseph took the paddling canoe out to the reef, where they fished, and then they smoked their catch over a fire and wrapped it in banana leaves.

When the sun was getting low in the sky, Retawasiol went up to his canoe house and lay down. He slept until the darkening sky revealed the first star, and then he came down to the beach where the others had finished the preparations for the voyage.

The fully packed *proa*, covered with pandanus mats to protect it from the sun, sat at the edge of the water. Joseph and Napu sat with the men around the fire eating and talking quietly. When they saw Retawasiol emerge from his *utt*, they fell silent and waited.

The old man approached them, looked at the canoe, and said, "The stars have stopped fighting and will not fight again for a while. This means the weather will be good. It is a good time for voyaging. The spirits of the ancestors came into my dreams and have told me that the soldiers will come back soon to look for the American with the blond hair and to take my canoe. We must leave tonight; we must leave now."

Carrying the Spirit of the Voyage in one hand, he went to the canoe, pulled off some of the matting, and slowly climbed onto the outrigger platform. He took a piece of rope and lashed the Spirit of the Voyage onto the mast and then looked down at the others who had gathered around the canoe. "It is time," he said, and he waved his hand out toward the sea.

But then he stopped and seemed to listen, and without turning and looking, he said, "It's too late; they are here. Joseph, go away from the fire, go back into the jungle. Hide yourself."

They all peered out toward the distant, dark horizon and saw what the old man had only sensed: there was a warship. It was just a few lights on a black streak on the edge of the water, but Joseph felt his heart stop. They had waited too long to leave. He was caught, trapped.

Retawasiol still did not look where the others were looking, but again said, "Joseph, go now. Go to the middle of the island. Cover yourself with leaves. And ask the spirits to help you so the soldiers will not find you in the dark. And take this. It will protect you. "

He untied the Spirit of the Voyage from the mast and handed it down to Joseph. Joseph looked out to sea and then up at Retawasiol. He took the Spirit of the Voyage from him and slowly backed away from the fire, away from its glow, and moved up the beach and into the shadows of the jungle.

When he had disappeared into the trees, Retawasiol gave more orders: "Get the *tuba* ready. This captain likes *tuba*. I have drunk it with him many times. It makes him happy and it makes him forget. It will give us a chance."

With great effort, Retawasiol climbed down from the canoe and joined the others by the fire. "Remember," he said, "Napu is my grandson. He is here to take care of me. We were getting the canoe ready to go fishing. We're leaving in the morning."

Then they watched as the warship drew closer and stopped a half-mile off shore. After a short time, a small boat was launched from the ship, headed toward the island. In a few minutes, in spite of the growing darkness, it was close enough to see five men on board.

By the time they approached the beach, the men in the launch were mere shadows. Just before the bow touched the sand, the shadow at the helm cut the engine, while the shadow in the bow jumped out and held the boat steady. A third shadow waited until the boat was nearly on the beach before he stepped out into the shallow surf. He gave orders in rapid Japanese and then walked up the beach to the fire.

He stepped into the circle of firelight and glanced around at the gathered men. Wearing his officer's hat, pistol and sword at his side, he bowed slightly. "Good evening," he said in English.

No one replied. They stared into the fire and continued to pass the coconut shell cup full of *tuba* from hand to hand.

Douglas Arvidson

"I see you have my canoe down at the water. But it is not ready to be taken aboard my ship as I ordered." The captain laughed, then put his hands on his hips and looked from face to face before settling on Retawasiol.

Without looking up at the captain, Retawasiol said, "We needed it to go fishing. We need to eat."

"You have two canoes here. I don't think you need this one, too, for fishing. But I am afraid there is no time now to worry about canoes. Ha! Ha! I'm being called away by my superiors. I must join the battle in the Mariana Islands to defend the homeland from the Americans who are even now attacking the island of Saipan and killing our people.

"So—I'm not here to get my canoe. I'm here on a more important mission: to find the American spy. I have good reason to believe he is on this island. Ha! Such spies with their radios have caused many problems for our military efforts."

He turned and spoke to the four sailors who had pulled the launch up on the sand. When he was finished, the men took pistols from their belts and walked up the beach toward the trees, shining their flashlights into the gloom. "It is not a big island. I think they'll have no trouble finding him. When they find him, I have told them to shoot him."

"Captain," Retawasiol said, "we have no American spies here. What is there to spy on? There are no Japanese soldiers. Just birds and coconuts and a sick, crazy, half-blind old man. And though I have tried, I have never been able to make a radio out of a coconut. We only know how to eat them and drink *tuba* from them. And so, while your men are searching, I invite you to drink with us from our coconut. We are your friends and it will be our way of saying goodbye. Until you return, of course, and we hope that will be soon."

Retawasiol nodded at Raumwele, who stood up and brought the cup of *tuba* to the captain. The captain studied the broken coconut shell that held the drink for a long moment, but then he took it. Before he drank, he nodded at Retawasiol and then at each of the others in turn, including Napu, who was sitting by Retawasiol's side. Then he tipped his head back, and instead of sipping, he gulped it down and handed the empty shell back to Raumwele.

"Good, that's good," Retawasiol said, smiling and nodding. "We have just harvested our *tuba* yesterday, so we have a lot of it.

Raumwele dipped the cup into the rusty bucket of *tuba* and handed it to Retawasiol, who sipped at it and passed it to Napu. Napu felt his stomach rise up at the smell of it, but he took a small sip and passed it along. When it had passed around the circle of seated men, Raumwele again filled it and brought it to the captain.

The captain took the cup, but this time, instead of drinking it down, he began walking down the beach away from the fire. When he reached Retawasiol's *proa*, he took a sip and then, with a sudden movement, pulled his sword from its scabbard. He took another sip and said, "Maybe I should just take a small piece of the canoe with me, just to remember you by."

The light from the fire played off the shiny black wood of the hull and he raised his sword as if he was going to chop a piece from it but stopped himself and lowered the sword. "I'd forgotten," he said, "that *proas* are sacred. They carry the spirits of your ancestors in their wood and in their sails. I would hate to have those spirits angry with me. They might take revenge. Ha!"

He lifted the cup to his mouth and drained it, tossed the cup down onto the sand, and then again swung his sword up high, this time bringing it down hard on the side of the canoe. But at the very instant the steel blade struck the wood, there came a flash of lightning and a roar of thunder and the sound of gunshots and screaming from the dark jungle of the island.

Napu felt the pain of terror shoot through his body: *They found Joseph. They're killing him.* He started to jump up but felt Retawasiol's hand on his shoulder and heard his fierce whisper: "No! Do not move."

The captain stared at the jungle and then at the blade of his sword. Before he could say anything, there were more shots and more screams and then shadows burst from the dark edge of the trees and came running down the beach. The four soldiers stumbled and fell as they scrambled toward the water, and just as they reached the boat, there was another heavy thunderous roar and a ragged arc of lightning ripped the sky above them.

Still they screamed and the captain examined the blade of his sword as if the lightning might have come from it. He looked back at his men and they screamed something at him in Japanese and began pushing the boat away from the beach. The captain began yelling at them but they did not listen. One of them got the engine going while the other pushed the bow around out toward sea. When the captain realized they were going to leave him behind, he ran out into the water, waving his sword, and threw himself head-first into the launch. A moment later they were speeding away, the sound of their engine diminishing into the darkness.

Napu jumped to his feet and ran up the beach toward the jungle, calling out Joseph's name. As he disappeared into the trees, it began to rain. Soon a heavy downpour put out the fire and left Retaswasiol and the others in complete darkness. They sat and waited, not speaking.

But then the rain stopped and the stars came back and the beach glowed again in the loom from the night sky, and they saw two more shadows come out from among the trees and walk down the beach. Joseph and Napu approached the circle of men and sat down among them. No one spoke until Retawasiol said, "Tell us, Joseph, what happened?"

Joseph's voice came to them out of the darkness of his shadow: "I pulled leaves and branches down over me and hid under them, but I forgot about the Spirit of the Voyage. I guess it was sticking up through the leaves. Then I heard the sailors coming through the trees. They were yelling, 'Hey, Joe! Hey, Joe!' and they were shining their flashlights and then they shined them on where I was hiding and I thought they had found me then, but then there was that big flash of lightning and the thunder and they started screaming and shooting and I waited to get shot." He stopped for a moment and they could hear him breathing, and then he said quietly, "But they missed. Then they ran away, still screaming."

"Let me have the Spirit of the Voyage," Retawasiol said, and Joseph reached across the darkness and handed it to him.

The old man ran his hands over the smoothness of the root until he found the old bullet wound. Now, beside it, was another gash, raw and splintered and new. He handed the stick back to Joseph and said, "Anyway, it was a good time to have a thunderstorm."

Chapter 32

Before the moon rose above the horizon, they set sail. Joseph tied the Spirit of the Voyage to the mast again, while Napu took the rest of the protective mats off the canoe. When the men began pushing the *proa* down its path of palm fronds, they jumped off and put their shoulders to the hull and it slid slowly down the steep slope of beach and into the water. While the men held the canoe to keep it from drifting away, Napu and Joseph climbed onto the outrigger platform. Retawasiol nodded toward Napu and pointed to the helm and Joseph understood that he was to climb down into the hull and be the first to bail out the water that splashed in.

But first they ran the sail up the mast and tied off the lines. Only then did Napu move to the helmsman's place on the end of the canoe. He put the rudder in the water, and when he was ready, Retawasiol pulled in the line that adjusted the set of the sail, and the canvas filled with the wind.

The canoe quickly picked up speed and moved out across the small distance to the deep reef and then over it and out to sea. Before he slipped down into the deep V of the hull, Joseph saw the men on the beach watching them through the increasing darkness. One of them held a palm frond up into the wind, a wish for good voyaging. He knew that when you were leaving on a voyage it was dangerous to look back at someone watching from the shore because they could cast a bad spell on you, but he trusted these men from Puluwat. And then he felt the sea take them in its arms, the swell lifting them and dropping them smoothly and gently. By now it was a familiar and comforting sensation.

It was nearly dark. They all looked up at the stars. Retawasiol had said it was nearly four hundred and fifty miles to Saipan in the direction of the stars of Setting Little Bear—*Doloni Mailob Balefang*. At first they set this course, but then, after a short time, Retawasiol took a heading more to windward, which Joseph realized was because of the current and to allow for the canoe's drift.

It seemed that Retawasiol had been correct: the stars had stopped fighting and the wind and the sea were at peace. With the breeze holding steady from the east, the great Pacific swell carried them on its smooth back. There was little water for Joseph to bail out, so he climbed up next to Retawasiol.

They sailed this way through the night, Napu and Joseph taking turns at the helm and at bailing. And they watched Retawasiol as he adjusted the sail, using it to steer the canoe to windward, and when the old man was too tired to sit up any longer and needed to sleep, they shared this task, too.

*****

When the dawn came, it came quick and hot. The seas stayed thick, ruffled into small wavelets as the breeze carried the *proa* along. With the stars gone, they steered by using the angle of the canoe to the swells, and they used the sun, too, and they watched behind them at the wake the *proa* was leaving in the water to judge the current, which Retawasiol said was not much.

Now Napu and Joseph took turns sleeping for short periods while Retawasiol was able to handle the sail. By the end of the day, they found they could fall asleep immediately after closing their eyes and wake refreshed some two hours later. And so, though they had no clocks, the watch schedule was set: a time to sleep, a time to steer, and a time for sitting down in the hull bailing.

They were joined by a pod of porpoises that raced ahead of the canoe and then around it, leaping from the sea in small arcs, their sleek bodies cutting the water cleanly. They dove under the hull and disappeared deep into the endless blue and then shot upwards and into the air, twisting in the wind, and then landing and disappearing again.

As Joseph had learned, after two days at sea, the moments that mark time blended together, seeming to fold into themselves, and there was no need to understand it. Only the sun arcing through the blue heavens and the moon's quick race through the slowly wheeling stars spoke of the passage of something infinite and indefinite.

Toward the end of the third day, as the shadows cast by the seas were lengthening and the sun's glare on the surface of the sea was painfully bright and the porpoises disappeared, they saw something rising and falling on the swell ahead of them.

"Look," Joseph said, pointing. "What's that?"

"A small boat," Napu said.

He steered the *proa* toward it. As they approached, they saw that it was a small, rubberized raft of some sort and there did not seem to be anyone in it. But when they got closer, they could see that indeed there was something inside it, something lying on the bottom.

When the canoe came up alongside the raft, they couldn't believe what they saw: a body dressed in uniform, its flesh nearly gone, only the skeleton remaining. A skull stared up at them. The skin had peeled away in black patches; the eyes were empty sockets; the lips were drawn back, black and tight and dried against the yellow-brown of the teeth.

Joseph felt the hair on the back of his neck stand up and his mouth went dry. Napu let out a long moan. They called to Retawasiol, but the old man seemed to be sleeping and would not wake up.

For long moments they stared, and as they stared, the sea lifted the canoe and the raft up together and together dropped them down again, and the brilliant sun glared against the surface of the water and off the face of the dead.

"What do you think happened to him?" Joseph said.

"I don't know. He died of thirst, maybe. It doesn't look like he had any water."

"Do you think he is Japanese?"

"I—I—no, look at his hair—it's blond."

Joseph reached up and felt his own hair and after another moment of silence said, "Look. See those things around his neck? All the soldiers wear them. They're called dog tags. My uncle had some. They have the soldier's name on them."

Again, for long moments, they stared at the dead man as the sea lifted them and dropped them and there was the sound of the waves slapping against the hull of the canoe and the sound of the rubber raft rubbing against it.

"Do you think we should—should we get them?" Joseph asked.

They were looking down into the life raft as it bumped up against the side of the canoe, and now Joseph, who had been tending the sail, reached down and grabbed the line on the side of the raft and tied it to the canoe to keep it from drifting away.

"Maybe his family—if he's an American—maybe they would want to know. That's what dog tags are for. So the guy's family will find out that he died."

"How are we going to get them?" Napu asked.

The silver dog tags were visible lying against the dried, blackened skin and bones of his chest where his uniform top was opened.

"I think I might be able to reach them from here," Joseph said, but he hesitated until the *proa* began to pull away from the raft. As he leaned out over the water, the sea lifted the canoe and the raft jerked away. Joseph felt himself losing his balance and he grabbed at one of the lines that supported the sail, but could not stop his forward motion.

As he tumbled downward, his body fell against the line he had tied to the raft and the raft was pulled hard up against the side of the canoe again and he fell into it. He landed on top of the dead man, and he could feel the bones give way under his weight and hear them grinding against each other inside the uniform.

He screamed and pushed himself against the side of the raft, trying to get away from the dead man, but the raft was small and the bottom was soft and the corpse rolled up against him.

He stopped struggling and lay still. The dead man's skull was pressing against his chest and its body against his arms. He looked up and saw that the line holding the raft to the canoe had come undone and he was drifting away.

"Bring the canoe back here!" he yelled. "Hurry!"

"I can't," Napu yelled back. "The sail is loose now. I can't steer and Retawasiol won't wake up. There's something wrong with him."

Joseph watched as the distance between the canoe and the raft increased. The dead man pressed against him and the dog tags had fallen against his own bare chest. He grabbed for them and pulled. The bones in the dead man's neck separated and the tags on their chain came free in his hand. Joseph pushed himself up and rolled out of the raft into the clean blue of the sea.

He went under for a moment and, when he broke the surface, he saw the *proa* drifting away from him. He began swimming, his arms thrashing at the water. He could see Napu standing up next to the mast calling to him and he could see Retawasiol's still form lying on the platform and the sail fluttering loose in the wind.

For a moment it seemed as though he would not be able to catch up with them, but then the distance began to close and after several minutes, he was up alongside the *proa* and Napu was reaching down for him and pulling him up onto the outrigger.

He lay sprawled in the sun, breathing heavily. For a long time he did not speak and then he heard Napu say, "You okay? That was something, Joseph. That was really something. It scared me pretty bad."

Joseph sat up. He could see the raft off in the distance and then he remembered the dog tags. He still held onto them with one hand. He read the name stamped in the bright metal. "His name was Miller, J.R. He was a Catholic—like my uncle."

Then Joseph looked at Retawasiol. He had not woken up during all the yelling. Joseph touched his shoulder and softly spoke his name. He moaned and his eyes flickered open for a moment and then he was quiet again.

"I guess he's just really tired," Joseph said, and he gazed out across the water, gleaming black, the raft outlined in dark red by the setting sun. Then above the raft he saw the first star. He put the dog tags around his neck and grasped the line that controlled the sail. "We'd better get going."

Chapter 33

Two days later, it was not birds that told them they were getting close to the island of Saipan, but planes. Joseph first heard them through the fog of sleep and when he sat up, the drone of their engines seemed to echo off the far horizon. "I heard an engine," he said. And then he heard something else: Retawasiol's soft, hoarse voice beside him. "Planes," the old man said, "war planes."

He had not moved in those last two days except to drink from the coconuts Joseph and Napu held to his mouth. But now, with great effort, he pushed himself up and pointed off toward the northwest. Joseph could not see the planes but he did see the low, gray silhouette of a ship.

"And there's a ship, there, too," Joseph said. "It's not a cloud."

"But look there," Retawasiol said, his voice hoarse and weak, "There are clouds. Napu, tell me about that one there."

Napu was sitting on the stern of the canoe steering, his feet resting on the rudder, his hands grasping the top of it where a curved branch formed the tiller. "There is an island over there," he said. "The cloud is sitting over it. It is a dark green island, because I can see the reflection on the bottom of the cloud. It is probably Saipan."

"Why do you think it is Saipan?" Retawasiol croaked on wheezing breaths.

"Because it is a high island. I can see the outline of the mountains through the cloud."

It was true. The outline of a high island was just visible through the bottom of the cloud that sat low on the horizon.

"Are we going there—to Saipan?" Joseph asked.

"We will have to," Retawasiol said. "We need more drinking nuts for the voyage to the island where the world was born from the fires in the mountain."

"But what about the war? What about the soldiers?"

It was Joseph who asked the question. The men from Puluwat had said there was a terrible battle on Saipan between the Americans and the Japanese.

Retawasiol seemed to think about this for a moment and then he said, "While I was sleeping I have been talking it over with the spirits. We have decided that we must go there—to Saipan. The spirits say they will watch over us."

And indeed, the current and winds seemed to be one with the spirits, because without much steering, the canoe was carried in the direction of the big cloud that sat on the green mountains of the island.

*****

As they got closer, they began to see the war. What they had thought were just clouds, were clouds joined by billowing plumes of smoke and dust; what they had thought was one ship, were many ships; and what they had thought was thunder, were exploding bombs. Nature had been suspended and then replaced.

As the sun went down, it turned the black clouds of battle red, and the red smoke drifted out over them and the smell of things burning and the thump-thump-thumping of big guns firing continued throughout the night. In the morning, with the smoke low on the water and the blueness of the water ruined by ash and debris, they saw a body.

It floated face down past the slowly moving *proa*. But it was not a soldier; it was a woman, they could tell that much, and she was wearing a kimono of many bright colors and her black hair floated on the surface of the water in waving tendrils and the back of her neck was white against the darker sea.

Napu and Joseph glanced at Retawasiol but the old man had fallen asleep, his face turned up toward the sun, and so they turned to the woman again and watched until she disappeared in the wake of the canoe.

And then they saw another one, and then another, and then another. None was a soldier; only a few of them were men. They were women and children, some face up, some face down. Some wore flowered kimonos, some simple dresses. Sometimes a woman held a child in her arms and small crabs scuttled across their bloated faces.

Neither Napu nor Joseph could speak. They watched the dead float past them and they watched the smoke from the island climbing up toward the place where the spirits looked down on them, and they heard the roar of explosions and saw the flash of fire.

"We can't go there," Napu finally said.

"No. We can stay here for a while. Until Retawasiol wakes up. He'll decide what to do next."

They set about configuring the sail so that the wind blew around the canoe and over it but did not move it and this way they drifted on the current. Still though, the sea was carrying them toward the island.

Many times planes flew over them and circled them and from the markings on their wings, they knew they were Americans. But the planes did not shoot at them and always flew off and disappeared into the glare of the sun and the smoke and the dust.

All day they drifted and Retawasiol did not wake up and he did not move and his face stayed facing up toward the sky like the dead floating past them.

"Napu, do you think Retawasiol...." He stopped himself. He did not want the old navigator to hear him.

But Napu understood and he whispered, "I can see him breathing."

They watched Retawasiol's chest and saw it moving up and down.

"Try to wake him up," Napu said.

Joseph let go of the line that controlled the sail and touched Retawasiol's shoulder, softly at first, and then, when he did not respond, with more force, but the old man lay still.

"We've got to decide what to do," Napu said, "Look; we're drifting toward those cliffs. We'll get smashed against the rocks."

"Let's sail around there, toward the beach," Joseph said. He pointed toward a place where the cliffs ended and a narrow beach began.

But the war was there, on the beach. They could see men running and things that looked like tanks burning and shells exploding.

"It is too late," Napu said. "We can't sail away now. The wind and the current...."

Joseph hoisted the sail and then set it so the canoe picked up speed and began moving toward the beach. "Let's get in there, see? Under the end of that cliff. It looks like a small cave or something."

He pointed and Napu pushed on the rudder with both feet and the canoe turned and pointed toward it.

And then the *tam*, the big, smooth piece of wood on the end of the outrigger, exploded. There was a sharp sound of wood splitting and splinters hit their faces.

"We got hit!" Joseph cried out. "Someone's shooting at us!"

Napu kept his feet on the big rudder. "Keep down! Stay down!" he yelled.

"I've got to watch out for Retawasiol!" Joseph yelled back.

"No, help me steer! Keep the sail in tight."

Joseph glanced down at the old man, who had not responded to the sound of the canoe getting hit. He pulled in on the sail and felt the canoe pick up speed.

They were now moving parallel to the shore, sailing toward the beach. The *tam* had a big hole torn in it, but still it did its job, keeping the canoe balanced against the wind. As they drew closer to the beach, they could see soldiers lying on the sand in strange positions, bodies and arms and legs twisted impossibly around themselves. They lay in heaps everywhere and the air was filled with the acrid smell of smoke.

Bullets began hitting the water around them and twice more there were splintering sounds and pieces of wood were torn from the hull of the canoe but they kept it on course. Between the end of the cliffs and where the beach began, there was a small place where there seemed to be no reef and the water was calmer. Without thinking of how it would happen, without the planning that Retawasiol had taught them was so important, they sailed the *proa* through this place and toward the shelter of the overhanging cliff.

Chapter 34

They did not take the sail down. Instead, they ran the canoe fast and hard up across the reef and into the shallow water on the other side of it and then under the cover of the low cliff. Through the sounds of the war, they could hear the hull crunching as it bumped along on the rocks. When the canoe stopped, Joseph let go of the line and the sail ran out and started flogging in the wind. He jumped into the water and held the bow of the *proa*. Napu had left his place at the helm and was sitting by Retawasiol. The old man still had not moved, had not woken up.

"I don't know what's wrong with him," Napu said. "He just keeps sleeping."

"Let's get him on the beach."

"No, no. Let's leave him here. I don't think we can get him off. He's safer lying where he is. I'll cover him with a mat."

Napu put a mat over him and then he grabbed a line and jumped into the water next to Joseph. The canoe was being lifted and dropped by waves and every time it came down, it hit the rocks. Together they pulled it around so that it was in a place where the water was calmer. They tied it off on a rock and left it there and went as far up against the cliff as they could and curled up against the rocks.

Around them on the cliffs were bushes and broken trees and everything was covered with a fine gray dust. The air was filled with the war: the sounds and concussions of shells exploding in the distance, drifting palls of smoke, and the strange, sweet smell of things rotting. Down the beach they could see burned-out tanks and out at sea, beyond the reef, the gray hulls of ships.

They huddled together and listened and watched the canoe as it bobbed slowly in the water. Under the woven mats, Retawasiol lay still.

"What do you think we should do now?" Joseph asked.

Napu did not answer. He was staring out at the canoe and seemed to be listening. "I think I hear him."

"Who?"

"Retawasiol."

"I don't hear anything."

"He's calling to us."

They both listened but Joseph could only hear the sounds of planes and bombs and, nearby, the waves on the reef.

"I'll check on him," Joseph said.

They both waded back out into the water and Joseph climbed up onto the canoe. He lifted the mat off of Retawasiol's face and the old man looked up at him and moaned.

"He's...he's awake," Joseph said.

"He needs water, bad," Napu said, and he climbed up on the canoe. They chopped open the top of a coconut and worked together to get Retawasiol sitting up enough to swallow. Joseph held his head and Napu put the coconut to his lips. The old man struggled to swallow, but kept drinking until the nut was empty.

"How are you?" Joseph asked, but Retawasiol's eyes stayed closed and he became quiet.

"I think he went back to sleep," Joseph said.

"But it's good; he drank a lot."

"Should we stay here with him?"

Napu studied the beach and the low cliff, the broken trees and the dust-covered bushes. In the distance there was always the sound of the war. Then he saw the root of the nunu tree, the Spirit of the Voyage with its sleeping face and its ragged bullet holes, tied to the mast, and he said, "Yeah, let's stay here. It's better than lying on the rocks."

"Let's get under the mats."

They pulled the mats over them and lay quietly, feeling the *proa* rising and falling gently. Now, in the semi-darkness of the covering mats, the war seemed further away and the smells changed from smoke and death to wood and sea. After a while, Joseph heard his mother's voice and he called out to her and then he heard Napu and realized he had been dreaming.

*****

They slept for a long time with the war raging around them. And then it was dark again, and the sound of the war diminished and then faded away. They sat up and pulled the mats off and checked on Retawasiol. The old man lay still, breathing lightly. Overhead, stars had filled the sky.

Napu said, "We need to try to get him to drink some more."

They opened the last of their coconuts with their machetes. They held up Retawasiol's head and poured the water into his mouth. At first it ran out the corners and down his chin, but then he started to drink and he finished the nut. Again they spoke to him, but he did not answer. They lowered his head onto the mat.

Joseph and Retawasiol shared the last two nuts and Joseph said, "I'm still thirsty. We've got to go and get more nuts."

The darkness had folded over them like a thin, cool sheet. The air was quiet and among the stars, a full moon spread its milky light down through the clouds and set the beach aglow. Looking out across the lagoon to sea, the war seemed to have disappeared.

"Maybe the war is over," Joseph said.

"I don't know. I guess it could be."

"I'm going to go and get some coconuts now," Joseph said, "You can see them all over the ground where the bombs blew them off the trees."

"You'd better let me go," Napu said. "The Japanese will shoot you because you got blond hair. They will know you're an American."

"Maybe the Japanese will," Joseph said, "but the Americans won't. If you go, they both might shoot you." He did not wait for an answer. He slid over to the edge of the platform, slipped off into the water, and waded to shore.

Chapter 35

At first he crawled along in the sand and through rocks and broken bushes, but after a few minutes, when nothing happened, when no one shot at him, he stood up. He waited, holding his breath and wondering what it would feel like to get shot: would he feel it or would he just be dead?

When he could not hold his breath any longer, he let it out and took in another. He began to pick his way along in the moonlight, moving slowly and stopping after every step to listen. The war seemed to have moved off into the distance. He occasionally heard what he knew must be gunfire but what sounded like popcorn popping, and sometimes a flash lit up the dark jungle that rose far above him on sheer cliffs. His bare feet felt the dust and the broken things that lay all around.

Extending back from the beach, it was mostly bushes, but here and there a coconut tree grew up among them. Their tops had been blown off; he could see their broken silhouettes in the dim light and he made for one. He was right: underneath the trees, the ground was scattered with coconuts. He knelt down and felt for them with his hands and made a pile of them and then he found another tree and made a pile of nuts under it. When he had done this for three trees, he gathered up half a dozen nuts, tied them together with their stems, and dragged them back to the beach.

Standing in the water, he called in a loud whisper, "I'm here. I found lots of them." He waded out to the canoe and handed them up to Napu. "How is he?"

"The same. He's still asleep."

"Okay, I'm going back for more. We'll try to get the canoe loaded up before morning."

"I'm going with you this time," Napu said.

"What about...."

"The canoe is tied up to the rocks. He'll be okay for a little while. We can get a lot more together. Anyway, I can't let you go out there alone." Napu slid off the platform into the water and together they waded ashore.

"Follow me," Joseph whispered. "I didn't see any soldiers."

Joseph led Napu back along the way he had come. After a few steps on the moonlit beach, they moved inland until they came to the second tree with the pile of nuts beneath it. They gathered them up, tied them together, and made their way back to the beach. When they had waded out to the canoe, they saw that Retawasiol still had not moved.

"He's still breathing," Napu said.

"What do we do if...."

"The spirits will decide when that happens. He wants to die on the island where the fire comes out of the earth. The spirits said he must do this so we need to get him there. We need to leave as soon as we can."

"I think we just need to make one more trip and the canoe will be full," Joseph said.

They went back to shore and again made their way up the beach and back onto the battlefield. The moon was getting low in the sky; its milky light etched the torn bushes and trees with shadows and shone softly on dark jungle that led up to the distant cliffs. It was very quiet and the breeze felt cool on their skin.

"Here," Joseph said, "here's the last pile."

So they started picking up nuts, bending down and cradling them in their arms, and when they had them all gathered up, Napu said, "That's all we can fit into the canoe. Let's go. We got enough."

No sooner had these words been uttered than there was a huge flash of white light followed by a shattering explosion overhead that knocked them both to the ground. They lay among the dropped coconuts, for a moment blinded by the bright light, while above them and around them the explosions roared and continuous flashes lit up the sky. Then the sounds of men screaming and rifle fire rose up and blended with all the rest.

Joseph called out to Napu but it was impossible to hear if he answered. He lifted his head and saw Napu lying close by, holding his hands over his ears. He crawled over to him. "Are you all right?"

Napu did not answer him, but he reached out and grabbed Joseph's arm. Then they both lay huddled together, pressing themselves against each other and to the ground, pressing their faces into the dirt, their hands and arms over their heads. In the distance, the screaming of the men continued and overhead and all around them the exploding shells lit up the sky and the land and the concussions slammed into them.

*****

They lay like this for a long time and for a long time the sky was bright with exploding shells and the roar of the battle was all around them. Pieces of hot metal rained down on them, burning them, and the earth shook and rose and fell under them. There was always the sound of rifle fire and of men screaming and they choked on the dust blasted from the earth.

Then, with a painful, infinite slowness, the war seemed to diminish and move away, and after a while there was the sound of it in the distance, and then it was replaced by a stillness that lifted the night from them.

Napu touched Joseph's shoulder and said, "I think it's morning now. Are you okay?

"Yeah, I think so," Joseph said, and then he spat. "My mouth is full of dirt."

"Mine, too."

There were no more explosions, but the sky was getting bright; it was dawn and they were not dead. Still, they were afraid to move. They waited, lying curled up around each other until the first hot rays of the sun touched their skin.

Joseph lifted his head saw that Napu was covered with dust, his hair and his body were gray with it and, through the dust, his body and face were smeared with dried blood.

Napu looked back at him. "You are....gray," and he stopped speaking and Joseph said, "You, too."

They pushed themselves up and gazed around. The land was no longer the land they had come to from the sea. The coconut trees were shattered and gone and the trees of the jungle that had risen toward the base of the cliffs were gone, too, and everything was gray with dust.

Around them were piles of things that were torn up and twisted and broken and covered with dust, and when Joseph said, "There are lots of dead men," his voice sounded flat and very far away and the hot air and sunlight seemed to suck the sound out of the words. Around them, lying in heaps, were the bodies of soldiers, both Japanese and American.

From behind them there was the sound of quick, heavy footsteps and a shadow fell over them. They turned around slowly, their eyes struggling to focus through the sunlight and the horror. A soldier stood over them, pointing his rifle. Joseph felt his heart stop. Far away he heard Napu gasp. Now maybe they would die.

They waited and then the soldier said, "Stand up."

They stood up and the soldier kept his rifle pointed at them.

"Who are you?" the soldier asked.

Neither of the boys spoke. The soldier looked very tired and was covered with dust and his uniform was torn and his helmet was pushed back on his head, revealing a bloody bandage.

"You speak English?" he asked.

Joseph nodded. "I'm an American," he said, and still he could not believe it was his own voice, so small and flat and far away. The ringing in his ears was loud.

"So am I," Napu said. "We're from Guahan—from Guam."

"Guam?" the soldier said. "How in Sam Hill did you get here?"

"On a canoe," Napu said.

Before he could say anything else, another soldier came up behind the first one and then another one. They emerged from among the torn and broken bushes and dust like specters, the rays of the sun coming in behind them. They all looked like the first soldier, filthy with dust, their eyes deadened by exhaustion.

The first soldier said, "I found them lying here, sergeant. They don't got no rifles. Nothin'. Say they're Americans from Guam. Came here on a canoe."

The sergeant stared at the boys dressed only in their filthy loincloths and smeared with blood and dust. He looked at the boys' hair that reached down past their shoulders. "Civilians," he said and then he pointed at Joseph and said, "Where'd you get those dog tags?"

Joseph had forgotten about them. He reached up to his neck and touched them. "There was this guy in this raft—out there." He pointed out toward the ocean. "You want them? You can have them. I was gonna give them to someone because we figured...."

But the sergeant was no longer interested. "Where are you from?" he asked.

"Massachusetts."

The sergeant laughed. It was a hard laugh and he started coughing and then he said, "Massachusetts? You're not much more than a boy. How did you get here in the middle of a war?"

"I was in Guam with my uncle when the Japanese came and he got killed and...."

His voice trailed off. It seemed too long ago. He did not feel like he was from Massachusetts anymore and the only image of his uncle he could remember was of his face as he lay dead in the water with *A Boy's Picture History of the World in One Volume* lying on his chest.

"No, how'd you get here? On a battlefield. What are you doing here?"

Joseph felt like he was talking from inside a drum, his voice echoing around inside his head. "We needed coconuts."

"Coconuts? What for?"

"To drink. On the canoe. We're sailing to the island where the fire comes from the mountains and—"

But the sergeant was no longer listening. "Well," he said, looking past Joseph and Napu, "It looks like we licked 'em. Last night was their last bonsai charge. We killed 'em good last night. And listen, you'd better not go back to Guam anytime soon. We're going there next. We're gonna kill 'em good there, too, pretty soon."

Then he turned and walked away and the other soldiers did, too, but before he left, the first soldier said, "You want to go back to Massachusetts, kid, follow the sergeant. You hungry?"

The boys could not think about food. They just stared at him.

"If you are, just look along the beach there. There's all sorts of C-rations washed up and lying around. Help yourselves. A lot of our guys won't be eating them anymore." He turned and walked off the way the others had gone.

Chapter 36

Soldiers carrying stretchers appeared around them as if from nowhere, and started picking up the dead. They took them down to the beach and then along the water's edge where there were boats pulled up on the sand.

Without knowing why, the boys watched this for a long time and then Napu said, "Retawasiol," and his voice, too, was far away and came to Joseph through a fog of exhaustion and confusion.

"Retawasiol." Joseph repeated the word, trying to make sense of it.

"He...." Napu looked at Joseph, but the words seemed to be stuck in his mouth.

What had come before the battle—Retawasiol, the canoe, the sea—started coming back to them, slowly, in pieces, and they began walking back toward the canoe.

They followed the men carrying the stretchers, picking their way among the blasted rocks and trees and bushes. When they got to the water it was brilliant with sunlight and splashed and gurgled on the sand and rocks just as it had before the war had found them. But in the daylight, it did not look like the place they had come ashore last night. "Where is it?" he asked.

Joseph did not answer him. Instead, he stood in surf and stared out across the reef and then up and down the coastline. Then he said, "It must have been around here somewhere."

"There were rocks and kind of a small cliff," Napu said.

"There it is," Joseph said, and he pointed up the beach where the reef came in close and met the rocks.

They walked up toward it. "Yeah, there's the canoe," Joseph said, and it was all coming back to him now, through the fog of the battle and the visions of the dead. "It's still okay."

He started running and Napu came up beside him and they ran together down the beach and when they reached the canoe they saw that Retawasiol was no longer lying on it.

"He's gone," Napu said and to Joseph his voice still sounded like it was coming from another place far away.

"No, he's got to be here somewhere," Joseph said, and he again felt a terrible fear rise up inside him. "He's got to be here."

They splashed across the rocks to the canoe and stared at the outrigger platform as if its emptiness had been a deceit of their exhaustion. The pandanus mats that had covered Retawasiol were still there, spread about in disarray, but the old man was gone.

"Look," Joseph said, "the Spirit of the Voyage is gone, too."

The Spirit of the Voyage had been lashed onto the mast but was no longer there.

Without saying anything, Napu started wading toward the shore and then he said, his voice quiet, "Here he is."

Joseph waded up behind him and saw Retawasiol lying half in the water and half out of it, his head resting on a patch of sand. The Spirit of the Voyage was cradled in his arms.

They kneeled in the water beside him and Joseph felt his wrist for a heartbeat like his mother used to do to him when he was sick.

"I think I can feel something. Is he breathing?"

"Yes," Napu said.

"It must have been the Spirit of the Voyage that saved him," Joseph said. "It must have carried him here."

"Let's get him back to the canoe."

Joseph took the Spirit of the Voyage from the old man's arms and stuck it into his belt. Then Napu took his shoulders and Joseph his legs and they lifted him up and carried him out to the *proa.* Napu held Retawasiol's head above water while Joseph climbed onto the outrigger. He grabbed the old man's shoulders and together they got him out of the water and lay him on the outrigger platform.

"We've got to get some coconut water in him," Joseph said and he stopped, glanced down at his waist and then at his hands, and said, "Our machetes. They're back—back there. We forgot them."

Napu was standing in the water holding onto the *tam* and now he rested his head on it for a moment but then said, "I'll go and get them. You stay here. We can't leave him alone again."

Joseph watched as Napu waded slowly back to shore. The sea had washed away the dust from his body but his black hair was still gray with it and his back was covered with cuts and blood ran down from them. When he reached the shore, he did not look back. He walked down the beach and then disappeared into the broken land.

*****

While he was gone, Joseph watched Retawasiol breathe. The old man lay face up, and the skin of his chest was stretched tight across his ribs as they rose and fell slowly. His eyes were closed and his face was like a tight, brown mask, his lips drawn back from his small, brown teeth. Joseph tried to remember how long it had been since Retawasiol had fallen asleep, but time had become something incomprehensible, something he could no longer trust.

He had just covered Retawasiol with a mat when he heard Napu call him from the shore. He was carrying both machetes and in his arms he cradled what looked like half a dozen cans. "I found the machetes. And I found these. It's food. Remember, the sergeant said we could have them? They said we could take all we wanted. There are lots of them on the beach."

Joseph slipped off the canoe and waded ashore. He took his machete from Napu and slipped it into his belt and then took some of the cans. They were drab green and one had *U.S. Army Rations C, B-Unit* printed on the side and the others said, *M-Unit*. They had a small key on the top for opening them. The boys carried the cans out to the *proa* and put them down into the bottom of the hull.

"I don't think we can get Retawasiol to eat until he wakes up," Joseph said. "And I was thinking, we've got to get him to that island right away so . . . you know. So he can die."

Joseph had not whispered the word "die" and now his eyes met Napu's and then he glanced down at Retawasiol. The old man lay as he had been, breathing slowly and softly. "Yes, you're right. He has to die there. We must make sure of that. It's what the spirits want. We've got to go tonight." Then he looked at Joseph again and said, "Do you want to go back to Massachusetts like the soldier said?"

"No," Joseph said quickly and then he hesitated and said, "I can't remember much about it anymore. I don't have anyone there to go to. This is my home now. Here, on this canoe. Besides, you are my only brother, my only family."

Napu nodded and said, "Good."

*****

They washed off in the sea and examined each other's wounds. They both had many small cuts and burns and scrapes on their backs and chest and legs, but nothing seemed too serious. They opened a coconut and Joseph held Retawasiol's head up while Napu poured some water into his mouth. The taste of the coconut water seemed to wake him a little and he swallowed it. They poured more and more until the nut was empty.

"What do you think we should do now?" Joseph asked. He was looking up at the shore and at the smoking, shattered jungle that climbed up the distant cliffs. The war seemed to be over. The wind came fresh from the east and carried away the smell of it. "Retawasiol said the island where the fire comes out of the earth was under the *star-that-does-not-move*."

Napu nodded. "Yes," and he pointed out toward the sea. "There," he said. "If the wind holds like this, we can make it."

"But he didn't say how far."

"He said we will know it. When we see it, there will be no mistake about it."

Joseph opened a coconut with his machete. He held the nut up and turned it in his hand as he chopped the top off. When it was ready, he offered it to Napu, who took it and drank it all while Joseph opened another nut.

When they were full of coconut water, Napu said. "We should go now while the war is quiet."

Chapter 37

They covered Retawasiol with mats and tied the Spirit of the Voyage to his arm so he would not be alone in his dreaming. Then they put the spars up and tied them off and they both got into the water and pushed the *proa* out away from the rocks and the low cliff.

When they climbed on board, they could feel the wind and, without discussing it, Joseph climbed back to one end of the canoe and got the big rudder set up. When he was ready and with the wind and the current already carrying the canoe away across the water, Napu ran the sail up.

The *proa* moved fast then, out over the shallow water, and they found an opening in the reef and steered for it. The sea was brilliant with sunlight. The war seemed far away and the gray shadows of the warships on the horizon were like distant clouds.

When they hit the surf on the reef, the canoe rose up to meet it and the spray washed over them and the sail flogged for a moment but then it filled with wind again and they rushed through the opening and out into the sea.

Then they both looked back at the island rising huge above them. The jungle was bright with dust, and the tops of the trees were all blown off. The sheer cliffs rose up toward the scudding clouds and the rising, swirling smoke. The beaches were littered with the stuff of battle: burning tanks sent up rages of black fire, and thousands of smaller things, cans of food and helmets and rifles and the packs of dead soldiers were dark spots on the white sand. They turned away, back toward the sea.

"Did you see the current?" Napu asked.

"Yeah, right now it's pushing us up the island. I think when we get out farther, it will change."

Together they guided the *proa* out and away from Saipan. Napu adjusted the sail and Joseph kept his feet on the long rudder and his hands on the tiller. The big Pacific swells greeted them and lifted the canoe and they rode up on them and then slid down their backs and the wind was steady from the east. They passed among the warships and the sailors watched them and sometimes pointed rifles at them and the boys stared up at the sailors waiting for what might happen and once they saw a flash from a muzzle and a bullet hit the water near them and a moment later there was the sound of the rifle.

When Joseph called out to the sailor and said he was from Massachusetts, the sailor seemed to notice his blond hair and he put the rifle down. Other sailors came up along the rail and watched as the *proa* skimmed by.

So they picked their way through the maze of ships and sometimes a plane would circle them and then come down close and look them over but no one shot at them again, and after awhile both the ships and island were disappearing in the haze and they were alone.

It was then, after the last ship was gone and only the faint trace of the island could be seen, gray-blue above the horizon, that Joseph felt the crushing weight of fatigue sweep over him. His head hung down and his eyes burned and he began hearing things, like singing and voices and people speaking to him.

He looked at Napu and saw that his head, too, seemed to be sagging under a great weight. "We need to sleep," he said. "It's okay, now, I think."

Napu shrugged his shoulders. Retawasiol's still form lay under the mats. "I guess we have to. I can't do anymore."

They hove to, configuring the sail again so that the canoe sat in the seaway without moving, just drifting. Joseph climbed over to the outrigger and they each opened a coconut and then Joseph said, "I'm hungry, too. We've got to eat. Let's try these things."

He got a can of the C-rations the soldiers had given them and opened it. The smell of it came up to Joseph's nose and he put his face close to it.

"What is it?" Napu asked.

"I don't know. It doesn't smell too bad, though."

He stuck his fingers into it and pulled out a wad of food and put some of it on his tongue. He tasted it and swallowed and put his fingers in the can again and this time took out a big wad of it and stuffed it into his mouth.

*****

They slept through the day and into the night and sometimes they would be awakened by a plane flying low overhead or a ship passing and they would sit up and watch it and then lie down again and later they were not sure if it had really happened or if they had dreamed it. When they woke, finally, it was dark and the stars hung over them, thick as a celestial blanket, but it offered no comfort and the wind felt cold and the light from the stars came from far away and was very lonely.

They were hungry again but before they ate, they got Retawa-siol to drink another coconut and they made certain he was comfortable. Still, though, the old navigator opened his eyes only while he was drinking and he did not seem to see anything and he did not speak and much of the water ran down the corners of his mouth.

"I don't think he is sleeping," Napu said. "I think he is in a coma, like my grandmother was before she died. That's what the doctor said."

"I never heard of that before," Joseph said. "It's like he's kind of half asleep." Then he said, "We'd better get going."

They put up the sail again and this time, Napu sat on the end of the canoe and put his feet on the rudder and took the other end of it in his hand. Joseph kept the sheet in his hand and adjusted the sail. They found the *star-that-does-not-move* low on the northern horizon.

"I feel a current," Napu said, "from there." He pointed toward the west. "Let's steer up and keep the star there."

They set the *proa* on a course that kept the North Star just off the leeward bow and the swell coming at them at an angle from the east-northeast. As the night passed and the stars wheeled over them, they only had to keep this heading.

During the night, the wind held steady and the seas slowly built so that the canoe rose high up each crest and they could see far off through the night with the stars igniting the tops of the seas as they broke and sometimes they would hear the heavy engines of passing ships. They didn't sleep, but at regular intervals they changed positions, taking turns at the helm and at the line that controlled the sail, and sometimes they would tie this line off and go down into the bottom of the canoe and bail out the water that sloshed in.

At the first paleness of morning, they could see the shadow of a high island off to the east and birds flew around the canoe as they went out to feed for the day. At first they thought this might be the island where the spirits came out of the mountains with the fire, but there was no volcano and no fire coming from the earth. As they sailed past it, they saw no signs of people, Japanese or Americans or islanders, and the surf pounded hard on the rocks of the shore, warning them off.

All day they sailed without stopping to sleep and still the wind held and they steered by the memory of the *star-that-does-not-move* and how it was that the swells had come under the canoe when they had last seen it. By afternoon they saw seabirds and at the same time, they saw another high island rising from the waves and their hearts jumped. They steered a course for it and by evening, they were approaching it. But it was a small island, and again, there were no signs of any fire or volcanoes nor of any people.

"I don't know," Joseph said. "Maybe there isn't an island where the fire comes from the earth and the spirits of the ancestors live. Maybe it was just a legend—or a myth. Maybe it was a myth. My uncle used to say that some things were just myths—you know, not really true. Just old stories."

"No," Napu said, "I think Retawasiol was right. I think there is an island up here just like he said."

"Well," Joseph said, "We've got to keep going now, anyway. We can't go back to the war."

When they were in the lee of the island, the wind dropped off and they stopped for the night. Again, they configured the sail so that the canoe only drifted slowly and again they forced Retawasiol to drink most of the water in a coconut. They opened more of the cans of Army food and ate their fill and then drank from a couple of coconuts. When they drifted off to sleep, the moon had risen and the stars were again spread out above them, vast and cold and unknowable.

They got under way before dawn. The *star-that-does-not-move* was small and bright above the horizon and they set their course by it as before and watched the swell that came from the east and kept it under the *tam*. When they cleared the island, they saw the current pushing the trace of the wake left by the canoe and they knew that in order to steer straight, they would have to point the canoe up higher than the star path.

Before morning began to make the stars fade, Joseph thought he saw something far ahead in the water that were not stars. They were too low in the sky and seemed to be a different color. Yet he did not want to believe that they were fires. What would they do if they were fires?

But then Napu said, "Look there. Fires."

So they were fires, just a few small specks glowing above the waves, and behind the fires the shadow of an island was forming in the dawn. The darkness of it rose high above the tiny yellow-orange glows and they could see that it was not like the other islands they had just passed. It was not even like Saipan, the highest island they had seen. It was much higher.

As the morning came in over them, they could see that the island had mountains that were shaped like cones—like the volcanoes in *A Boys Picture History of the World in One Volume*. Retawasiol was right—there was an island where the spirits came out of the earth.

"There are people there," Napu said.

"I never thought about that," Joseph said. "I just figured it was an island where spirits lived and—and nothing else."

They were quiet for a long time as the *proa* continued to cut through the seas and the morning overtook them. As the sun emerged, bright and hot from the sea, it revealed the island to be full and green and the greenness ran up the sides of the volcanoes to the tops and here and there brown cliffs broke through the green and plunged down into the ocean.

"It's very beautiful," Joseph said, but Napu, who was at the helm, was quiet until finally he said, "The people who made the fires—they could be Japanese. They could be...."

That was when they heard the planes. The sky was suddenly alive with the drone of their engines and their shadows skimmed across the blue sea as if they were sharks swimming just below the surface. They flew in low and the roar of the engines became a scream and then the bombs fell on the green island and plumes of smoke and dust rose up and then the thunder of the explosions reached out to them on the *proa.*

Chapter 38

"We should turn around and go back to that other island. The one we just passed. We didn't see anyone there. And there were coconut trees with lots of nuts." Joseph heard himself yelling the words although Napu was sitting just behind him.

"We can't do that. This is where Retawasiol wants to die," Napu said, his voice calm underneath the thudding of the bombs. "It would make his spirit angry if he does not die here."

They were approaching the tip of the island where the seas from the windward side met the seas of the leeward side and formed a current and where the waves were confused and had no rhythm. Above them, the war planes rose up and plunged back down and there was the sound of rockets and then the now-familiar smell of war reached them.

As they came in under the cliffs they thought they could see shapes of huge figures living in the brown lava rocks that rose up from the sea and Napu seemed to forget about the war for a moment. "Spirits," he said, pointing. "See them? Just like in the nunu tree. They live in the rocks."

And indeed the ancient brown lava seemed alive with writhing forms, part animal, part human, and the boys' imaginations played with them and made them move and speak.

"I think they know," Joseph said, "that we are bringing Retawasiol and the Spirit of the Voyage to them." He looked at the old navigator who lay quietly under the mats, his eyes closed. "Look, they are watching us. And they are protecting us, too. The bombs can't hurt us now and the soldiers can't either."

*****

As the war planes continue to pound the island with bombs, Joseph and Napu sailed along the ragged coast. They passed small indentations that offered no safe haven but finally, rounding an outcropping of rock, a small bay fringed by a curve of black sand beach opened up. They turned into it but the smoke-filled breeze coming down from the island was against them so they dropped the sail and began paddling. When they reached the shore, they still had not seen anyone, but still the roar of the planes and the blasting of the bombs went on and they could see flames coming from far beyond the beach.

As the dust and smoke drifted down on them, they jumped off the canoe and waded up onto the sand holding the canoe by two lines. The two of them would not be able to pull the *proa* up onto the beach so they did the best they could using the breaking swell to lift it up on the sand until it seemed secure.

In front of them, the beach extended up and gave way to a field of short grasses and thickets of ironwood trees. Scattered across the grass and among the trees were burned-out trucks and a small fighter plane whose fuselage had been torn apart by bombs. To the left, the beach rose up to meet more ragged volcanic cliffs, but to the right, where it curved back toward the sea, there were rock formations that became a low cliff. On top of this cliff, someone had built a rock cairn and below the cairn was what appeared to be a small cave.

"Look," Joseph yelled, "I think it's a cave. I'm going to take a look. We can stay in there until the planes leave."

"Be careful," Napu said, "Be really careful."

Joseph ran up the beach to the bottom of the cliff. He clambered up the rock until he was at the cave and then disappeared inside it.

It was not really a cave. It was more a deep, long overhang that went back into the rocks. But even before he ducked his head down to go into it, he had heard the sound of something scratching inside and then a metallic clicking sound and the sound of something breathing. But it was too late to stop; he was already halfway inside.

After the bright sunlight, it took him a moment to be able to see the soldier standing in the shadows. Then he saw that he was very young and his eyes were wide with fear and his face was very dirty as he aimed down the length of the rifle he had pointed at Joseph's chest.

They stared at each other and Joseph thought, *Now. Now I will die. But I can't do that until I warn Napu. I've got to warn Napu.*

But he could not move and the Japanese soldier seemed frozen, too, and Joseph saw that there was a long bayonet on the end of the rifle and the sharp point of it was nearly touching his bare stomach.

Joseph started to back out of the cave. He kept his hands out in front of him, out at his sides. He had moved only inches when the soldier seemed to find his courage and began speaking rapidly to him in Japanese and as he did so, he began wagging the end of the rifle. His voice was high-pitched and Joseph realized the rifle was moving because the soldier was shaking.

Then Joseph heard Napu calling to him from the beach and at the same time he heard the heavy sound of a plane close overhead and Napu's voice was swallowed by the roar of its engine. A mo-

Douglas Arvidson

ment later, there was an explosion. The soldier winced and Joseph lurched backwards, tripped on a rock, and fell out into the sunlight.

He landed heavily on a rock and his head slammed hard on the ground and a sharp pain shot through his back. He rolled away and tumbled off the cliff and down the face of the rocky outcropping he had just climbed up. When he stopped his fall, he was back down on the edge of the beach lying on his back, the sun glaring down into his eyes.

The fall had knocked the wind out of him and as he gasped for air, he felt strange, as if he had drifted away from the world for a moment, and then he saw Napu looking down at him and he tried to focus on his face. "A soldier," he said, "I saw a soldier up there. He has a gun . . . ."

He watched as Napu stood up slowly and looked up at the cave. Napu did not say anything, but stared above them and then Joseph heard something very strange: In the middle of the bombs and dust, Napu spoke loudly in another language, not the Chamorro language of his people. His voice sounded strong and clear and he seemed to be speaking very slowly.

Joseph pushed himself up to his hands and knees and then sat back. Above him he could see the soldier's head as he lay on the edge of the rocks. He was pointing the rifle at them but he answered Napu in rapid Japanese.

"What did he say?" Joseph asked.

Napu ignored him and spoke again to the soldier and the soldier answered him in a voice that sounded small and frightened. They spoke this way, back and forth, while the soldier pointed the rifle at them and the planes strafed and bombed the island behind them.

Then Napu said, "He says he is the lookout here and he's going to shoot us and cut our heads off. I told him we have a sick old man on the canoe. He is filled with the spirits of the ancestors and he has come very far to die here. I told him that the spirits of the ancestors are with us and they will not like it if he kills us. Then he said there are very many more soldiers here, on the island, and they will kill us. Then I said the spirits of the ancestor are guarding us and the old man and that the soldiers and the planes and bombs cannot hurt us and the spirits live on this island and come out of the earth at night and will take revenge on him if he cuts our heads off. I told him that they will eat him if he kills us and they will eat all the soldiers if they do not let the old man die on the island."

175

Chapter 39

Then they were all quiet for a long time. The soldier kept his rifle pointing down at them from the rocks and the planes swirled above them and dropped down from the sky and more bombs exploded. The earth shook with the concussions and the air was split open by the sound and the acrid stink of things burning filled the wind.

Napu did not duck or lie down, but stood at the water's edge, next to where Joseph lay, and waited for what would come next. The waves came up and washed over Joseph and when he opened his eyes the world seemed to be spinning over him. He felt the water stinging the raw scrape on his back as he lay in the sand, and the sun was hot on his face.

He watched the small white clouds skittering and turning across the blue of the sky high above them as if they did not care about the planes and he could see the silhouette of the soldier against the bright sky and then he saw something else. A shadow came up next to the soldier. It seemed to be the shadow of a man who was much bigger than the soldier and it was not standing on the ground but floated in the air next to him and behind him and then over him and through him and the soldier was swallowed up by the shadow.

Then it all seemed clear to Joseph and, despite the pain that jabbed into his back and the throbbing of his head, he pushed himself up from the sand and stood up slowly. He put his hand on Napu's shoulder. "It's okay now," he said. "It's okay to get Retawasiol off the canoe and take him up to the cave."

Napu turned his head and looked at Joseph and then looked back up at the soldier and said, "What do you mean? How do you know?"

"I saw the shadow of the Spirit of the Voyage. He is behind the soldier and now the soldier can't shoot us and the bombs can't hurt us."

Napu was confused. He glanced at Joseph and then at the canoe and then back up at the soldier.

"Napu, listen to me. I saw the Spirit. His shadow moved over the soldier. He is now protecting us. That's why the soldier can't shoot us and none of the bombs have hit us. We didn't even get hurt in the middle of a battle on Saipan. Now I know why."

Napu thought for a moment longer and then said, "Anyway, we can't wait. If he's going to shoot us, he will shoot us. If the planes are going to bomb us, they will bomb us. There is nothing we can do about it. We must do this for Retawasiol. He is a sacred man who taught us the secrets of the star paths."

They turned their backs on the soldier and the bombs and went back to the *proa*. The old navigator was lying under the mats. His eyes were nearly closed and the skin on his face was drawn back tightly across the bones of his cheeks.

Napu opened a coconut and held the old man's head up and tried to get him to drink. "He won't drink any more," Napu said. "He feels cold."

Joseph got on the *proa* and together they tried to get Retawasiol to drink but the water just ran out of his mouth. Joseph felt for his pulse. "He's still alive," he said. "We got him here and now—now it's time for him to join the spirits of the ancestors. They are waiting for him up there. I think—I think it would be good to put him in that cave. It's a good place—a good place to be, you know?"

"Let's go," Napu said. "We'll put him in the cave and put the Spirit of the Voyage next to him to keep him company."

Very slowly and carefully, they lowered Retawasiol off the outrigger and carried him to shore. They ignored the soldier who stood aiming his rifle at them from the rocks and now the planes and the bombs seemed far away as they carried the old man up over the rocks to the base of the cliff and then up the broken path to the cave. When they came to where the soldier was in the path still pointing the rifle at them, they stepped over him and walked past him and the soldier made no move to stop them. They stooped low and brought Retawasiol into the cave and lay him on a bed of fresh dried grass that the soldier must have been using as his bed.

Napu stayed with Retawasiol while Joseph went back to the canoe and got more coconuts and their machetes. While the soldier lay still in his place on the rocks and watched, and with the war sending dust and smoke over them and the concussions from the bombs beating against them, they sat in front of the cave and opened the nuts and drank.

"Did you say anything to the soldier?" Joseph asked. His voice was calm and his heart felt brilliant and soft and clean.

"I told him the ancestors will reward him for this."

"You never told me you could speak Japanese."

Napu shrugged. "My grandmother was half Japanese. She spoke it with me sometimes. I did not want you to know that—that I'm part Japanese. I was ashamed."

"It's okay now, though, you know," Joseph said. "It's good now that you are part Japanese. Maybe it saved our lives."

Napu shrugged again. "It's the spirits of the ancestors who are keeping us safe. Anyway, we got nothing to do now. Just wait for the spirits of the ancestors to come for Retawasiol. Then we can leave."

*****

All day the planes came, wave after wave, and the bombing and strafing continued, and all day Napu and Joseph sat just outside the cave and watched the old man's face for some sign of life or of death. His breathing was shallow and when Joseph checked his pulse, it was very faint. Sometimes they tried to get him to drink from a coconut, but the water just ran out and down his face. Then, when the sun was going down behind the volcano that towered over the island, and the shadows slid out from the edge of the forest to the beach and then across the bay to the edge of the cave, Joseph could find no pulse at all in Retawasiol's wrist and he had stopped breathing.

"I think the spirits came for him," Napu said, looking out at the approaching darkness and it was then that the bombs stopped falling and the planes left and the sun began to go down behind the volcano. The dying light was red and its redness fell over them and covered them with red dust and they breathed in the red sunset smoke.

Throughout the long vigil, the soldier had watched them, keeping the rifle aimed at them and not moving from where he was lying on the edge of the escarpment that led up to the cave and the boys continued to ignore him.

Now, with the old navigator dead and the night settling in around them, Joseph had an idea. "Let's build a rock wall around Retawasiol. We can build it up to the ceiling of the cave. Like a real tomb that I saw in the book. It would be easy and there are lots of rocks around here."

"But," Napu said, "we need to bury him first. I don't think the rocks will be enough for—you know."

"I was thinking," Joseph said, "we could do what the Vikings did? Put him on the canoe and set it on fire and push him out to sea. But—"

"But he's not a Viking."

"No. He's an islander. What do islanders do?"

"On Guahan, we always bury people when they die."

"Okay, let's bury him." Joseph glanced around the cave. "But there's not enough dirt here. We'll have to carry it up from the beach. We'll have to use sand."

"We can use mats from the canoe. Pile the sand on the mats and carry it up."

"But we can't work in the dark," Joseph said. "We'll have to start a fire."

Now the young soldier had gotten up and was squatting on the rocks where he had been lying. He was watching and listening, holding the rifle across his legs. When the boys stood up, he stood up too, and followed them down to the beach. But first, he set the rifle down on the rocks. When he was standing near them, Napu spoke to him in Japanese. He seemed to think for a moment and then nodded and walked away up the beach.

"What happened?" Joseph asked. "Where is he going?"

"I don't know. I told him what we are doing and how we had to make a fire."

"Maybe he's going to get the other soldiers."

"I don't think so," Napu said, "Or else he would have gotten them by now."

They got the mats off the canoe and lay them on the beach and piled sand on them. It was dark but the stars were brilliant through the moving clouds and a small moon rose in the east. When they carried the first mat filled with sand up the rock escarpment to the cave, they found the soldier bending over a small flame. As they watched, he nursed the flame into a blaze that lighted up the cave and the flames flickered across Retawasiol's body.

They dumped the sand on the floor of the cave and put the mat over the old man. Before they covered his face, Joseph said, "I think we must be sure he's dead before we bury him." He took Retawasiol's wrist in his hand and felt for a long time and then lay his ear against his chest. "Yeah, I guess he's dead."

Then Napu reached out and put his hand on Retawasiols' forehead and then he leaned over and put his own forehead against the old man's and held it there for a moment and when he sat back up there were tears in his eyes and when Joseph saw this, his own eyes welled up and he said, "He taught us the star paths and how to live with the sea. And he saved us, you know? If it wasn't for him, the Japanese would have cut our heads off."

When he had said this, he glanced at the soldier who squatted near the cave entrance, and then he covered Retawasiol's face with the mat.

Then they all worked together—Napu, and Joseph, and the soldier, too—going back and forth to the beach and piling the mats with sand and carrying them up to the cave. They gently poured the sand over the mats until Retawasiol's body was completely covered with a thick mound of it.

"Now," Joseph said, "we can build up the wall."

They started gathering rocks and stacking them up around the mound of sand, but the wall was ragged and uneven and was in danger of falling down. After a few minutes of watching them, the soldier said something in Japanese and Napu stopped. The soldier moved over to the wall and took down the stones they had put up. He lay the stones out on the ground and sorted them according to size and shape and then began stacking them up around the mound of sand.

It was soon obvious that he knew what he was doing. The rocks he chose seemed to fit together of their own accord, interlocking so as to make the wall tight and strong. So while Napu and Joseph went out into the night gathering rocks and picking up driftwood to keep the fire going, the young soldier worked by firelight. After several hours, had built it up to the ceiling and then, when he had tapped the final stone lightly into place, the entire structure was tight and solid. He turned towards Napu and Joseph and, with a solemn look on his face, he bowed deeply.

"A ceremony," Joseph said, "We need to have a ceremony. And we forgot the Spirit of the Voyage. Shouldn't we have put that in with him?"

Napu thought for a moment. "What would he have wanted us to do?"

Now there was a long silence as they both thought about this and then Joseph said, "I think he is already with the Spirit of the Voyage. He doesn't need the nunu tree root any more. I think he would want us to keep it with us. We still need it."

"And," Napu said, "if Retawasiol is with the Spirit of the Voyage, he will be with us too, then—always. We can take him with us."

Joseph was looking at the soldier, who was rocking back and forth on his heels as he squatted by the fire. "He looks really tired. Ask him if he wants a coconut to drink."

Napu spoke to the soldier in Japanese and held out an open nut. The soldier looked at the nut and then looked around behind him as if there might be someone watching from the darkness outside the cave, and then nodded. Still, he did not move forward to accept it and Napu set it on the ground between them.

He spoke to the soldier again and the soldier stared into Joseph's eyes and then took a quick glance at the rifle that he had leaned against the wall of the cave. But now the soldier seemed to think for a moment and then he reached for the coconut and drank until it was empty.

"Ask him if he's hungry," Joseph said. "We've got more of those cans of Army food."

When the soldier nodded, Joseph opened three cans of the C-rations. He kept one and gave one to Napu. When he handed one to the soldier, this time he did not hesitate; he began eating with his dirty fingers, digging the food out and stuffing it into his mouth.

As they ate, Napu and Joseph studied the soldier as if for the first time. He was very young, not older than they were, and very thin. His uniform was torn and dirty and he wore a ragged cap on his head that had a small flap of cloth on the back that covered his neck. His eyes were tired and he seemed to have a bad cold, struggling to breathe through his mouth as he filled it with food.

"Let's have a ceremony like we had before—on our island," Joseph said. "A fire ceremony. I'll get the Spirit of the Voyage."

He finished his C-rations and, licking his fingers, stood up and left the cave. A few minutes later, he came back carrying the Spirit of the Voyage. When he leaned it against the wall of Retawasiol's grave, the flames seemed to reach out toward it and the whole fire seemed to expand and burn brighter.

While Joseph did all this, Napu had been rolling coconut fiber rope on his thigh. Now he held it out and said, "I made this. We can do the same thing we did before—tie our arms together over the fire."

Joseph nodded at the soldier. "What about him?"

"What about him?" Napu said. "He did not know Retawasiol. He is not a navigator. He said he was going to cut our heads off."

"But he didn't. And he helped us bury him. He built the wall and then he bowed to him."

"What about the spirits?" Napu asked. "Won't they be angry if we put him in the fire ceremony?"

Joseph looked across the fire at the soldier, who was still squatting with his eyes closed. When he felt Joseph looking at him, he opened them and stared back.

"What's his name?"

Napu spoke to the soldier, and the soldier said one word: "Kiki," and closed his eyes again.

"I don't know if we are his prisoner or if he is ours," Joseph said.

"No one is a prisoner if they are with the spirits of the ancestors," Napu said.

"Then we need to put him in the fire ceremony."

Joseph said this and stood up. The soldier looked up at him.

"Tell him about the ceremony."

"I will try but I don't think my Japanese is good enough."

Napu began trying to explain the ceremony to the soldier. He held out the coconut fiber rope and tied it around his arm. He pointed at the Spirit of the Voyage and said Retawasiol's name and then turned his face upwards as if he were looking at the sky. When he was finished, the young soldier just sat quietly looking at him.

"Well, let's just do it anyway," Joseph said.

Napu stood up and they reached across the fire and, working together, they wrapped the rope around their forearms and let the end of it dangle down into the fire.

"Wait," Napu said. "We forgot the stuff for the spirits. You know, the food and other stuff."

"It's kinda dark to find all that now," Joseph said. "Let's open another can of food. We can put some on the fire and eat the rest. I'm still hungry."

They had one more can of C-rations and Joseph opened it and set it by the fire. When the soldier saw this, his eyes widened and he moved closer.

"I guess he's still hungry, too," Napu said.

"Tell him that after the ceremony, we'll eat the rest of it. Tell him we need to offer some to the spirits."

When Napu spoke to him this time, he called the soldier Kiki and this seemed make the soldier happy. His face relaxed and his whole body sagged down. His eyes gleamed in the firelight and the rifle with its bayonet leaning against the cave wall behind him seemed to be forgotten.

Napu and Joseph pulled small threads from the rags of their shorts and each pulled a hair from his head. Napu cut open a co-conut and carved out some of the white meat. They found a few small shells lying on the cave floor and put all of it in a small pile near the fire.

"I think we're ready," Joseph said and they stood up again and joined their arms together.

The soldier said something in Japanese and then stood up. He ripped a small piece off his uniform and pulled a hair from his head. He bowed deeply again as he had before Retawasiol's tomb, and then set the rag and the hair on the pile of offerings.

"What did he say?" Joseph asked.

"He said he wants to do it to."

"Okay," Joseph said, and he nodded at the soldier.

They took some of the offerings from the pile and stood next to the fire. All three of them put their forearms together while Napu tied the rope around it. Then they moved so that they were each standing at a corner of the fire, their arms over it. Napu let the end of the rope hang down into the flames and he said a chant in his own language. Joseph remembered a chant to the spirits that Retawasiol had taught them and now he said it slowly, his eyes on the burning rope. Then the soldier said something in Japanese, his voice high-pitched and clear.

When he had finished, Napu pulled his knife from his belt and cut the rope and let it drop into the fire. Then they started walking slowly around the flames and Napu started chanting Retwasiol's name in rhythm with their footsteps and Joseph started it, too, and then finally, Kiki began repeating it with them as their shadows played on the cave walls and the wall that formed the old navigator's tomb.

After a long time, when the fire had burned down and the darkness began creeping into the cave, Joseph said, "I'm hungry. Let's finish the C-rations."

Chapter 40

They ate the last of the C-rations, passing the can around and taking turns digging the meat out with their fingers. The smoke and dust of the bombing was gone and the night sky was clear.

Napu stepped out of the cave and looked up and said, "They are all there tonight. All of them."

Joseph knew what he meant and he went out and stood next to Napu and together they stared up at the sky and spoke the names: *Wenewenen Fuhemwakut, the star-that-does-not-move; Mailap Anefang,* the star of the north that controls the Universe, even the Earth; *Ukunik,* the tail of the fish; *Moll,* the star of the big waves and strong currents; *Mwerikar,* the rainy season star when you do not climb trees; and *Mailap,* called the big bird of the east.

They remembered them all and they said them out loud and then Joseph said, "It is time to go." Then he stopped and thought for a moment and said, "We should see if Kiki wants to go with us. He is our brother now and the planes will kill him if he stays here. He can sit in the bottom of the canoe and bail out the water."

"No," Napu said. "We don't have enough food or coconuts."

"We can stop at those little islands and get more. It'll be okay."

Napu glanced at the soldier and then turned away. "We can't trust him. He might try to kill us."

"I don't think so, Napu. He'll understand that we're saving his life. He won't hurt us if we save his life. He can't."

Napu turned to the soldier who had come out of the cave and was standing next to them. He spoke to him in Japanese.

The soldier listened. He, too, was looking up at the stars and then he said something and Napu spoke to him again and then the soldier was quiet and Napu spoke to Joseph: "He said many of the soldiers here have been killed by the American planes. There are not many left and many of them are wounded. There is not much food."

"Then he'd better go with us."

"He said he must die with honor—here, with his comrades."

"Tell him we have spoken with the spirits of the ancestors that live in the fire and in the stars. Tell him they are sick of this war and they don't want anyone else to die. Tell him they want him to come with us. Anyway, he's too young to die—at least on purpose."

Napu said this to the soldier and the soldier, who was just a shadow in the dark next to them, was quiet. Joseph went back into the cave and came out holding the rifle and he pointed it at the soldier and stuck the bayonet against his chest and said, "Kiki, you are now our prisoner. You have to come with us."

The soldier jumped back and put his hands in the air and Napu translated what Joseph had said and the soldier cried out and Joseph pushed the bayonet against him and said, " Tell him to get down to the beach and on the canoe."

Napu spoke to the soldier and the soldier spoke back and his voice was cracking as he spoke.

"He said you can kill him. Then he will not have brought dishonor on his family and his ancestors."

"Okay," Joseph said, "but tell him I don't want to kill him up here near Retawasiol's grave. That would not be good for his spirit. I want to kill him down on the beach. Tell him I promise to kill him if he'll go down there."

Napu translated the words and the soldier kept his hands in the air and turned around and as he walked down through the rocks, Joseph kept the bayonet against his back. When they reached the water Joseph said, "Tell him I've changed my mind. I want to kill him on the canoe."

But the soldier did not wait for Napu to translate. He spun around in the darkness and lunged at Joseph, trying to impale himself on the bayonet. But Joseph had lowered the rifle and the bayonet was pointing at the sand and the soldier landed on Joseph instead.

They went down in the sand together, rolling and kicking at the edge of the water and the soldier got on top of him and Joseph felt his hands reaching for his throat. Then he felt the soldier being lifted off of him and he saw Napu punching at him, hitting him in the face, and the soldier went down into the water and Napu jumped on top of him and began punching hard down at him. But they had rolled into deeper water and the soldier's head went under the surface and Napu's fists slammed into the waves and then found the soldier's face under them and kept slamming into it. The soldier arched his back and thrust his head up and for a moment his face came up out of the water. He gasped for breath and Napu hit him again and again his head went under.

Joseph got to his feet and pulled Napu off the soldier, grabbing him from behind and falling backwards into the water and then they were fighting, Joseph and Napu, rolling in the surf and yelling at each other before they both stopped at the same moment and sat gasping in the darkness.

The soldier had pulled himself up from the water and was clutching at the side of the canoe, choking and struggling to breathe.

"Come on," Joseph said, "Let's get him onto the canoe now."

"We can't take him with us," Napu said. "He tried to kill you."

"No, he didn't. He could have killed us a long time ago. He was trying to kill himself. We can't let him die here, Napu. Come on. Help me."

Joseph did not wait for Napu. He grabbed the soldier from behind and tried to lift him up and push him onto the outrigger but the soldier was too heavy. Then Napu was there helping him and together they got the soldier onto the canoe and he rolled onto his side on the outrigger platform and started vomiting.

"Let's go," Napu said. "The wind is with us."

"Wait," Joseph said and walked back up onto the beach where he could see the shadow of the rifle lying on the sand at the edge of the water. He picked it up and grabbed the bayonet and swung the rifle around over his head and let go. It flew end over end in a high arc out into the bay and hit the water with a heavy splash. A moment later, the reflected light of the stars had gathered over where it had disappeared beneath the surface. Then he said, "We forgot the Spirit of the Voyage. It's in the cave. We can't leave it here. We need it now."

"I'll get it," Napu said and he ran up the beach and up onto the rocks.

*****

They sailed out of the bay and out onto the dark sea and the wind carried them over the rippled surface of the big ocean swells. They could see fires from the bombing burning on the island and smoke came to them as they moved past the final tip of land. When they were out of the lee of the island, out from under the protection of the rocks, the sea became the sea again, boisterous and unruly.

"Where are we going?" Joseph asked.

"I am like the spirits," Napu said. "I'm sick of this war."

"Me too," Joseph said, "but we don't have any choice. We have to go back to Guahan. You know that. The old ghost, the taotaomo'na—we've got to do it."

Napu was quiet and there was only the sound of the wind running through the rigging and over the sail and the sound of the waves slapping against the hull, and then he pointed up toward the sky and said, "Look, there it is—the fire star."

He meant the bright red star, Antares, the heart of the Scorpion. He and Joseph watched it for a long time and then Napu said, "I think we should sail toward *Machemelotow,* the setting Southern Cross. That will take us close to Guahan and then we can watch for birds." He was quiet for another minute and then said, "You remember what that Amercian soldier told us? That they were going to Guam next? There will be war there, too."

"Okay, then," Joseph said, "we can wait somewhere. Give them a few weeks. We don't want to get caught up in the middle of another battle. We need to rest anyway and we need more coconuts. We can stop at the next island. The one right over there."

He pointed into the dark toward something they could not see but knew was there—the small, steep island they had passed on the way to the island where the fire comes out of the mountains.

"No," Napu said, "There are people there. We saw fires, remember? Probably soldiers. There were some small islands we passed coming up. There might not be anyone there."

"But what's going to happen to Kiki when we get to Guahan?" Napu said. "If the American soldiers have killed the Japanese, maybe they'll kill Kiki, too. And if the Japanese are still there, maybe they'll kill us."

"The Spirit of the Voyage will protect us on Guahan just like it did here," Joseph said. "And Kiki is not our prisoner. You've got to tell him that, okay? Make sure he understands. We just didn't want him to die."

"I'll tell him," Napu said, "but do you think he's going to believe me?"

Joseph did not answer the question. It hung in the air between them as he looked back up at the great constellation Scorpio and at its blood-red heart and felt the sea under them and wind all around them.

Chapter 41

They sailed past the first island just after dawn and just after dawn the planes came back. They heard the steady drone of their engines high overhead and then the bombing started again, and even though they were thirty miles away now, they could hear the sound of the explosions under the whisper of the wind.

But this did not hold their interest for long. The sound of the planes woke Kiki, and he sat up and stared at Joseph and Napu, his face filled with fear and confusion and one of his eyes swollen from Napu's punches. Napu quickly spoke to him in Japanese, telling him that he was not their prisoner but that they had only wanted to save him from the American bombs. "We didn't want to die and we didn't want you to die. You could have killed us, but you didn't. You helped us." Napu said, saying it in Japanese and then repeating for Joseph in English. "We want to be friends."

Kiki did not respond to this. He stared at both of them until Joseph held his hands up and said, "Look, no weapons. We don't want to hurt you." But Kiki turned away from them and sat watching the shadow of the faraway island they were leaving behind and then at the dark, steep flanks of the smaller island they were now passing.

But after a few hours, Joseph offered him a coconut to drink and after he had finished it, he started examining the canoe. He studied the sail and how the hull moved so easily through the water and when he saw a fishing line and a lure wrapped around a stick, he asked Napu if he could fish.

After a short time of trolling, a fish struck his lure and pulled the line out taut until it was vibrating in the wind. He showed no excitement as he slowly wound it back around the stick, brought the fish to the side of the canoe, and lifted it on board.

"It's a barracuda," Napu said. "In our Chamorro language it's called an *alu*." He repeated it to Kiki in Japanese.

Kiki did not look at him, but said softly, "*oni-kasamu*."

"Yes," Napu said, "that's right. That's what my grandmother called them."

Napu, who was handling the line that controlled the sail, glanced back at Joseph, hesitated, and then handed Kiki his knife and Kiki cut the fish up. They ate it raw and shared two coconuts. Kiki watched closely as Napu lopped the top of them off with his machete and then he drank deeply when Napu handed one to him. Once he was finished eating, he sat quietly, studying the island they were approaching.

"Do you think he believes us now?" Joseph asked.

"I think so. He could have killed us just then—with my knife," Napu said.

*****

They sailed all day, putting both islands behind them until they disappeared below the horizon. But as the afternoon wore on toward dusk, the wind diminished and the *proa* barely moved through the water. They did not see any more land.

"I'm too tired now. We should sleep and wait for the stars," Joseph said, "so we know where we're going."

"What about him?" Napu said, meaning Kiki, but not looking at him.

"What do you mean? He can fish, or sleep if he wants to."

"I don't mean that. Our machetes and knives are just lying there. He could . . . ."

"Napu. I'm not worried about that. Like I said, he could have killed us many times by now. He could have shot us, or stabbed us with his bayonet, or called for the other soldiers—but he didn't. Besides, look, there is the Spirit of the Voyage, right there, looking at us. He will keep us safe. Tell Kiki that we have to sleep for a while but that he's on watch. If he sees anything, wake us up."

And so they configured the canoe in the wind so that it would only drift, and Napu lay down on the mats on the *lepep* on the leeward side of the mast, while Joseph stretched out on the platform on the windward side, near where Kiki sat.

*****

Later Joseph would have no memory of sleeping, no memory of dreaming, no memory of feeling the ocean under the canoe, no memory of his hunger or thirst. It seemed he had just closed his eyes when he heard the sound of a strange, insistent voice and he was immediately awake, his mind aware of every detail, grasping to understand.

He opened his eyes. Kiki was standing over him, a machete in one hand, and Joseph's knife in the other. The pale, red light that played off his face was either sunset or dawn. Behind Kiki's face, far past him and past the mast and the *proa's* rigging, stars hung in the translucent air.

Joseph did not move. Kiki glanced down at him and then over at Napu and he shook the machete in the air and yelled words that Joseph could not understand. Joseph held his hands up and said, "What, Kiki? What?"

Kiki yelled again and swung the machete up over his head and Joseph yelled, "No!" and rolled away toward the edge of the outrigger until he was nearly on the *tam*.

He heard Napu's voice: "It's a ship, Joseph! Kiki sees a ship!"

Then Joseph realized that Kiki was using the machete to point. He held it up so that the blade went out toward the horizon and Joseph's eyes followed it and he saw the gray hulk of something coming at them through the water.

It was still far off, but he heard the rumble of its engines just as Napu said something to Kiki in Japanese and Kiki looked back at him and then lay down on the outrigger. "Cover him with the mats, Joseph!"

Joseph watched the approaching ship again and then sat up and started piling the mats on top of Kiki. When he was covered, Joseph sat on top of the pile and waited. The ship came out of the gloom slowly. It was at least a mile away but it was coming straight at them and they could see its outline against the horizon and see the white bow wave glittering in the sun. They were helpless. There was no wind: the *proa* bobbed up and down on the seas going nowhere.

"Let's sheet in the sail," Joseph said.

"We don't have time. There's nothing we can do," Napu said.

And it was true. The ship was coming down on them quickly, and Joseph realized that it was dawn because as it came on, the light was growing brighter and he could see dark markings on the hull but he could not tell if it was Japanese or American.

They waited as the ship closed on them. Joseph sat on the pile of mats that covered Kiki, and Napu stood next to the mast, his hand on the empty sail. The rumble of the engines grew louder and they heard clanking sounds and then the rush of the sea as the huge hull cut through the water. As it came over them, they saw no one on the deck and no lights and then the *proa* was lifted up by the bow wave and thrown up into the air. It seemed to spin on the edge of the outrigger and the *tam* went under the surface and the *epep* on which Napu was standing shot up into the air and as Joseph clutched at the benches at the base of the mast, he felt Kiki slip out from under him and saw Napu flying over him, his arms outstretched. A moment later, they both disappeared into the warship's roaring, foaming wake.

Chapter 42

The canoe came down hard with a loud slapping sound. Joseph heard the squeal of the coconut fiber lashings as they took up the strain. Still, it hung together and for a moment Joseph was alone on the *proa* as the sun came up over the horizon with a brilliant suddenness that silhouetted the ship as it moved away.

Then he saw two heads bob to the surface. Napu's face spun around as he searched for the canoe and Joseph yelled out at him. He swam to the side of the *proa* and grabbed the *tam*. "Kiki!" Joseph yelled down to him, "He's right there! He's right next to you!"

And indeed, Kiki's head was only a few feet from Napu but his face was under water even though his arms were thrashing at the surface. And then Joseph saw why: he still held the machete in one hand and the knife in the other.

"Grab him," Joseph said, "but be careful. He's still got the knife and the machete."

Napu held on to the *tam* with one hand and reached for Kiki with the other. He grabbed one of his arms and pulled him toward the outrigger but Kiki was swinging wildly and the knife plunged past Napu's face and stuck into the *tam*. Joseph crawled out toward them and pulled the knife out of the *tam* and tossed it into the hull of the canoe and then grasped Kiki's arm. When Kiki swung the machete out of the water with the other arm, he lost his grip on it and it flew past Joseph and onto the outrigger. Joseph dove for it before it could slide off into the sea.

He dropped it in into the hull, too, and turned and watched as Napu struggled to get onto the platform by climbing on the *tam*. But now Kiki was also trying to climb back aboard the outrigger and their combined weight pulled the *tam* and the outrigger below the surface.

"Napu," Joseph yelled out, "one at a time! Get on one at a time! You're too heavy!" As he said this, he crawled out onto the *epep* on the other side of the mast to try to balance the canoe.

Napu slid back into the water next to Kiki and got Kiki's arms on the *tam*. With Napu pushing, Kiki was able to pull himself onto the outrigger where he lay stretched out, breathing hard as he hung onto the partly submerged platform.

"Kiki!" Joseph yelled, and he motioned for him to come to the middle of the canoe. When Kiki had pulled himself up next to the mast, the *proa* righted itself and Napu was able to heave himself up out of the water and onto the outrigger.

*****

Napu and Kiki lay on the outrigger platform until their breathing slowed and then they lay still with their eyes closed and let the sun dry them out. Joseph watched the ship disappear over the horizon, a gray shadow on the dazzling water. When he turned the other way, he saw another shadow on the horizon: the top of a small, high island. At the same moment, he felt a breeze touch his skin.

"Napu. Are you all right?"

Napu did not move, but said, "Yeah, I'm okay."

Kiki lifted his head and watched the horizon for a moment and then lay back down. Napu spoke to him in Japanese and Kiki answered him.

"Kiki says he's okay, too. He wants to know what happened to the knife and the machete."

"Tell him I got them. They're in the canoe."

Napu spoke to Kiki and then moved up and sat on the bench next to the mast. "We have a breeze now," he said. "We need to get going. Do you see any damage?"

"I haven't looked, but we need to check. I thought the *proa* was going to come apart when the bow wave hit us." Then he pointed and said, "Look over there. There's another island. It looks pretty small. Maybe it's too small for soldiers and we can stay there for a while."

Then Napu said, "You know, we slept all night while Kiki was on watch. He didn't kill us. He saved us."

As he said this, he moved back to the helm and got the rudder in the water and Joseph pulled the sail up and sheeted it in and the canoe began to glide over the building seas.

*****

It took the rest of the day to reach the island. They did not see signs of anyone living there and when they drew close enough they could see why. The shoreline was all steep cliffs that plunged into the water and the seas broke hard on the tumbled rocks; there did not seem to be any protected bays where they could safely leave the *proa*. When they explored the north side, though, they found a small indentation where the water was protected from the full pounding of the waves, and it was here that they pulled the canoe up against the shore.

They inspected the coconut rope lashings that held the *proa* together and found that in many places they were worn nearly through and in some places had parted completely. The *tam* had loosened and needed to be repaired before they could sail again.

With the outrigger and the *tam* pulled up on the rocks and the hull floating safely in the water, Joseph and Kiki set about exploring the island while Napu cleared a small place for their camp. They found coconut trees and pandanus growing in the narrow gullies that ran down the island's steep slopes, and as Joseph cut the nuts from the stalks, Kiki opened them and they drank their fill. They then cut pandanus leaves for weaving more mats and carried the nuts and the leaves back to the *proa.*

"Let's make a fire," Joseph said.

"I don't know," Napu said. "What if the pilots see the smoke? They don't know we're Americans and they might start bombing us."

"Well, Kiki found a breadfruit tree. It would be good to be able to cook some. Maybe if we just made a small fire, after the planes are gone."

"Yeah, that might be all right," Napu said.

Kiki sat on his haunches, listening impassively to their conversation, and when Joseph started collecting wood for the fire, he stood up and helped him and then watched as Napu made a bow and used it to spin the stick in the notch of a palm stalk. When the fire was built up, they put some breadfruit on the coals to roast.

While Napu and Joseph watched them cook, Kiki started fishing from the rocks along the shore. They had saved some of the meat and guts from the barracuda; it had stuck to the canoe when it dried so it had not been washed overboard when they were hit by the bow wave of the ship. Now he used it for bait, standing out on a rock and swinging the line over his head and casting it out away from the shore. In a few minutes, he walked into camp carrying three fish on a stick that he had put through their gills.

Napu studied them and said, "*Satmonetiyu*, goat fish. Good eating."

Now for the first time, Kiki smiled and bowed slightly. "*Osuji-himeji*," he said, and Napu nodded and said, "Yes, that's what they are called in Japanese."

At that moment a large, black cloud that had been approaching the island released its rain. They had been sitting under the *proa's* sail, which they had spread over the small clearing where they had made their camp, but now they moved out from under it and stood in the downpour. They rubbed their bodies clean with coconut meat and let the rain wash them off and then they filled all their empty coconuts with water as it poured off the edge of the sail.

While they were bathing, Joseph noticed that Kiki was laughing and he asked Napu to ask him why. Kiki listened to Napu and then laughed again and answered him: "Only because I am happy," he said, "that's all."

Chapter 43

They decided to stay on the island until the war was over and they soon settled into a routine. During the day, they gathered coconuts and fished. They wove mats from pandanus leaves and long strands of rope from the husks of coconuts and used it to make repairs on the *proa*. And they watched as the American planes flew over them and for the next hour they listened to the far-away sound of the bombing. At those times Joseph always thought of the old navigator lying in his tomb behind the wall Kiki had made, and he hoped the war would be over soon so that his spirit could get some rest.

In the evening, after the last of the planes had returned to wherever they had come from, they built up the fire from the remaining coals and cooked breadfruit and roasted and smoked the fish. Sometimes Napu and Joseph spoke quietly to each other and sometimes Napu would speak to Kiki in Japanese and Kiki would listen and think for a long time before answering with one word before falling silent again.

And they looked at *A Boy's Picture History of the World in One Volume*. Joseph had rolled it up and tied it with coconut husk rope and now he unrolled it and they opened its torn, water-stained pages and studied the pictures of the great men and events of history. When Kiki saw the picture of a Samurai warrior, he looked at it for a long time but said nothing.

They explored the tiny island whose single volcanic peak rose hundreds of feet above the sea. The lower reaches of its steep sides were pounded by the crashing surf, but above that, it was mostly green, covered with grasses and bushes and there were no signs that anyone had ever lived there.

One evening, with Kiki walking in the lead, they were returning to their camp after a day of fishing on the windward side. They had just crossed the top of the island's volcano when Kiki stopped and held his hands out at his side to stop the others.

Joseph and Napu came up beside him and peered over his shoulder. Sitting below them on a narrow ledge that faced the sea was a Japanese soldier. He was leaning against the back of the ledge looking out over the water, his back towards them, his hat pulled low on his head, his rifle lying across his legs.

They watched him for a long time, not daring to move, hardly breathing. But neither did the soldier move, and when a cloud passed over the sun and broke the spell, Napu said, "He's dead."

They watched for another minute, waiting for something, but there was nothing. When Kiki stepped down onto the ledge and peered at the soldier, his face turned pale. Joseph and Napu stepped down beside Kiki and saw that the soldier was a skeleton. Like the skeleton Napu and Joseph had found in the rubber life raft, its dried skin was black and pulled tight over the bones of its face. The soldier's hands still clutched at the stock of his rifle and next to the charred remains of a small fire was an open book, its torn and yellowed pages riffled by the wind.

Kiki knelt in front of the soldier and read a metal tag that hung on the soldier's neck. Then he bowed and said, "Akira."

Then he spoke to Napu in Japanese, which Napu translated: *This is my friend, Akira. His name means "intelligent," and he was. He wanted to be a mathematician but they sent him here, to be a lookout, like me. And so now he is dead—as I should be.*

Kiki said nothing more. He bowed again and stood up and started to walk back down the mountain.

"Doesn't he want to bury him?" Joseph asked.

Napu spoke to Kiki and Kiki said, *"No. He loved looking out over the sea."*

"Wait," Joseph said, and he turned around and walked back to the dead soldier. He took the dog tags he had found on the dead American soldier and put them around the Japanese soldier's neck. "There, they can be together now forever, up here in the wind, looking over the sea."

After that, Kiki was quiet and never smiled when he brought fish back to camp. He spent most of his time sitting alone, staring out across the water.

*****

When the moon had nearly run though its cycle, Napu woke one morning and said, "It's time now. I think we can go home to Guahan. Maybe the war is over there, too, like on Saipan." And then he looked up at the island rising above their camp and said, "And there are not many more coconuts left here."

They made their preparations. They loaded the canoe with green drinking nuts and the empty nuts they had filled with fresh rainwater. They cooked breadfruit and smoked fish and stowed them in the hull and they got the sail back on and checked the new lashings on the *tam.* They had taken the Spirit of the Voyage from the canoe and stuck it in the earth next to the fire and now, when dusk promised the stars, they tied it back on the mast and pushed the *proa* down into the water. Then they climbed on board and hoisted the sail.

It was rainy season and many of the clouds were thick and black and carried downpours. Thunderstorms far off on the horizon flashed and glowed with lightning, blotting out many of the stars, but Napu and Joseph knew what to do. There was just a sliver of moon and the stars were bright among the clouds and they watched for a clear place in the sky. They found a star they knew well and using the position of that star, they knew from where *Tan Up*, the rising Southern Cross would come, and then they knew where it would become *Tolon Up*, setting Southern Cross, and that Guahan would be there, under it. They knew that from here, Saipan lay under *Wenenewenen Up*, the Southern Cross when it sat straight up, and that by using *etak*, they would always know where Saipan was as they sailed toward Guahan. As they left the island, they watched for the current and adjusted for it and the breeze was good from the east-southeast and the sail filled and they felt the *proa* begin to move.

Napu sat at the helm and Joseph adjusted the sail, and when it was necessary, Kiki bailed out the water from the hull. And at that moment, leaving the island, Joseph saw a big piece of bamboo floating past the canoe and for a moment his heart stopped. Retawasiol had told them that there are many signs to look for when setting off on a voyage, omens of luck, good or bad. He had said that seeing a piece of bamboo adrift near the canoe was a sign of trouble.

Joseph glanced at Napu. He had not seen it. Joseph took in a deep breath and said nothing.

But the *proa* seemed to be alive, and when Napu did look at Joseph, Joseph smiled and nodded at the Spirit of the Voyage where it was tied to the spar, facing forward, and they understood something: it was good to be back at sea, good to have the *proa* moving over the swells, good to have learned what Retawasiol had taught them — it was good to be navigators.

They sailed through the night and through the next day and the next and, though the sea was endless, they were seldom alone. The air was filled with airplanes that sometimes dove in low and circled them but then climbed up again and disappeared into the haze, and warships were always somewhere in sight, steaming in convoys across the far horizons. Sometimes the ships came close, but they never gave any indication that they saw the tiny canoe with its small, brown sail. And as long as there was wind, they could steer the *proa* away from them.

The wind was fickle, though, and thick with moisture. It would blow for hours, but then a squall would approach and the wind would swerve around to the south and the squall would bring heavy rain and the wind would come at them in strong gusts. At these times, they took the sail down and wrapped themselves in pandanus mats and waited, letting the canoe ride it out as they bailed the water from the hull.

At night the squalls moved around them and it seemed as though the war had lifted itself from the earth and had moved into the sky. As they huddled together under the scant protection of the pandanus mats, the lightning arced overhead and then began striking the water all around them, igniting the air with brilliant streaks that hissed and exploded and silhouetted the rigging against the dark water. And above it all, the air shuddered with the concussions of the thunder and the seas seemed to be sucked up into the vortex that swirled around them.

But it was not the war and the squalls soon passed leaving the sky clean and filled again with stars. Then they felt the breeze steady again on their wet skin, and they ran the sail back up and found the fire star, the red heart of the Scorpion, and set sail, following the Southern Cross that Retawasiol had called the Trigger Fish.

Chapter 44

Then, at dawn of the fifth day, the war was all around them again. It started early in the morning with the sound of thunder, yet looking toward the horizon they saw only blue sea and a sky scattered with white clouds. But it was a sea filled with ships and the thunder and the flashes of lightning were coming from them and the concussions came through the air and off in the distance they could see the flat, dim outline of land.

"Guahan," Napu said, and as they sailed slowly toward it, they watched the shells from the ships exploding on the island and the smoke and dust rose up in great palls.

"What are we going to do?" Joseph asked. "The war is still here."

"I don't know," Napu said, and he let the sail run out so that the wind fell out of it and the canoe stopped and began drifting.

All day they watched as, in the distance, the fire came out of the guns on the great, gray battleships and the sun was bright on the plumes of dust that rose up from the land and the heavy whump-whump-whump of the explosions rolled out to them across the blue ocean swells.

When night came, there was no moon. The shelling continued anyway, and the flashes of the guns seemed to echo off the sky and off the stars and come back again and light up the air around them. Joseph lay down on the *epep* and closed his eyes and listened, and when he drifted off into a light sleep, it was filled with the sounds of war and he heard voices yelling things he could not understand.

Then amid the yelling he heard Napu's voice and he tried to answer him but his voice would not work, but he felt Napu's hand on his shoulder and his voice in his ear. "I think we should go around to the other side. There's that little bay we came out of, you know? I don't think the war will be there."

Joseph sat up. There was no sound but the slapping of the waves against the hull. The breeze was light on his skin and the sky seemed to sag under the weight of the stars.

"What?"

"That little bay," Napu said. "The war has stopped. I think we can go there now."

Joseph was staring at the island. It was just a black loom in the distance with the yellow glows of many fires scattered across the darkness. The shelling had stopped.

"You think it is? You think it's over?"

"I don't know. Maybe the American ships killed all the Japanese soldiers."

Joseph looked at Kiki. He was sitting on a bench and leaning against the mast staring off into the night.

"Is that the place we started from?"

"Yeah. We can go in there and maybe we'll be safe until we know the war is over. We can go back up into that little river in the jungle."

"Maybe that's a good idea," Joseph said. "We can stay there until we figure out what's going on. It's a pretty good place to hide, back up in that river."

Napu explained to Kiki what they were doing, but Kiki sat and stared at the island and did not respond. He moved away from the mast and sat on the *epep* while Joseph hoisted the sail and Napu went back to the helm.

The breeze was light and the *proa* moved slowly through the darkness. They moved in close to shore and they could see small fires burning all along the coast and the acrid smell of smoke blended with the sweet odors of the jungle. All night they heard the heavy engines of ships moving around them but saw only shadows and the phosphorescence of their wakes. Toward morning the breeze faded and as the dawn pearled the air, they saw they were only a few hundred yards off the coast. Their *proa* ghosted through the water, barely moving.

Napu saw them first: ships, hundreds of them, big and small, all around them as if they were congealing slowly from the wet heat and darkness. They made no noise, but from their silence came a whisper as if great, coiled beasts had gathered together and were breathing in unison as they waited to strike.

There was nothing to do. The breeze was dead and the *proa* drifted. Napu told Kiki to lie down inside the hull. He had just moved to do this when it all started. There was a high whistling sound and then another and another and the morning exploded.

At the first barrage, shells began detonating all around the *proa*, and then a huge explosion lifted it out of the water. It spun around in the air and came down at an angle. The *tam* hit the water hard and the outrigger was crushed in on itself, folding over on top of the hull. Napu and Kiki were thrown into the water away from the canoe, but Joseph, who clung to the mast, was caught between the outrigger platform and the spars.

All around them, the water was white and the air was stunned with the concussions of the shells. The ships that had surrounded them with silence were now moving, heading toward the shore, and the great whispering of their presence became the roar of their engines that filled the spaces between the explosions.

Joseph felt himself get lifted with a force that snapped his face down on the hull, and then he was being twisted in the air and something came down on him, crushing him and driving him below the surface. A sudden and terrible pain tore through his back and into his chest and he tried to breathe but the water was over him and the pain burned through him.

Napu came to the surface, struggling to swim in the fury that raged around him. He could not see the *proa*. Boats carrying soldiers toward the shore were all around him, their gray hulls immense and wild, racing over him. He dove under and heard them go over him and felt the water against him and waited for the propellers to cut into him. But a moment later he was still alive, and a moment after that, too, and he dove again and came to the surface again and then he felt his hand come against the broken wood of the *proa*.

He clung to it. The men driving the landing craft saw the hull of the canoe and avoided it. Napu watched them as they moved toward the beach and he heard the whine and whistle of the shells coming from the batteries on the shore and felt the explosions tearing at the water around him.

He saw Kiki first, on the other side of the broken canoe, hanging onto the place where the rudder used to hang down into the water. Then he saw Joseph, lying on the canoe under the outrigger, trapped between it and the hull and the rigging. He was facing down, his head under water, and the morning light played off his bright blond hair that floated on the surface in sparkling ringlets.

Napu climbed up next to him, lifted his head, and put his face against his. He called to him, "Joseph! Joseph!"

Joseph began coughing and then he gagged and vomited and Napu held his head up and put his feet against the outrigger and pushed. The outrigger lifted up and Joseph's body slid away from the hull and into the water. Joseph tried to swim but then cried out in pain. "I can't—I can't move my arms."

"I've got you," Napu cried, and he put one arm around Joseph's chest and held onto the hull of the canoe with the other.

"Kiki can't swim," Joseph sputtered, and Napu saw blood coming out of his nose and out of his mouth and he coughed again and spit up more blood.

"It's okay," Napu said. "He's here. Kiki's here. We've just got to hang on here. Just hang on."

They stayed together, clinging to the smashed hull of the *proa* as wave after wave of the fury of the war passed by them and then onto the shore. The boats full of soldiers kept coming and the shells kept hitting the water.

"I'm going to swim us to shore," Napu said. He spoke to Kiki in Japanese and they both pulled on the outrigger. It came away from the canoe with the *tam* still attached to it and he put an arm around the *tam*. With his other arm around Joseph, and Kiki hanging onto the side of the outrigger platform, he began swimming, kicking them through the water.

"The Spirit of the Voyage," Joseph called, "and the book."

Napu looked back at the canoe. The Spirit of the Voyage with its sleeping face was floating in the water, still tied to the broken mast. It was looking up at the sky, the newly risen sun reflecting on its dark face.

"I can't get them now," Napu said.

"We need them now. You've got to get them. I can hang on here."

Blood was coming from Joseph's mouth and nose and running into the blue water and spreading out in a dim red cloud. Napu slid the *tam* under Joseph's arms. "You okay? Can you hang onto that?"

"Yeah, I'm okay."

Napu swam around the outrigger platform and back to the canoe. He saw the book, rolled up and tied with a piece of rope, floating under the water down in the hull, and he grabbed it. But the mast, with the Spirit of the Voyage tied to it, was far below the surface. He could see it and tried again and again to dive down to it, but he was too exhausted, too out of breath, to reach it. He swam back to Joseph. "Here," he said, and he put the book on the platform in front of him. "I can't get the Spirit of the Voyage. I tried. I just can't reach it."

"But we've got to have it," Joseph said, his voice soft with his weakness. "We need it to protect us."

"I know, Joseph. I tried. I couldn't get it. I just couldn't get it."

Napu again wrapped one arm around the *tam* and one arm around Joseph and started swimming. As he swam, he could see the shore and see the war moving along it and up it into the distant mountains. The sunlight glowed off the smoke and dust from the exploding shells and green of the jungle, too, and the sound of the explosions ran down from the tops of the sharp peaks and spread out across the water.

The outrigger platform floated just under the surface and as Napu swam, he pushed it before him, one arm around Joseph. Kiki clung to the other side of it, but he was afraid of the water and, in his panic, kept trying to climb onto it. He did not seem to understand Napu's instructions to just hang on. Finally, exhausted, he stopped struggling and grabbed it and allowed his body to float.

Joseph closed his eyes and imagined that the Spirit of the Voyage was still with him. He saw its bulging eyes open and it looked at him and he knew everything was good and slowly the fear left him. The pain in his chest and the sounds of the war both seemed to grow smaller and move away together as if they were two parts of the same thing. He felt Napu's arm around him and felt him swimming and heard his breathing. After a while, he started to feel cold and he had no strength left and when he could no longer hold onto the *tam*, he let it slip away.

When Napu felt Joseph let go of the *tam*, he wrapped his arm tighter around his body. He turned him over to make sure his face stayed out of the water, but when he spoke to him, Joseph no longer answered.

The shelling did not stop and the war seemed to be all over them and all around them. Napu swam among dead soldiers floating face down, their olive drab uniforms crimson with their blood, and the water around them red with it. The shells were bursting over them, and bullets struck the water sending up small white geysers and sometimes the bullets skipped across the water like the flat shells he and Joseph used to skim on the calm water of the lagoon. Then his hands and feet touched the sharp coral of the bottom.

Kiki felt the bottom, too, and stood up. Napu yelled for him to stay down in the water, but instead, he continued to stumble forward. As the bullets struck the water around him, he walked up onto the shore and Napu watched as he disappeared into the rising billows of dust and smoke.

Napu spoke to Joseph again, but Joseph did not answer. He kept Joseph's face above the water and saw that his mouth was full of blood and his eyes were open wide as if he was staring upwards in amazement that among all this, even during a war, the sky was still blue and the clouds still moved through it, white and pure. And then Napu started crying and he held Joseph close to him and they lay together in the shallow water until the war moved away from the sea and up into the mountains.

Epilogue

"Joseph, Magahet, you boys wake up now."

The boy named Joseph rolled over and opened his eyes. His father was smiling at him, yet it was a serious smile, the smile he used when he meant business.

"We're ready now. It's time," he said. "Wake up your brother."

The boy began rubbing the sleep out of his eyes and then he remembered and his heart jumped and he took a quick breath: today, for the first time, he would be the navigator on an ocean voyage.

From his sleeping mat, he could look out from under the low eaves of the canoe house and see the nearby water of the cove, still gray in the first dim light of morning. "How is the wind?" he asked.

"Good. It will be a good day. And good stars tonight."

He watched as his father pulled back his long, gray hair and tied it behind his head with a piece of coconut fiber rope and then stooped over and left the *utt.*

His younger brother was asleep near him, stretched out on his mat, his mouth open, breathing deeply and slowly. There had been too much excitement last night as final preparations for the voyage were finished. There had been a fiesta at the canoe house with a lot of food and even music. Family and friends had come both to wish them well on the voyage and also to celebrate Joseph's eighteenth birthday. Afterward, they had not been able to get to sleep and had sat out on the beach until past midnight naming the stars and challenging each other to remember the star paths.

Now Joseph touched his brother on the foot and chastised him. "Come on, Magahet, get up. Father and I have been up for a long time waiting for you. Maybe we'll have to leave you here. Maybe we shouldn't take you on this voyage. Maybe you're too little."

The boy opened his eyes and for a moment struggled against the confusion of sleep. Then he said, "What do you mean? I've been awake waiting for you."

Joseph laughed and said, "Yeah, sure. You were snoring so loud I thought there was a typhoon coming."

His brother yawned and said, "I was just pretending to be asleep because I didn't want to wake you up. I know you need your beauty sleep pretty bad."

"Yeah, sure," Joseph said, "not as much as you do. Come on, hurry. We got to beat Isa to the canoe."

Then they were laughing and racing each other to the water.

*****

But they were too late. A moment later, they were standing knee deep in the cove next to their father, their hands touching the sides of the *proa* that had been readied for launch. In the pearly light of first dawn, it was a beautiful thing, sleek and newly painted a shiny black and red, its mast etched against the sky.

Looking down on them from the outrigger platform, was their sister. "Did you boys get enough sleep?" she asked. "I hope we didn't wake you too early."

Joseph's answer was sheepish. "Yeah, sure. When did you get here?"

"A long time ago. I brought you breakfast."

"Oh, yeah. Good. Thanks."

Now all three of them waited. They knew what must come next. Their father walked back to the canoe house, ducked inside, and re-emerged a moment later carrying two things he always kept inside the sacred *utt*, things the children had grown up with, about which they had heard many stories.

One was what was left of a thick book. Its covers were gone, its fragile pages stained and torn. It was rolled up like a scroll and tied with a piece of rope. The book's title, though, was still legible across the top of the outer page: *A Boy's Picture History of the World in One Volume.*

In his other hand he carried a piece of wood that he said was a root from a nunu tree and that looked like it had been carved into the grim image of a sleeping man. The man's eyes bulged under his closed lids and in one side, close to each other, there were two jagged holes.

These things were brought with them every time they sailed the *proa* and now they watched as their father brought them down to the canoe once more. He handed them to Joseph and climbed up on the *tam* and across the outrigger platform and sat down next to the mast. He reached down and Joseph handed them up, first the book and then the carved stick. They waited in silence as their father set the book down inside the hull and then lashed the stick to the mast.

Then Napu stood up on the outrigger and they all bowed their heads. He began slowly, rhythmically, speaking in the ancient language of his people: "Spirits of the ancestors, we ask for your blessings for this voyage. Watch over this canoe and watch over the brave young people who steer her over the sea. We ask for a steady wind, a fair swell, and many birds to guide us by day. And especially we ask for many stars in a clear sky to guide us by night."

He stopped and stared up at the sky. His children were silent, watching, waiting. After a long moment, Napu smiled and said, "Let's go!"

*****

They had practiced this many times and knew what to do. They took the protective palm leaves off the canoe's eyes and then pushed the *proa* down over the path of fronds to the water. It slid easily and floated gently on the small waves of the cove.

When the canoe was pointed out toward the sea, they climbed on and hauled up the sail. With Joseph at the helm, Isa controlling the set of the sail, and Magahet down in the hull ready to bail water, they adjusted for the wind and the canoe moved quickly away from the shore.

Ahead they could see the glimmer of the first sunlight on the open ocean. This morning the sea beckoned with a vast serenity and when they skimmed out between the rocks of the breakwater, they felt the swells lift the *proa* and then drop it down and then lift it again in a great, endless rhythm. Then Isa, and Joseph, and Magahet all looked at their father because he said these swells were the ocean's soul and when he first felt them they would tell him if it was a good day to start a voyage. They knew he was also looking for a piece of bamboo floating on the surface. If he saw one, it would be a bad omen and they would not begin the voyage that day. If the news was good, he always smiled. And now he smiled and they could once again concentrate on sailing.

*****

They sailed all day as the sun arched overhead from horizon to horizon. They all took turns at the helm and at controlling the sail. But only Isa and Magahet spent time sitting down in the hull bailing out the water that splashed in; this was not like other days when they sailed the canoe out and then brought it back to the cove. This was not a day to practice shunting the spars and holding a course using the swells and estimating the current. This was their first voyage to a far distant island, and Joseph was to be the navigator. Only he stayed either at the helm or on the bench near his father, next to the mast, and watched the sea and the sky and gave commands to the others in a soft, strong voice.

When the sun was about to drop below the horizon and the sky to the west was becoming red and the sky to the east was growing dark, their anticipation increased, for there was always a competition to be the first to see the first star. And it always happened suddenly. Joseph, or Isa, or Magahet would shout out, "There it is!" and Napu, the father, from his seat at the base of the mast, would say, "And what star is that. It has a name," and that was easy because it was always the star called "the light of the flying fish," the brightest star in the night sky.

But tonight the sighting of the first star was not a game. It meant the voyage was starting in earnest. The heading of the canoe was adjusted for the exact star path to be followed and all Joseph's concentration was focused on keeping the *proa* on this course. As the sky darkened and the full night came over them, the wind abated, but the swell was faithful from the east and the heavens were true, wheeling above them in eternal grace.

As darkness engulfed them, Napu, too, was filled with his own anticipation, but it was not for the sight of the first star. What he waited for came slowly, rising imperceptibly from the distant, dark edge of the sea. It was the great summer constellation called Scorpio and at its heart, the red supergiant star called Antares.

They all knew this, too, and when it emerged from the sea, Joseph said, "There it is, Father, there's your star—the fire star."

Then Napu would lie down and close his eyes and remember as they sailed the *proa* toward the edge of the world.

About the Author

Douglas Arvidson grew up on a small family farm in New England. After serving in the military and finishing graduate school, he spent nearly thirty years overseas, teaching, traveling, and writing, including eleven years living on a sailboat on the island of Guam. It was during this time that he studied the ancient methods of traditional navigation. His international prize-winning short fiction has been published in Paris, Prague, and in literary magazines in the United States. He now lives on the Eastern Shore of Virginia. You may visit his website at douglasarvidson.com and for insights on the writing of this novel, please go to brothersofthefirestar.blogspot.com.

About the Cover Illustrator

Rob Scarborough is a graduate of the Savannah College of Art and Design and works commercially as an artist and graphic designer. See more of the illustrator's work at his website: www.scarboroughconcepts.com.